D1560132

FIGHT

Jeff Elkins

Copyright © 2020 Jeff Elkins

All rights reserved.

ISBN: 9798629701453

ALSO BY JEFF ELKINS

Grab (a Watkins and Howe Adventure)

Steal (a Watkins and Howe Adventure)

Mencken and the Monsters

The Twelve Commandments

Becoming Legend

Mencken and the Lost Boys

Saving Deborah

Mark and All the Magical Things

7 Nights in a Bar

My Top Five In No Particular Order

DEDICATION

For all my Edna Karr Cougars.
You continue to inspire me every day.
Second to none.

And for Wendy.
Love you Babe.

CONTENTS

Chapter One	1
Chapter Two	7
Chapter Three	14
Chapter Four	23
Chapter Five	29
Chapter Six	37
Chapter Seven	45
Chapter Eight	58
Chapter Nine	63
Chapter Ten	73
Chapter Eleven	77
Chapter Twelve	84
Chapter Thirteen	92
Chapter Fourteen	100
Chapter Fifteen	103
Chapter Sixteen	111
Chapter Seventeen	115
Chapter Eighteen	121

FIGHT

Chapter Nineteen	128
Chapter Twenty	136
Chapter Twenty-One	141
Chapter Twenty-Two	146
Chapter Twenty-Three	152
Chapter Twenty-Four	157
Chapter Twenty-Five	167
Chapter Twenty-Six	175
Chapter Twenty-Seven	185
Chapter Twenty-Eight	194
Chapter Twenty-Nine	200
Chapter Thirty	208
Chapter Thirty-One	220
Chapter Thirty-Two	231
Chapter Thirty-Three	235
Chapter Thirty-Four	237
Chapter Thirty-Five	248
Chapter Thirty-Six	256
Chapter Thirty-Seven	261

ACKNOWLEDGMENTS

Special thanks to my editor Bethany Hockenbury.
Thank you for making my work readable.

Also, special thanks to the amazing cover designer,
Elizabeth Mackey.

CHAPTER ONE

There was a lot that Charlie didn't understand. He didn't understand why the secretive group of powerful people met at cheap Chinese buffets, he didn't understand why they all entered through the back doors of the establishments like they were avoiding paparazzi even though the restaurants they picked were always empty, and he didn't understand how they'd all found out about the Chinese Food Club in the first place. But Charlie didn't care. None of that mattered. All that mattered to him was that he knew the club existed, he knew that his best friend, Anderson Siltmore, was a member, and he knew that he desperately wanted to join.

Charlie took the right turn slowly, wondering if Anderson knew he was following him. Charlie loved Anderson's car. Anderson had paid close to 9 million for the black Maybach Exelero. Powered by twin turbo V12 engines and capable of speeds up to three-hundred miles per hour, the sloping rear was unlike anything Charlie had ever seen. It had even been featured in a Jay-Z and Beyoncé video, but none of that was what made Charlie salivate over it. What made Charlie envious was that only one Maybach Exelero had been built. It was, therefore, a visible statement of wealth and power. If you could buy that car, you could buy anything in the world.

Anderson took a left down a one way street, and Charlie followed. They were moving out of the city now and closer to the southwestern suburb of Catonsville, which confused Charlie. No one of Anderson's status lived in Catonsville. It made him wonder if he'd been made. Maybe Anderson was driving him out to the middle of nowhere for fun? That's something Anderson would do and then deny later. Charlie could hear him now, "What do you mean I lost you in Catonsville? Why would I be in Catonsville?"

Charlie knew Anderson wasn't smarter than he was. He didn't work harder or have some special gift Charlie was lacking. By Charlie's estimation, the only reason Anderson was out-earning him was the Chinese Food Club, and that's why Charlie had to become a member. No matter what it cost.

Charlie slowed down. He'd seen on YouTube that it was important to leave at least four car lengths between yourself and the person you were following. Plus, Charlie wasn't worried about losing the Exelero. It was impossible to miss. As long as Anderson didn't become purposefully evasive, Charlie knew he would be able to spot the car.

Charlie followed Anderson down another one-way street and found Anderson easing into a restaurant called "The Lucky Star Buffet." It looked like every other cheap, takeout Chinese food place Charlie had ever seen.

Before Anderson could get out of the car, Charlie gunned his engine and whipped into the parking spot next to his friend. Bounding from his vehicle, Charlie began laughing and ranting before Anderson could even open his door, "Hey, Andy. This is funny. Wow. I can't believe you're here? I mean, this is crazy! You come here too, huh? The Lucky Star? So good. Am I right? I love this place so much. I mean, egg rolls? And, um, rice? So good. What are the chances, right? Wow. It's crazy running into each other like this. Am I right?"

As Anderson stepped from his car, a surge of jealously raged through Charlie. Anderson was tall and impeccably fit. All his suits were exquisitely tailored, his salt-and-pepper hair was immaculately coiffed, and he never wore a tie. He had the perpetual look of someone on vacation off the coast of Italy. "Charlie, you shouldn't be here," Anderson said with the tone of an older brother scolding his younger sibling.

Charlie laughed nervously and stammered, "What? I can eat here. There's no law against a guy loving a good Chinese buffet. I mean those egg rolls? Right? And the, um, the dumplings? Pow! Am I right? So good. That's why I'm here. The food. So good."

Anderson put his hand on Charlie's shoulder and squeezed. Charlie winced and looked down to avoid Anderson's gaze.

"Look, I'd love to invite you in, but you know the rules," Anderson consoled.

Charlie's gaze drifted to the black Lexus SUV that was pulling into the parking lot. "Who's that?" he asked.

"How would I know, Charlie? I'm just here for lunch," Anderson said with a dismissive sigh.

A driver hurried out of the driver's seat and opened the back door. A long-legged woman in a white dress stepped from the vehicle and walked toward the back door of the Lucky Star Buffet.

Charlie's mouth fell open. "Is that Michelle Dives? Do you know Michelle Dives? She's, like, the new Oprah. You have to introduce me! Come on, man! You need to get me in with Michelle!" Charlie begged.

"I'm just here for lunch, Charlie," Anderson said again.

Reaching up and grabbing Anderson's shoulders, Charlie demanded, "I need you to let me in. Right now! Take me in there! You know how much I need this. Come on!"

"I thought you said you were here for the food," Anderson said with a grin.

"I mean it, Andy. You take me in there right now or… Or…. Or we're done. I mean it. Do it or I'm cutting you off. No more Good Time Charlie for you! Nope! It's over between us."

"Look, Charlie. It's not personal. It's just business."

"Don't quote the Godfather at me! You owe me. You owe me this. And I need it! I'll tell. I'll tell Alicia. Don't think I won't. And she won't like it."

Anderson gave Charlie a look of pity and said, "We both know telling her won't win you any points."

"Damn it," Charlie said, stomping his foot. "You can't keep me out. You have to let me in! Don't do this to me."

"I'd love to take you in, Charlie. Lunch with my best friend would be great," Anderson said.

"Really? Man, you are the best. That's awesome!" Charlie exclaimed. A giant grin filled his face.

"Oh, wait. There's just one thing. Did you bring the million dollars for the buy-in?" Anderson asked, feigning concern.

Charlie stammered and looked down, "No. I mean, you know I don't have that right now because all my cash is tied up in those investments I told you about. But I'm good for it. You know I'm good for it. I mean, if you let me in, I can get it. I just need a little more time."

"I'm sorry, buddy. You know how the world works. You have to pay to play," Anderson said with a shrug.

Charlie laughed, hoping it would hide his desperation. "But you have it. Right? And we're friends. Right? So, like, maybe you could just spot me? You know I'm good for it. I mean, you've lent me money before, I think. So you know I'll pay you back. Come on, man. I need this. I need to get in that room."

Anderson shook his head and said, "You know that isn't how this works."

Another car pulled into the lot. This one wasn't fancy. It looked like an unmarked police car. An older man in a blazer stepped from the vehicle.

"Who's that?" Charlie asked.

"How would I know? I'm just here for lunch, Charlie," Anderson said with another sigh.

"Look, Andy. Stop dicking around! I need this. You know I need this. You better let me have it or else!" Charlie demanded.

Anderson squeezed his friend's shoulder again and said, "I know you need it. And if it were up to me, I'd let you in without hesitation. But there are rules for a reason. Now look, I've got to go. I'll see you tonight? Let's grab dinner. Woodberry Kitchen? I'm buying."

Charlie sighed. He could feel a knot forming in his chest and tears building in his eyes. He sniffed like he had a cold and started backing toward his car. "Yeah. It's okay. You're right. I guess I just need to get the buy-in. I'll figure it out, I guess. Rules are rules. I know. I get that. We've got to stick to the rules. So, I'll see you tonight. Okay? Woodberry Kitchen," he stammered as he backed away.

"See you tonight," Anderson said, as he walked away.

Once his friend's back was turned, Charlie wiped his eyes. Taking a deep breath, he yelled after Anderson, "I'm going to get that cash! You'll see! I'm going to get it and then you'll have to let me in!"

JEFF ELKINS

"Go get it, Charlie," Anderson called with a wave as he walked toward the rear entrance of the building.

Charlie got in his car and let the engine roar. He looked at himself in the rearview mirror. His red eyes and flushed cheeks ignited a vein of rage in his chest. He was so tired of being weak. "You're going to get that money. You're Charlie Michaels. God-Damn-Good-Time-Charlie Michaels," he told himself. He let the engine of his car roar and glared at himself in the mirror. "We'll figure it out. We'll get it. We're God-Damn-Good-Time-Charlie Michaels."

CHAPTER TWO

Holding tight to Sarah's hand, Moe eased her way through the line to a small table against the window. It didn't matter what time of year or day, The Charmery ice cream shop was always crowed. Locals and tourists came at all hours to experience the spot's whimsical creations. Located at the end of a strip of eclectic stores on 36th Street in the heart of the Hampden neighborhood, The Charmery was a jewel in the crown of the traditionally blue-collar but gentrifying community.

There were only four tables in the shop and a scattering of extra chairs, which wasn't a problem because most customers got their ice cream to go. Moe moved around the table and took the seat against the window. Sarah, pulled out a chair for the soft teddy bear she was carrying and placed the stuffed animal in the seat. She then took a seat next to it, leaving an empty place at the table for Stacie.

Not sitting down, Stacie asked, "Okay. I'm buying. What does everyone want?"

"I can't see," Sarah said, trying to read the menu over

the crowd.

Moe said, "I'll read them for you. Tell me when to stop. Pure Vanilla. Maryland Mud. Old Bay Carmel. Malty Vanilla Chip. Tell Tale Chocolate."

"Stop!" Sarah exclaimed with glee.

"Tell Tale Chocolate?" Moe asked.

"Yep. And Pure Vanilla for Mr. Bear," Sarah said with a smile, motioning to her stuffed animal.

"One Tell Tale Chocolate, one Pure Vanilla, and I'll get the Peanut Butter Pie," Moe said to Stacie.

"Coming right up," Stacie replied as she eased through the crowd back to the end of the line.

Moe looked at the smiling young girl. Unlike when Moe had first met her at the psychiatric hospital, Sarah appeared to be thriving. Her hair was freshly cut short, her clothes seemed new, and there was a restored vibrancy to her that Moe had only seen in her memories. Even so, the attentiveness of her eyes betray a wisdom only earned by witnessing things of no six-year-old should ever witness.

"I like your haircut," Moe commented.

"I got to pick it myself. Ms. Kolwalski said I could."

"It's nice. I also I like the shoe laces you picked out today. They're very pretty," Moe said, commenting on the bright pink laces Sarah had run through her Converse. The laces had come from the box of laces Moe had given the young girl as a present.

"Thank you. I look at them like you told me to, and then I think about happy stuff," Sarah said.

"How's the new house?" Moe asked. After helping Sarah find her voice again, Moe had helped to move her into a foster home on a large farm in the county.

"We have horses," Sarah said with restrained enthusiasm.

"What are your horses' names?" Moe asked.

"My horse is Buttercup. She's nice. But there's another horse that's not nice. Tornado. Johnny likes him though. And Dempsey is old, so no one gets to ride him," Sarah explained.

"Do you get to ride Buttercup?" Moe asked.

"No. Right now I just get to brush her. I have to brush her a lot and check her saddle. I'm good at brushing. I like brushing her legs. I think I might get to ride her soon though. She is so big. She is probably, like, as tall as this room."

"Well, that is really tall," Moe laughed.

"Yeah. And she goes really fast. She won't go fast with me though. Ms. Kolwalski said Buttercup is a good horse and she won't go fast until I'm ready so I don't need to be scared because Buttercup knows how to be nice to little kids like me."

"Well that's good."

"Yeah. And we have chickens too. And I get the eggs and bring them inside, and we eat them. But don't worry. The eggs don't have babies in them yet. We eat them before that."

"That's good. I'd hate for you to have to eat a baby chicken," Moe said.

"That would be sad. So we don't do that. We eat them before there are babies in them."

"That's good," Moe said with a smile. "How do you like your new school?"

"It's okay. I like gym. That's fun. And my teacher is nice. Her name is Ms. Lad-wal-ace. I can't spell it though, so don't ask," Sarah said, shaking her head.

"I won't. I promise," Moe said.

"It has a nice playground too. It's new. That's what Ms. Lad-wal-ace said. She said it's new so we should play on it a lot to break it in."

"It sounds like a great school," Moe said.

"Yeah. I like it. And the kids are mostly nice. Some of them aren't, but most are."

Moe smiled. "That's good. It's good to be at school with nice kids."

"Yeah. I miss my old school though," Sarah said, looking down at her shoe laces.

"You do?"

"Yeah. It didn't have a new playground or anything. But. It had nice kids too. And I miss my old house. It didn't have horses. But." Sarah looked down at the table and bit her bottom lip.

"It was a nice house," Moe said.

"Yeah. I miss it," Sarah said, as a she wiped a tear away with the back of her hand. She reached over and took the bear from the chair next to her, wrapped her arms around it, and laid her head on it.

"Now, who is this? I don't think we've been properly introduced."

"This is Mr. Bear. He's my new friend," Sarah said, her head still resting on the stuffed animal.

"He looks really soft," Moe said.

"I get to take him everywhere. Ms. Kulsi said if I get sad or scared, I should just hold him because he will help me."

"Who is Ms. Kulsi?" Moe asked.

"She's the pretty lady that comes to the house on Tuesday. I talk to her about how I feel about stuff."

Moe felt tears build behind her eyes. She swallowed to push them back. "And. You've been feeling sad?" she asked.

Sarah sniffled and squeezed Mr. Bear. More tears came. "Yeah," she said. "I get sad a lot."

Unable to keep them at bay, tears began to slide down Moe's face as well. She reached across the table and rubbed Sarah's arm. "It's okay to be sad about your mom and dad," she said.

"Yeah," Sarah said, her head still resting on Mr. Bear.

They sat for a moment, crying together. Sarah broke the silence and said, "Can you help me see them? Like you did before?"

Moe smiled. "Sure," she said, and she held out her hand. Sarah took it, and Moe closed her eyes and enter Sarah's memories.

She opened them, and she was standing in a bathroom on a wooden step stool. She was wearing Minnie Mouse pajamas. They weren't Sarah's favorite, those were the Superman ones, but they were all that was clean.

Moe looked up at the mirror above the sink and smiled.

Sarah's reflection smiled back.

She stuck her tongue out and laughed at how she looked. She knit her eyebrows together and then raised them. She blew her cheeks up and crossed her eyes, and then she laughed. She started crossing her eyes and jumping up and down on the stool.

Her dad's voice came from downstairs. "Are those teeth brushed yet?"

Moe stopped jumping, grabbed her toothbrush off the sink, and started brushing her teeth.

"Use toothpaste," her dad yelled.

Moe sighed, rolled her eyes, ran the tooth brush underwater and brushed some more. She didn't like the taste of the toothpaste her mom got, and she'd told them that she wasn't going to use it. They'd never know.

Moe tapped the toothbrush on the side of the sink, put it back into its holder, and ran to her room. She grabbed the book Harry Potter book off her shelf and laid down in her bed. "Ready!" she yelled.

"Coming," her mother called.

She listened as her mom came up the stairs. It wasn't

like her dad. His steps were loud and stompy. Her mom seemed to float.

"Did you get the book?" her mom asked, as she entered the room.

Moe sighed at the sight of her. She was so beautiful. Sarah liked how her hair fell around her shoulders. Sarah hoped her hair would do that too, someday. Moe held up the book with a grin, and her mother laid down next to her.

"What chapter are we on again?" her mom asked.

"Mo-om. There's a book mark," Moe said, rolling her eyes.

"Oh. Right," he mom said with a smile.

Her mom turned to the middle of the book and began to read. Moe nestled into her side and listened to the words hang in the air. She didn't understand all of them, but she liked lying next to her mom.

When the chapter was over, Moe yawned and turned in the bed. Sarah's mom flicked off the light and gently began to sing while she stroked Moe's hair.

"Tu-ra lu-ra lu-ral. Tu-ra lu-ra lie. Tu-ra lu-ra lu-u-ra. That's an Irish lullaby," her mom finished. She stood and walked slowly to the door. "Good night, beautiful girl," her mother said, like she did every night.

"Good night, mommy," Sarah replied.

"I love you. I'll see you in the morning," her mother said.

"I'll see you in the morning," Sarah replied.

Then her mother disappeared, and Sarah was alone. She closed her eyes.

Moe opened her eyes. She was back in the ice cream shop. Sarah let go of her hand and picked her bear back up. They sat for a moment, silently crying together.

Moe took a deep breath and wiped her eyes with her hand. She wanted to comfort the child and say that everything would be okay, but she knew the worst thing she could do was give Sarah false hope. "I'm sorry," was all Moe could offer.

"I miss them a lot," Sarah said.

"That's good. You should miss them," Moe replied.

Sarah looked up at Moe and asked, "Are you and Ms. Stacie going to catch the people that hurt my mom and took my dad away?"

Tears began to escape Moe's eyes again, and her jaw tightened. This was a promise she knew she could keep. Reaching over to touch Sarah's arm again, she said, "We're going to catch them all. And we're going to make them pay for what they did. I promise."

Sarah nodded and put Mr. Bear back in his chair. She looked at her shoe laces again and then up at Moe. "Thank you," she said.

"For what?" Moe asked.

"For being my friend," Sarah said with a shrug.

"Ms. Stacie and I love you very much," Moe said.

Sarah grinned and shrugged again.

Returning to the table, Stacie noticed the tears in Moe's eyes, and said, "Wow. Looks like you two have been talking about some serious stuff." She placed a tray on the table that contained eight different cups of ice cream.

"That's more than we ordered," Moe said with a laugh.

"Look. We are three strong, beautiful, confident women and one very soft bear. Why would we limit ourselves to just one flavor each? We should eat as much ice cream as we want. We've earned it," Stacie said.

Picking up a spoon and taking a bite of the creamy and rich peanut butter scoop, Moe looked at Stacie and said, "We haven't yet. But we're going to."

CHAPTER THREE

Moe ran her hand across the bar. It was sandy. She did it a second time, letting the grit slide across her palm.

"The sand keeps the bar from getting water rings on it," Ami said, as she took a swig from her beer. Dressed in her standard outfit, a green t-shirt, black sweatpants, and combat boots, Ami had complained the entire trip to the hole-in-the-wall bar that, as the tech expert on the team, she didn't actually have to be here tonight. Moe knew she had come because Moe had asked, and Moe was grateful.

"Well, it just makes it look dirty," Stacie said, also taking a sip of her beer. She grimaced as she swallowed and passed it to Ami. "I've never understood the fascination. What do you think the chances are that the bartender could put together a good martini?"

Moe looked down the dimly lit space at the old man behind the bar. His fingers were covered in band aids, and there were no less than six stains on his flannel shirt. As he wiped his nose with his sleeve, Moe said with a laugh, "I don't think this is a martini kind of place."

Stacie shook her head in frustration and said, "After we do this, you owe me a real drink."

Moe smiled at Stacie and rubbed her back. The ex-actress wasn't just her partner, she was also her best friend, and Moe was happy they were a team. "You got it," Moe said.

There was a celebratory commotion as Johnny Cash's "Cocaine Blues" began to play in the background. Moe turned on her stool to watch the reaction of the room. The dimly lit bar was surprisingly full. Most of the patrons were men who looked weary from a long day's work. There were a few women scattered around. Everyone seemed to be gathered with different groups of friends. Moe was thankful there were so many people around. It made blending in easier.

The door opened, and Moe turned to see Francine enter. The thin professional bodyguard was the only person in the room wearing a suit. Walking to them with military precision, she took the stool next to Stacie, motioned to the bartender for a beer, and said, "Ladies."

"Thanks for coming, Francine. I know you are busy. I appreciate you taking time to help us with this," Moe said.

"Of course. Anything for my favorite people," she said, as she slipped the bartender a twenty and took the beer from him. "When is the mark showing up?" Francine said, as she swiveled in her chair to watch the room.

"His credit card said he's here every Tuesday by 9:30," Ami said, as she finished her beer and started drinking the one Stacie had passed her.

"He's late," Francine said.

"He'll be here," Moe said.

"It would be easier to wait if the location were more up to our standards," Stacie said, tracing a pattern in the sand on the bar.

"Probably better you aren't drinking. You need to be sharp," Francine said in her typically mothering tone.

"Why do you get to drink, and I don't?" Stacie complained.

"My job is safer than yours," Francine said.

"I don't know that that's true," Moe said.

With a genuine look of concern, Stacie turned to Moe and asked, "Are you sure you want to go through with this?"

Her earnestness gave Moe pause. She knew what Stacie meant. Part of what held Moe's world together were her rules. She didn't take cases that would hurt people, she didn't carry a gun, and she didn't take people's memories against their will unless she absolutely had to. Looking down at her drink, Moe said, "The rules aren't set in stone. Desperate times and all that."

"I've got your back. I just don't want you to do something you'll regret," Stacie said.

"This is for Sarah," Moe replied. Saying the six-year-old foster child's name ignited a fire in Moe's chest. She was willing to do whatever it took to catch the men who had kidnapped Sarah's dad.

The door to the bar opened again, and a tall man stepped through. In his trench coat-length leather jacket, his goatee, and his sunglasses, he so matched the stereotype of drug-dealing thug, it almost seemed intentional. Moe's mind raced with the memory of the man standing in Sarah's house, holding down Sarah's dad, as Sarah's mom lay lifeless on the floor of their home. It was a memory Moe had received from the next door neighbor. Through the neighbor's eyes, Moe had watched this man drag Sarah's dad from the house and stuff him in a van. Thankfully, Sarah had been hiding in her closet upstairs when murder of her mother and kidnapping of her father had happened, so the young girl had missed all of it.

Moe's heart raced as images filled her mind of Sarah's mom, lifeless and unmoving, her blood pooling around her head. "That's him," Moe said.

Without turning away from her beer, Ami began to remind the team of the details she'd gathered, "Giovani Corbi. Mid-level thug. Drug dealer – mostly heroine. From his arrest record, it seems like his primary job is driving up to New York, picking up the dope, and driving it back down. Grew up in Brooklynn Park. Dropped out of Ben Franklin High School his junior year. He's been arrested three times, mostly for minor offenses. Over the past fifteen years, he's spent seven on the inside."

Moe looked down at her shoelaces. Wine red had been the right choice. She liked how the silver flecks of glitter sparkled in the dim light as she moved her feet left and right. She felt her confidence building in her chest. They could do this. Tonight, Giovani was going away for a long time. "Everyone knows their job?" Moe asked.

Stacie turned on her stool to face the room. "We got this," she said.

Francine took a long drink of her beer, draining the glass. There was a faint cracking sound as she stretched her neck to the right and then the left. She rolled her shoulders and said, "See you out back." Standing, she marched out the front door.

"Wait for me," Ami said, as she drained the last of Stacie's beer, stood, and followed Francine out.

Moe and Stacie watched as Giovani joined a group of men in the far corner of the room. They celebrated as he sat down at their table, patting him on the back and laughing. Moe figured they were excited about the big score of black-market prescription drugs Ami had arranged online by anonymously putting Giovani into contact with a supplier in Philly. It was a big win for Giovani. He was moving up in the world.

"Remember, you need to get him thinking about the drugs. That way, when I go in, it will be fresh in his mind," Moe said.

"Right. That way you can take what is on top without poking around too much inside," Stacie said.

"Get in. Get out. And you be careful," Moe said.

"Please. My job is easy. You've got the rough part of this," Stacie asked.

"It's for Sarah," Moe reminded herself.

"For Sarah," Stacie said. Turning to the old bartender, she ordered two shots of whiskey. Taking a shot glass in each hand, she said, "Let's do this."

"I'll be right behind you," Moe said.

Stacie took a deep breath, flashed Moe her best seductive smile, stood, and crossed the room to Giovani's table. Putting one of the shot glasses in front of the thug, she toasted with him. They both threw back their shots, and the table cheered. Stacie motioned to the bartender to bring two more, and then she sat in the big man's lap. Watching the thug put his hands on Stacie made Moe's blood boil. While she knew it was all part of the plan, she didn't want that monster anywhere near her friend.

They took another shot. Then another. Then a fourth. Stacie took her time, luring him in. Finally, she leaned into Giovani and whispered something into his ear. The large man grinned with excitement and took his final shot. Stacie stood, took him by the hand, and led him down a hallway that led to the bathrooms and the rear exit of the bar.

Moe leaped to her feet and followed behind them. Turning down the hall, she felt the cool autumn air spilling in from the rear exit. Stacie made eye contact with Moe as she pushed the back door open with her butt and pulled Giovani into the alley with her. The thug was so completely focused on Stacie and the treat he thought he was about to receive that he was taken completely by surprise when Francine shattered his knee with a sharp kick. Before he could do more than grunt in pain, Francine finished her attack with a fierce right cross to his temple. Giovani swayed for a moment, and Moe thought Francine would need to hit him again, but then the huge man slammed to the asphalt.

Moe raced into the alley. Looking up at Stacie, she said, "You good."

"Please, piece of cake," Stacie said.

Ami stepped from the shadows of the alley and began searching Giovani's pockets. Retrieving the large man's phone, she took her own phone from her pocket and connected the two phones with a white cord. "45 seconds to finish the clone," she said.

"Do your thing and let's go," Francine said, looking over Moe's shoulder down the hall.

Moe knelt beside Giovani, placed her hands on his head, closed her eyes, and began to search his memories for the prescription drugs.

Eminem's angry, playful, fast-paced voice filled the car. The bass rattled the windows. Moe recognized the beat as "Lucky You." It was Giovani's favorite. He'd had it on repeat for the last hour. He bounced his head to the beat as he slowed the car and came to a complete stop at the stop sign. The last thing he needed right now was to get pulled over for something stupid, not with what he had in the trunk. This was his come-up. He couldn't screw it up.

The song transitioned to "My Mom." Moe considered switching it back, but Giovani decided that this one was good too. Moe crept the car forward through the intersection. Giovani was so ready to offload this stuff. He didn't like driving around with it. His phone pinged. Taking it out of his pocket, Moe read the message. It was from Big Mike. "Where the F is u. I aint wait here for u all day u said we party."

Moe smiled at the text and wrote back, "be there in 30." Giovani's mouth started to water at the thought of celebrating with everyone tonight. One way or another, he was going to get laid. He deserved it after this score. Moe slowed the car. She was here. Reaching for the visor, she pressed the button on the garage door opener. Three houses up, a garage door sprang to life and began to rise.

This was the moment Moe needed. She looked up and down the street, studying the block. The house was the fifth one on the block. Giovani knew the address was 128 Hilltop Road, but the garage was on the side street Lethbridge Road. It was Giovani's sister's house. She let him use the garage without asking any questions.

Giovani parked the car in front of the open garage. He sighed with relief; he'd made it. Tired of the current song, he pulled up his phone and hit the next button on Spotify. The comic beat of "Just Lose It" rang through the car, and Giovani laughed. It was like Spotify was reading his mind. Giovani had planned to wait to do anything until he got to the bar, but he told himself a bump right now couldn't hurt. Taking a small glass vial from his pocket, Moe screwed the cap off and tapped out a line of white powder on the dashboard. Holding one nostril with her finger, Moe snorted the line with the other. She clenched her teeth as a surge of energy ran through her veins. "Woo!" she screamed as her heart started to race. Giovani loved this feeling.

Jumping out of the car, she ran to the trunk. She looked up and down the street. It was as empty. Best hiding spot ever. No one was ever around. Popping the trunk, he looked at four boxes of pills. He knew each box had fifty vials of pills. His mind raced trying to do the math, but numbers were never his strength. It was the biggest score he'd ever seen. Moe grabbed the first box and jogged into the garage. She laid it in the back corner and snatched a tarp to throw over it. Then she remembered there were three other boxes in the car. She laughed and ran back to the trunk.

Moe pulled out of Giovani's memory. She had what she needed. She tried to stand, but fell backward. She could still feel the cocaine rushing through Giovani's blood. Her head was spinning. The aggressive sound of Eminem's voice rang in her ears.

Francine caught her before she fell. "Are you okay?" she asked.

Stacie came to Moe's other side and put Moe's arm around her neck. "This happens. Sometimes it's hard for her to pull out of the memory," Stacie said.

Moe shook her head and took a deep breath. She tried to push the cloud of the drugs and the bass of the music out of her mind. "The drugs are at 128 Hilltop Road in Brooklyn Park. In the garage around the corner on Lethbridge," she managed.

With her free hand, Stacie pulled her phone from her pocket and dialed. "Detective Mason? Yeah. We got it. You'll find the drugs in a garage in Lethbridge Road. The address of the house is 128 Hilltop Road in Brooklyn Park. Giovani is at a Freddy's Bar off Patapsco. He's in the back alley. Have fun with the bust." Stacie hung up and asked Ami, "You got what you need?"

Ami returned Giovani's phone to his pocket and said, "I'm good."

Moe could feel her blood slowing. The feeling of the cocaine was starting to wear off. She knew the last of the vial was in Giovani's pocket. She started to reach down for it.

"No you don't. Whatever else this guy is carrying, we can leave it for the cops," Stacie said, pulling Moe back up. "Nice work ladies. Let's get out of here. We'll meet back at the office. Help me get her to the car?" Stacie asked Francine.

"She okay?" Francine asked, as she put Moe's arm around the back of her neck.

"This happens when the memory is intense. She can get stuck in it. She'll be fine. She just needs to sleep it off," Stacie explained.

Moe let the two women guide her. Once in the back seat, she closed her eyes and fell asleep to the sounds of Eminem rapping about his mother's drug habit.

CHAPTER FOUR

Moe woke with the sound of Eminem pounding in her ears. She sat up in bed. Her heart was racing. She searched the room for her coat. She was sure there was more in the vial in the pocket. She began searching her sheets, running her hands through them and then tossing them aside. She knew there had to be more somewhere. Standing, she walked across the bedroom to the closet and looked through her clothes. She just needed a bump. Nothing big. Just something to keep the party going. Her heart beat in sync with the sound of "Just Lose It." She ripped through the hangers, throwing clothes to the floor in search of the jacket.

A soft whine caused her to pause. She turned to see Bosley sitting at the foot of her bed, a look of concern in his eyes. The sight of the adorable and loyal mutt helped her remember where she was. This was her and Stacie's bedroom. Her bed was behind her. Stacie's was against the opposing wall. This was her closest. Stacie's was on the other side of the room. The song in her head went silent. There was no coat. There was no cocaine. She didn't actually need a bump. It was just a remnant from the night before.

Moe walked to the bed and sat down. Bosley rested his chin on her lap. Moe took deep breaths in an attempt to slow her heart. She reached down and rubbed the dog's head.

"Good morning. How are you feeling?" Stacie asked from the door of the bedroom. She carried a mug of coffee in each hand.

Moe fell back into bed. "I've got Eminem banging in my brain, and I'm trashing my closet in search of cocaine," she said with a pathetic laugh.

"I turned your alarm off because I was going to let you sleep. Maybe I shouldn't have. I'm sorry," Stacie said, as she sat down next to Moe on the bed.

She handed the mug to Moe, and Moe took a sip. The warm bitterness of the coffee filled her chest and eased her mind. "Thank you for taking care of me," Moe said.

"You were pretty messed up last night. You looked like you were going through withdrawal," Stacie said.

"Giovani did some coke in his memory, which means I'll be doing coke over and over until it clears my head," Moe said, taking another sip of coffee.

Stacie gave her a nervous grin and asked, "Should I check you into recovery or something?"

"No. It's not actually in my system. I've just got the memory of it in my head. It'll fade, and I'll be fine," Moe said.

"Good," Stacie said, standing. "So get dressed. Theo Thalberg texted. He wants us to meet him in two hours for lunch. I'll get an omelet going for you. You need something in your system besides coffee and imaginary drugs," she said, as she walked out of the room.

"You don't have to do that," Moe called, her mouth watering at the thought of one of Stacie's omelets.

"What do you want in it?" Stacie replied from the kitchen.

"Ham, cheese, and mushrooms," Moe yelled back.

"I'm on it," Stacie said.

Reaching over to her bedside table, Moe picked up her phone and turned on "I Wish" by Stevie Wonder. The base line ran through the Bluetooth speakers that were positioned around their apartment/office. "Thank you, Ami," Moe said, as she bopped to the beat.

"The Will Smith version is better," Stacie yelled from the kitchen.

"No. It's not," Moe called back as she walked to the bathroom.

She gave herself extra time in the shower, letting the warm water run over her face after she shampooed, conditioned, and detangled her hair. As she dried it, she decided to go with a half-up-half-down. Using hair ties, she separated the back of her hair from the front and brushed the small hairs at her scalp. Using both hands, she worked the front section of her hair into a ball. She then let the back half of her hair fall free. Shaking it, she fluffed until it had more volume.

Happy with how her hair looked, Moe took the last step in her routine. Looking to the top right corner of her mirror where a picture of her mother, father, and four brothers was taped, Moe read the mantra typed at the bottom, "Your name is Moneta Watkins. Daughter of Amar and Rashida. Sister to Robert, Joseph, Calvin, and Lance. You grew up happy and strong. Remember the love. Remember the joy. Because no matter what is in your head, this is your story." With each word she felt the memory of the cocaine, and the boxes of pills in the trunk of Giovani's car, and the sound of Eminem fade away.

Looking in her closet, she decided to go with her t-shirt that displayed the logo of her favorite D.C. Comics villain, the Reverse Flash. The burnt yellow shirt with its black circle and red lightening blot in the center just felt right. She pulled it from the hanger and slid it on. After pulling on her jeans and putting on her shoes, she stepped into their living room.

While Moe had been in the shower, Stacie had changed the music to a sad Adele song. Sitting down at their small round kitchen table, Moe asked, "What happened to Stevie?"

Ignoring the question, Stacie set a perfectly constructed omelet in front of Moe and said, "Eat."

Moe took a bite. The eggs were fluffy, the cheese was melted but not gooey, and Stacie had seared the ham before hiding it in the middle. "Oh, this is perfect," Moe said.

"Speaking of perfect," Stacie said, as she took a step back to look at Moe and then ran into the bedroom. She returned with a dark grey blazer. The deep red threads running through it gave the garment a rich and unexpected visual appeal. "Put this on," Stacie said, passing it to Moe.

"I'm good," Moe said.

Stacie thrust the blazer forward and demanded, "Trust me."

Moe sighed, took another bite of the omelet, and grabbed the blazer. Sliding it on, she was surprised at how well it fit and how nicely it matched her t-shirt.

"You look marvelous, darling," Stacie said in her best aristocratic accent.

Moe laughed. "You know what, because you brought me coffee in bed and made me the perfect omelet, I'll do whatever you tell me to. Even wear a jacket."

"First off, it's not a jacket. It's a Tagliatore Farfetch blazer hand-crafted in Italy. Second, if I had known eggs had that kind of power over you, I would have started dressing you a long time ago," Stacie quipped as she sat down across from Moe and took a sip of her coffee.

"You love my wardrobe," Moe teased.

"No. I do not. If I make you another omelet, can I throw away half of your t-shirts?"

"Don't you even joke about that," Moe said, pointing her fork at Stacie.

She wolfed down the last bite of her omelet, took a quick sip of coffee, stood, and grabbed Bosley's leash off the kitchen counter. The dog responded by running to the office door.

"After you catch a glimpse of yourself in that blazer, you'll change your mind," Stacie said, sipping from her coffee.

"Not a chance," Moe called, as she and Bosley bounded down the steps.

Moe pushed open the front door to the building and sunlight splashed against her face. It was a surprisingly warm day for Baltimore in the fall. To the left of the door, Moe found Mr. Hudson, her landlord and the occupant of the first floor apartment. The heavyset old man was sitting on bench, cracking pecans with his bare hands just like he had every day that Moe had lived in the building.

"Good morning, Mr. Hudson," Moe said with a grin.

He grunted in reply as he roughly rubbed Bosley's head.

"Anything exciting happening in the hood this morning?" Moe asked.

"Nope. Normal day," Mr. Hudson said. He cracked another nut in his hand, pulled the shell away, dropped them on the ground, and then handed the meat to Moe.

"Thanks," Moe said, popping the nut in her mouth.

"What do you have planned for today?" Mr. Hudson asked.

"Well, I'm going to let Bosley pee on that tree over

there," Moe said motioning to the park across the street. "Then Stacie and I are going to meet with a new client. Then, we are going to join Robert, my oldest brother who happens to be with the FBI, and talk with a judge who is losing his mind. You?"

Mr. Hudson nudged the brown grocery bag next to him and said, "I'm going to sit here and eat this bag of nuts."

"Then what?" Moe asked.

"You mean if I finish them?" he asked.

"Yep," she confirmed, tugging the impatient dog who was now pulling on the leash in hopes of dragging Moe across the street.

"I guess I'll go inside and get some more," Mr. Hudson said.

"Sounds like we both have exciting days ahead of us," Moe said.

Mr. Hudson cracked another nut in his hand and said, "Mine sounds like more fun."

Moe laughed as she gave in and let Bosley lead her across the street.

CHAPTER FIVE

The restaurant wasn't much to look at. If Moe had blinked, she would have missed it. Located in the downtown section of the northern suburb of Towson, The Most Amazing Seafood was located in a strip of stores a block south from a huge mall.

"Are you sure this is where Thalberg wanted to meet?" Moe asked Stacie as she pulled the car into a parallel parking spot. The size and depth of the large store front window of The Most Amazing Seafood looked more suited to a pet store than a restaurant. There wasn't a flashy sign or decorative chalkboard out front. There was simply a banner along the top of the door that displayed the restaurant's name. The street was filled with bars and novelty shops designed to attract college students from the university down the street. The establishment was jammed between a temporary looking vape store and a weird looking shop simply called "Sports." This restaurant felt out of place, and Moe couldn't fathom what about it would catch the eye of a billionaire philanthropist like Theo Thalberg.

"This is the spot. I looked it up online while you were sleeping. It's got really good ratings," Stacie said, as she got out of the car.

"This is putting the phrase 'a diamond in the rough' to the test," Moe replied with a smirk.

In contrast to its exterior, the interior was a charming and intimate setting. The establishment consisted of four tables, each with four chairs around them. On the far side of the room was a cart filled with various fish and crabs laying on ice. Theo Thalberg and two women sat at the table to the right. Theo was dressed in light blue pants and a pink polo. The older woman wore a distinguished looking pantsuit, while the younger was dressed in plain black dress.

"Moe. Stacie. Come and join us," Theo called with a smile. Moe returned the warmth. She was happy to see Theo again. It was rare that she got a repeat customer. Few people had more than one mystery in life to solve, but Mr. Thalberg had so much money, Moe figured he could afford as many whodunits as he wanted.

Moe and Stacie crossed the room together and began shaking hands. First to speak, Moe said, "I'm Moneta Watkins. This is my partner, Stacie Howe."

"Dorothy Lumpum with Lumpum and Brumtum," the older woman said.

"Nice to meet you," Stacie offered.

The younger woman shook hands but said nothing.

"Take a seat. What would you like to drink?" Theo asked.

"Just a water," Moe said, pulling out a chair and sitting down.

"Sprite for me," Stacie said, taking a seat.

"PJ?" Theo called.

An older man dressed in an apron appeared through a door in the back of the restaurant. "You know what you want yet?" he asked.

"Not yet. Could my friends get a water and a Sprite?" he asked.

"Sure thing," the chef said, as he disappeared to the back.

"You're in for a treat. PJ is the best seafood chef in Maryland. Without question," Theo said.

The chef appeared with a glass of water and a can of soda. Placing it on the table, he asked, "Y'all want to pick out your fish?"

"We just pick it out?" Stacie asked, clearly charmed by the idea.

PJ recited a saying Moe felt like he had likely repeated a thousand times, "Take a look at the buffet. It's all fresh. I go down to the dock every morning. What they've got, I buy. They don't have it, I can't cook it. What you see is what I got. You pick it. I'll cook it."

"Would you mind if I order for everyone?" Theo asked.

Moe offered a shrug, a nod, and a smile.

Stacie said, "Sure."

"That's fine," Dorothy said.

The woman in black, whose name Moe still didn't know, remained silent.

"Excellent. We'll take the Bluegills. Fried and stuffed with the crab," Theo said.

"Like you always get them," PJ interrupted.

Theo continued as if PJ hadn't said a thing. "With sides of broccoli, asparagus, and..."

PJ cut in again, finishing Theo's sentence. "And mac-n-cheese. I made a batch for you this morning when I found out you were coming in."

"You know me so well," Theo said.

"I'll get started on it," PJ said, as he walked back to the kitchen.

31

"The whole place is just him?" Stacie asked.

"It is," Theo said with an excited grin.

Changing the subject, Moe turned to the woman in black and said, "I'm sorry. I haven't gotten your name yet."

"I'm so sorry. I got so excited about the food, I forgot to introduce you. This is Katie Scrasdale. She is the person I brought you here to meet," Theo said.

"It's nice to meet you," Moe said.

"Nice to meet you too. Although I wish it were under better circumstances," Katie said.

"What can we do for you?" Stacie asked.

Dorothy leaned forward, placing her elbows on the table. "We have a problem, and Theo thinks you might be able to help. My firm specializes in overturning wrongful convictions. Ms. Scrasdale's fiancé, Malcom Sennack, is currently wrongfully imprisoned for a murder charge."

Katie looked down at the sound of her fiancé's name.

Without pause, Dorothy continued, "If we are going to get a new trial, we need new evidence."

"That's where I was hoping you could help," Theo said.

"So far, my firm hasn't come up with anything substantial enough to challenge the conviction, but Theo assures me that you have connections and methods I don't," Dorothy said.

"Please. Please, help us," Katie blurted out. The second the words escaped her lips, tears began to form in her eyes. She wiped them away and looked down into her lap.

"I can't imagine how difficult this is for you," Moe said.

"Would you mind telling us what happened?" Stacie asked.

Theo and Dorothy both waited for Katie to speak.

When she didn't, Theo stepped in. "I've known Katie for most of her life. He father was a fraternity brother in college, and we've kept in touch since. I came to the hospital with Katie was born, so when Katie started dating a man who was launching a nonprofit, I of course got involved. And everything was going well. Malcom is incredibly intelligent and ambitious. He had big plans. The boy was a visionary."

"Thank you," Katie said quietly.

"He is a great man," Dorothy said, reaching across the table to pat Katie's hand. Moe could tell by the firmness of Katie's chin that she was trying not to cry.

Chef PJ quietly put a basket of assorted rolls and drinks on the table and then disappeared to the kitchen.

Theo took a sip of his water and continued: "I was immediately attracted to the boy because of his story. He hadn't had an easy road. He grew up in on the east side of the city in a poor neighborhood. Went to public schools. Had a few run-ins with the law when he was a teenager – nothing big, just typical teenage shoplifting and fighting. But he overcame all of that, graduated from Hopkins with a business degree, and started working to make his city a better place. I first met him at a fundraiser Katie invited me to. I think it was at the Waterfront Marriot? Or maybe Martin's North? I can't remember."

Interrupting, Dorothy said, "Two months ago, Malcom went to meet with his real estate agent, Charlie Michaels. When he arrived, he found the agent laying on the ground, near dead, stabbed multiple times. Malcom checked Charlie's pulse and then went to call for help, but as he stepped out of the office, cop cars surrounded the building. They had gotten a call from the office next door claiming they had seen Malcom running into the office angry and screaming. Even though they didn't find the murder weapon, the police believed they'd caught the killer in the act. A young man with blood on his hands was all the proof they needed. The trial was quick. I was not Malcom's representation then. His lawyer botched the defense, thinking the absence of a murder weapon would make it an easy case, but the jury didn't need a weapon. Malcom got twenty-years with possible parole in five."

"That's horrific," Stacie said.

"We'd like to meet him," Moe said.

"I knew you would. I told her you'd want to talk to him and do your thing," Theo said with a smile.

"I can get you a visit," Dorothy said.

"You said he was working to make the city a better place. Could you tell us more about that?" Stacie asked. Moe grinned at her partner. She loved that Stacie was already searching for leads.

Katie looked up and with a tentative voice she said, "Malcom built a mentoring program for men coming out of prison. It's called the Resurrected Tribe. The program provides men a place to live, vocational counseling, GED services, and a healthy community for accountability as they transition back into society. Malcom's dad spent almost all of Malcom's childhood behind bars. There are currently more than a hundred and fifty men in the program."

"And it gets bigger every month," Theo added.

"We were about to get married. We were two months away from our wedding day when they took him away," Katie said looking down into her lap again. "I wanted to go ahead with the ceremony while he was out on bail, but Malcom said he didn't want this to taint our wedding day. He was so sure they wouldn't convict him. He thought we should just hold off until everything had passed, but then the verdict was... The jury came back with a..." The words got stuck in Katie's throat as her eyes welled up with tears again.

"Don't lose faith. We're going to get him out," Dorothy said, as she put her arm around Katie's shoulder.

Chef PJ appeared with a tray carrying four plates, each holding a fried fish stuffed to overflowing with crab meat. He placed a fish in front of each of the members of the table and then laid down two platters of vegetables and a large bowl of mac-n-cheese.

Moe glanced down at the food. While it smelled and looked amazing, it felt weird to eat with such a heavy topic on the table for discussion.

Theo took up his knife and fork and cut into the fish in front of him. "We want to hire you to find new evidence that will allow us to open a new case. I'll double the fee I paid you before," Theo said.

Stacie glanced at Moe, and Moe nodded.

"Of course we'll take the case," Stacie said.

A spark of relief appeared in Katie's eyes. "Thank you. Thank you so much," she said.

Theo took a bite of the crab meat spilling from his fish. "Amazing," he said to himself as he savored the bite. Then he called to the chef who had disappeared in the back, "PJ! It's amazing!" Looking at Moe, he asked, "When can you start?"

"Right now," Moe said.

"Do you have any idea who might want to frame him?" Stacie asked.

"No one. Everyone loves Malcom," Katie said.

Dorothy smiled and passed a thumb drive to Moe. "It's good to have you on the team. My office has made copies of all the files we've collected, including the transcript of trial and transcripts of the interviews we've done. You'll find them all on this drive," she said.

"Thank you," Moe said, tucking the drive in the pocket of the blazer Stacie had forced her to wear.

Dorothy spread her napkin across her lap and added,

"I'll need regular updates from you. Anything you find will need to come to me right way. While you beat the streets, my office will continue to look for grounds for appeals."

Moe glanced at Theo, who said through a mouth full of fish, "I'm buying, but Dorothy is running the show."

"We'll let you know what we find," Moe said.

"Okay. Enough shop talk. Moe and Stacie can read the files and go from there. You all need to get into this crab before it goes cold," Theo said with a smile.

Taking up her glass of water, Katie held it high and, with a stiff upper lip, said, "A toast. To Malcom. May he come home soon."

Moe took up her glass and touched it to Katie's, "To Malcom's freedom."

"To Malcom!" Theo, Stacie, and Dorothy joined in.

CHAPTER SIX

Dressed in a perfectly tailored black suit with a red tie, Robert, Moe's oldest brother, looked like he'd just materialized from an advertising campaign for the FBI. As he stepped from his car, Stacie sighed. "He is just a beautiful man," she said.

Moe elbowed her and replied, "Gross. Stop ogling my brother."

"There's just so much there to ogle," Stacie laughed under her breath.

Moe pointed her finger in Stacie's face and said, "No. I mean it."

"Ladies," Robert said, as he walked to meet them.

"Robby," Moe said, using his childhood nickname because she knew he hated it.

"Moe, you look amazing. I expected you to be in your standard 'I just threw this on' t-shirt and jeans. The jacket is a nice touch," he said.

"I think she looks amazing in everything she wears," Stacie chimed in with a grin, not missing a chance to come to her friend's defense.

"You clean up well, Moe. You should do it more often," Robert retorted.

"So, are we going inside?" Moe said, motioning to the house in front of them. The colonial looking home was smashed between two houses with a more Bavarian style. Home to professors, doctors, and other highly educated members of society, the Guilford neighborhood was on the northern side of Baltimore, just above the Johns Hopkins undergrad campus. The community was known for its curving streets, lack of driveways, and the way its huge houses were jammed next to each other with almost no yard.

"Let's do it," Stacie said, bouncing up the walk ahead of them.

A grey-haired woman with mousy features and large glasses answered the door. "Can I help you?" she asked.

"Yes, ma'am. I'm Federal Agent Robert Watkins. I called yesterday?" Robert said, flashing his badge.

The woman's eyes widened with excitement and anticipation. "Oh yes! We've been expecting you! Please, come in," she said, motioning them into the house.

As Moe and Stacie followed Robert in through the entry hall to the kitchen, Robert said, "I appreciate you seeing us. I heard about your husband's retirement and needed to see it for myself."

"Well, he's out in the garden right now. Take a seat and I'll go get him," the grey-haired woman said, as she stepped past the kitchen table to a sliding door that led to a small back yard.

Moe, Stacie, and Robert all took seats at the kitchen table. "You sure this is connected to Lance?" Moe asked.

Lance, Moe's twin, had reappeared in town a few weeks ago after a long absence. While Moe's gift allowed her to relive memories, Lance's gave him the power to erase them, making him incredibly powerful and dangerous. Where ever Lance went, trouble followed, which is why Moe, Robert, and their other two brothers knew they needed to find Lance as quickly as possible and put a stop to whatever he was up to.

"That's why I asked you to come. It sounded like his handiwork to me, but it's hard to tell," Robert said.

"How did you find out about this? Do you know him or something?" Stacie asked, as she peered out the back window. The thin and dignified woman was talking with a man in blue jeans who was kneeling in a small garden.

"Judge William Marcus was my constitutional law professor in law school. Brilliant teacher. He had an encyclopedic memory of cases and decisions. It was like talking to a living Wikipedia of the law. That was before he became a judge and before I joined the bureau," Robert explained.

Robert stood when the back door opened, so Moe and Stacie followed suit. A silver haired man in blue jeans and a soil stained t-shirt entered the dining room. His wife followed behind him.

"Robert!" the man proclaimed with pleasure.

"Judge," Robert said.

"Not anymore," Judge Marcus said with a grin. "I assume you met Angie?"

"I'm sorry. With Bill's illness, I've been so distracted. I'm Angie, Bill's wife," the kind but troubled woman said, as shook Robert's hand.

"I'm not sick," the judge interjected. He motioned for everyone to take a seat at the long dining room table.

"It's nice to meet you," Robert said. Motioning to Moe and Stacie, he added, "This is my little sister, Moe, and her friend, Stacie. They are private investigators of sorts."

Moe reflexively frowned at the description, but she recovered quickly. As Moe sat down at the table, she couldn't help but notice how the chair creaked beneath her revealing the furniture's age. Taking a quick glance around the room, it appeared most of the Bill and Angie's furnishing were antiques.

"Can I get you something to drink? Or something to eat? Is it lunchtime yet?" Angie asked, looking at the clock. "Oh my, seems we've missed lunch," she added after seeing the time. Jumping up from the table, she moved across the room to the kitchen and began digging through a tall cupboard.

"I'm fine, thank you," Moe called.

"Me too. I'm good," Stacie added.

"So, Robert. What brings you here? I can't help you with a case. I'm retired," the judge said, as he took a seat.

"I heard you retired, and it felt early to me. I just wanted to make sure everything was alright," Robert said.

"Sorry to disappoint, but everything is fine. It was just time," the judge said.

Angie placed a plate of assorted cheeses and crackers on the table and said under her breath, "Now, Bill. Don't lie."

"What? I'm not lying," the judge replied, folding his arms across his chest.

"I heard you stepped down in the middle of a murder trial?" Robert probed.

"Yep. I was sad I couldn't finish it, but it was time," the judge said.

Angie grunted disapproval from the kitchen as she finished filling glasses of water.

Moe reached forward, grabbed a piece of Gouda, and popped it in her mouth. It was the expensive stuff, cold and creamy at the same time.

"But why in the middle of a trial? You always told us in class that no matter what happened, we had to see a case through to the end. That justice demanded it," Robert said.

"I did see it to the end. The end of my career," the judge said with a grin.

"You just don't seem old enough to retire yet. You could probably have another decade on the bench if you wanted it," Moe added.

As the judge positioned a slice of cheese between two crackers, he said, "Again, I'm sorry to disappoint you, but that's the thing. I didn't want another decade on the bench. I want to garden, and eat crackers and cheese, and binge watch TV. I can't tell you how many shows I've missed while I was working. So many good things to watch. I just started Game of Thrones. Have you watched it?"

Robert leaned back in his chair and folded his arms across his chest. "No," he replied.

As Angie placed small glasses of water in front of everyone at the table and then took a seat, she said, "Bill, this man is with the FBI. Isn't lying to the FBI a crime?"

The judge ate another cracker and said, "It's up for debate since this is a social call, but it doesn't matter because I'm not lying."

"We don't mean to pry, sir," Stacie urged with a warm smile. "We're investigating a criminal who has a history of erasing his victim's memories. We were hoping your retirement might give us some clues to his whereabouts."

"I'm sorry. I wouldn't know anything about that," the judge said.

"Bill!" Angie protested.

"What, dear? I said I wouldn't know anything about that," the judge snapped back.

"You can't hide it forever. Maybe they can help?" his wife replied, rubbing his arm.

The judge pulled away. "I don't need any help," he said.

"Judge Marcus, we need to catch this guy. We promise, whatever you tell us will stay with us," Robert said.

"It's good you went to the FBI, Robert. If I remember right, you were a less than average student," the judge said, leaning back in his chair.

"You were a tough teacher," Robert replied with a sheepish grin.

"If my memory serves, you received a C in my class. Isn't that correct?" Judge Marcus said.

"That's right," Robert said with a sigh.

"More interested in the attractive female students in the room than the beauty of the law."

"That sounds like me," Robert replied.

"You see, my memory is fine," the judge said with an air of victory. He popped another cracker and slice of cheese into his mouth.

"I did love your class. You were one of my favorite professors," Robert said with defeat.

"I wish I could be of more help. I'm sorry. I'm just a retired old man now," the judge said.

"You're a stubborn crotchety old jerk is what you are," Angie said under her breath but loud enough for everyone to hear.

"What's the standard penalty to lying to a federal law enforcement agent who is in the midst of a federal investigation?" Moe asked to confirm her suspicion.

Everyone at the table looked at Judge Marcus. He took another cracker from the tray and ate it.

"Judge?" Moe asked.

"Well, I don't know why you'd expect me to know that off the top of my head," the judge said.

"It's five years," Robert said.

"You must have tried hundreds of murder cases in Baltimore. What's the standard sentence for manslaughter in Maryland?" Moe asked.

"Am I being tested? Are you trying to test me? I was a judge longer than you've been driving," the Judge said, placing both hands on the table.

"Then you should know this, sir," Moe said.

"I don't have to play your games. I won't lower myself to senseless challenges. Besides, that's the type of statistic those of us who practice law look up when we need it. We don't just carry it in our heads. Why would we?" the Judge declared.

"Imprisonment for no more than ten years under the Maryland Criminal Code section 2-207," Robert said with a frown.

"Last chance, Bill. Either you tell them, or I will," Angie said.

"Fine. Fine. I just… I just don't want to talk about it," the judge said. He took a sip of his water as the whole table waited. Putting his glass down, he looked off into space, sighed, and said, "My memory is mostly fine. I've got everything, except… I can't remember anything about the law."

"The doctors thought it would be some kind of strange rapid-onset dementia," Angie added as she leaned forward to rub his back.

"But it's not. I'm fine. My mind is still sharp as a tack. I can tell you everything about today, and yesterday, and the day before. I can tell you that Robert was a horrible flirt when he was a student in my class. I can remember the day I met Angie and the blue dress she was wearing. I'm not hallucinating, hearing voices, or having problems reading clocks. My brain is fine," the judge said defensively.

"You don't need to lie about it, Bill. No one thinks less of you," Angie said.

"What's a judge worth who doesn't remember the

law," he said.

"I'm sorry, sir," Robert said.

"I don't want to talk about it. I retired. That's all there is to it," the judge said. There was a sorrowful look in his eyes that Moe recognized. It was the look of someone who'd lost something that no amount of searching would bring back. It was the look her brother Lance left in the eyes of every person he encountered.

"It's just your knowledge of the law?" Robert asked.

The judge looked down and said, "It's just my knowledge of the law."

"Would you mind describing the moment you knew it was gone?" Moe asked.

"They may be able to catch the person who did this to you," his wife urged.

"Fine. Fine," the judge said with a sigh. He took another drink before answering. "I had called a recess in the trial I was overseeing so I could review some new evidence submitted by the defense. I walked back to my private quarters. Then, the next thing I remember, I was sitting at my desk, all by myself, with this note in my hands. It's in my hand writing." The judge reached in his pocket and withdrew a small, folded piece of paper. He passed it to Robert. Robert read it and passed it to Stacie, who read it and passed it to Moe.

In crisp handwriting, the note read, "I had a choice. Forget or die. I chose to forget."

CHAPTER SEVEN

Moe sat on the couch facing the wall in the apartment that she and Stacie had decided to use as a work space. Bosley's head rested in her lap. She stroked the dog as she pondered the cases they were working on. The smooth sound of Janelle Monet's "I Like That" played through the speaker system. Moe had divided the wall into four columns with red yarn. Each column represented a case she and Stacie were currently working on.

The first column had five pictures in it, each one hung on the wall with clear thumbtacks. The top picture was of Sarah. Under the girl's picture were pictures of the four men a sketch artist had drawn based on Moe's memory. Through a neighbor's memories, Moe had witnessed the crew kill Sarah's mother and kidnap Sarah's father. Ami had been able to put names to three of the four men. Moe had drawn a black X through the face of Giovani Corbi since he was currently in jail and awaiting trial. Next to Giovani was a picture of Antonio Bainchi, a thick-necked low-level thug like Giovani. Next to Antonio was Damon Santobello, a thin, hook-nosed man that Moe currently had under observation. The final picture had a post-it note with a question mark in the top right corner. The shorter, rounder man had a goatee and wore glasses. Stacie had resorted to calling him "Three-Scar" because of the small scar above his right eye, the cut through the left side of his lip, and a third old gash that crossed the right side of his neck.

In the second column on the wall, there was a picture of Lance leaving the apartment. Moe's landlord, Mr. Hudson, had snapped it with a camera hidden on the roof of the building across the street. Under Lance's picture was a news clipping announcing Judge Marcus's retirement.

The third and the fourth column were both lacking in details. In the third column was a picture of Malcom Sennack and a single news clipping that described his trial. In the fourth column was a picture of Bruce Spiniker, the wealthy spoiled brat who had taken advantage of Stacie when she was in her early twenties, at the end of her acting career, and desperate to be acknowledged by someone. Bruce wasn't an official case yet, but Stacie had insisted his picture go on the wall just in case something came up they could use to put him in prison.

Stacie handed Moe a plate and joined her on the couch. Curls of steam rose off the broccoli, rice, and chicken dish Stacie had thrown together. "Thanks," Moe said.

Stacie took a bite from her plate and chased it with a sip from her glass of wine. "Gotta feed my girl," she said.

Moe reached forward, took her beer from the coffee table, and held it out to Stacie for a toast.

"To making all the bad guys pay," Stacie said, as she clinked her glass to Moe's bottle.

Moe took a swig. Looking at the wall, she said,

"We've got a lot of work ahead of us."

Swallowing a second bite, Stacie replied, "We've got this. Easy-peasy."

Moe took a bite of the rice concoction and was caught off guard by the smooth and tangy combination of soy sauce, orange zest, and butter. It took a minute to understand, but once it settled in, she liked it. "Nice," she said.

"I've got skills," Stacie replied with a grin.

A loud boom echoed through the room, causing Moe to jump and spill her beer. To both her and Stacie's surprise, the music in the apartment shifted to a heavy bass beat that shook the windows. It was joined by menacing trumpets. Moe jumped up and headed to the kitchen to get a towel to clean up her spill. "Did you turn this on?"

Stacie, matching Moe's shock, stood and said, "It wasn't me. I've never even heard this song before." She began searching for her to phone to see if she could change the tune.

A chorus of rappers filled the room, screaming about starting a riot. Stacie snatched her phone and began pushing buttons. Dropping to her hands and knees, Moe cleaned up her spill.

There was movement at the door that stopped both of them in their tracks. As the chorus hit a crescendo, the door flung open and Ami stepped through. Dancing to the music, she said, "What's up, bitches?"

"Of course we have you to think for this racket," Stacie said, rolling her eyes.

Ami pressed a button on the screen of her phone, and the music returned to its former calm. "What? A girl can't make an entrance?"

"Thanks for coming, and maybe next time go more happy and 'glad to see you' and less terrifying and 'prepare for battle' with the theme song," Moe said with a smile.

Ami walked to the kitchen and took a beer out of the fridge. "I will not be tamed," she said, as she popped the cap off on the counter. Walking over to the couch, she took a seat next to Moe. "Plus, it's from 'Spiderman Into the Spiderverse.' Who didn't love that movie? It's amazing. You should thank me for reminding you that it is a thing that exists in the world."

"Thank you?" Stacie said, as she took the spot next to Ami.

"You're welcome," Ami replied.

"I don't watch cartoons," Moe said.

"Yet, you know it's a cartoon," Ami replied.

"And you have a closet full of comic book themed t-shirts," Stacie replied.

"So, what'd you bring us?" Moe asked with a grin.

"Nope. Payment first," Ami said, holding out her hand and closing her eyes. Ami always demanded to be compensated with an entertaining memory Moe had collected.

Moe sighed and asked, "Fine, what do you want to see?"

"Oo! Me too!" Stacie declared with glee as she jumped up and moved to the other side of Moe. She also held out her hand and closed her eyes. "Make it something beautiful," she said.

"Hey! My payment, my pick," Ami complained.

"Fine. Just don't do scary. I don't need scary tonight," Stacie said.

"I'll ask for what I ask for," Ami retorted.

"You're like little children," Moe said, shaking her head. She took another sip of her beer, refusing to take the hands of her two friends until she absolutely had to.

"Okay. Not scary," Ami said, thinking. She and Stacie

still had their hands extended and their eyes closed.

"And nothing suspenseful either. And nothing like a roller coaster, because I just ate," Stacie said.

"Alright, princess. Ease back," Ami complained.

"And nothing where someone dies," Stacie added.

"Look, it's my pick," Ami asserted.

"Well, pick then," Stacie retorted.

"Fine. Not scary. Not suspenseful. No one dies. Well, then, I guess I want something heartwarming," Ami decided.

"Oo. That's good. That's what we need tonight. Some of that Hallmark channel stuff," Stacie affirmed. She sounded like a little kid who'd just been offered a cupcake.

"I'm not Netflix. I can't just conjure whatever content you want," Moe said.

Ami opened her eyes and cocked her head at Moe. "Then I can't tell you what I found out about all this mess on your wall," she threatened.

Stacie, her eyes still closed and her hand still extended in expectation said, "She'll do it. She just needs to complain a little first."

Ami closed her eyes and held her hand out again. "I demand something heartwarming," she said.

Moe looked at her two friends. They were lucky she loved them both as much as she did. She took their hands and said, "You two are ridiculous." Closing her eyes, she searched for the feeling in her mind. It took a bit. Heartwarming wasn't exactly something that came easily. After a minute, she found one they'd like. She pushed into the memory, bringing them along with her.

The wind blew across her face. The coolness of fall was coming on. Sweaters and jackets would be broken out of storage soon, and she couldn't wait. She liked the warm feeling of being wrapped in layers.

"What are we doing here?" Lance said, as he kicked at the dirt. Mom had to fight to get him away from his video game. He'd complained the whole way home about it being new and how he'd just reached a new level and how Calvin was going to ruin it. Moe understood. Being the youngest, it was rare that they got things that were just theirs. With Joseph and Calvin at football camp and dad having taken Robert back to college to get him moved into the sophomore door, the quiet house had been an unusual treat in the final weeks of summer. Moe had spent most her time reading and riding her bike, and Lance had been tied to the video game system he almost never got to use alone.

"We're here to help someone," their mother said with a smile.

Moe looked around. They'd driven twenty minutes outside of the city only to pull up to a McDonalds. Moe could see a few workers inside, chatting behind the counter, but besides them, the place was completely empty. On the drive there, every time she'd asked mom where they were going, her mother had said they were going to someone who needed help. After the third ask, Moe had given up. She knew that if her mother didn't want to tell her, there was no use in pushing the matter.

"You couldn't have just brought Moe to help? She likes to help. Why'd you have to drag me out here?" Lance complained.

"You'll see," their mother said in her all-knowing voice. It's the voice she used when she'd tapped into her gift. Moe's mom didn't see the future exactly. It was more like she saw versions of possible futures and how likely they were to happen. It was painfully annoying. How do you keep secrets like a normal middle school girl or have any life of your own when your mom could predict the future? "Don't wear that skirt today or the

50

boys will whisper about you in Mr. Ludwin's class." Or, "You need to study for another hour. Right now you're only going to get a C plus on that test." Or, "I don't want to hear that you were chatting in Mr. Hiser's classroom this afternoon. When your little friend Christi asks you about that show, you just tell her you need to focus." Moe hated it.

She looked at Lance. He was still looking down and kicking at the dirt. She felt bad for him. Of all of the siblings, he'd struggled the most with his gift. He couldn't seem to find the right time to use it. Every time he did, he seemed to mess it up, taking things from people they didn't want to lose. He'd tried to help a friend forget the soccer game they'd just lost and instead erased their ability to dribble. He'd tried to help their next door neighbor forget about mowing the lawn so they wouldn't be stressed about it, but instead he'd caused them to forget how to start a lawnmower. He'd tried to make a teacher forget that he hadn't turned in his homework, and erased her memory of the whole class. It had been a rough few months for her brother.

"Okay, here we go," their mom said with excitement, as a big white van pulled into the parking lot.

Moe watched as kids unloaded and went into the McDonalds. They looked like normal teenagers. There was one adult supervising. She wondered where they were coming from.

"They're on a church trip," her mother said before she could ask, which drove Moe crazy.

The kids were loud and laughing and joking with each other. They filed into the fast-food joint and lined up at the counter to put in their orders. The adult with them followed behind. He looked tired.

"Here's your chance," he mother said nodding to the van.

"What do you mean?' Moe asked, confused.

"Not you, dear. Lance. Here's your chance to use your gift to help someone," she said.

"Who?" Moe asked, looking at the long line of kids at the counter.

"Her," Lance said, motioning to the van.

Exiting from the van after all the other kids were gone was a short squatty girl. Her hair was cut into the shape of a bowl. There was something different about the way she moved. It was clunky and clumsy. Her eyes were slanted, her nose was flat, and a little bit of her tongue stuck out from her mouth.

"What's wrong with her?" Moe said.

"She has Down syndrome," he mother said with a warm smile. "Go and talk to her Lance. She could use your help," she added.

"What am I supposed to do?" Lance said, still looking at the ground.

"You'll know when you talk to her," mom said.

"This is stupid. I don't even know her," he protested.

"She won't care," their mom encouraged.

"I'm just going to mess it up," Lance said.

"Trust me," their mom urged.

"I can't do it," Lance said, stuffing his hands in his pockets.

Their mother turned, bent down, and looked Lance in the eyes. Touching his cheek, she said, "You need to understand that your gift is just a beautiful as everyone else's in the family and that it can help people too, if you choose to use it in the right way."

Lance sighed and looked at Moe for help. She smile back, silently telling him he might as well go for it because there was no telling mom no.

Hugging him, their mom said, "Your gift is beautiful, and you are amazing. You can do this. I know you can."

She let go, took a step back, said, "Now, go on."

Lance took a deep breath and trudged across the street. Moe hoped her mother was right and this would go as she expected. It didn't happen often, but on occasion, the outcome her mother was sure was going to happen, didn't. What if Lance made this poor girl forget her name or something? Moe knew he'd never forgive himself.

He crossed the parking lot, held out his hand, and introduced himself. Moe watched as the girl motioned to her arm and talked to him. She looked away from him and nodded her head as she spoke.

Lance looked back at their mother nervously.

"You got this, baby. Go for it!" she yelled back.

Moe watched as Lance touched the girl's hand and closed his eyes.

A few seconds later, the young girl grabbed him and gave him a big hug. "Thank you. Thank you," she said with a huge smile. Lance hugged her and then turned to run back across the street. Moe's heart filled with warmth at the site of his monstrous grin.

"What'd you do?" she asked when he came back.

"She'd gotten a shot this morning from her doctor and it really hurt. She couldn't enjoy the trip she's on because she couldn't stop thinking about it. So, I took her memory of it and it stopped hurting," Lance said.

Moe's mother held their hands as they walked back to the car. Moe felt like the warmth of her voice somehow added to her wisdom. "You two will have lots of choices to make. You will have to decide if you are going to help people or hurt them. I hope you will always make the choice that helps."

Moe made eye contact with her brother and saw her eyes in his face. She smiled, and he smiled back, and her heart leapt with hope for the future.

Moe opened her eyes, and the memory ended. She let

go of Ami and Stacie's hands.

"Didn't expect to get a nice vision of Lance. That was a pleasant surprise," Stacie said with a satisfied smile.

"He's what's on my mind," Moe said, leaning back on the couch. Staring at his picture on the wall, she wished she still had that kind of hope for her brother.

"That's the last time I ask for Hallmark memories. Super boring," Ami complained, leaning back with Moe.

"You can blame Stacie," Moe said, nudging her roommate.

"I shall," Ami said.

"I liked it," Stacie said, as she stood and took her plate to the kitchen sink.

"Alright, to business. You want me to go left to right or right to left," Ami asked, motioning at the wall.

"Left to right," Moe said.

"Saving the best for last," Stacie said, as she rejoined them on the couch.

Ami pulled a piece of paper from her satchel, passed it to Moe, and explained, "I had to bribe some guards, but I got you a visitation pass for you to see Giovani Corbi tomorrow. It's lawyers and family only right now, so you are going in as his cousin. He's at the Maryland Correctional Facility out on the west side of town. Your appointment is at 2:30."

"Perfect. Thank you. Do we need to pay you back for the bribes?" Moe replied.

"Please. I didn't offer them cash. I traffic in information, hon," Ami said with a grin. She then passed a manila folder with to Moe. Moe leafed through the pictures, holding them so Stacie could see while Ami talked. "Antonio Bainchi, or Big Tony, as his friends call him, has been a little more difficult to catch. He's more of a follower than a go-getter. Not the brightest bulb. He's just muscle for hire. No ambition. So I haven't been able to snare him in anything yet."

Stacie pointed to a picture of Tony in a boxing ring and asked, "Is he a trainer?"

"Yeah. Used to be an amateur boxer. He was just okay. Works out of a gym over in Dundalk. Gives lessons to teens and random other thugs from the hood," Ami said.

"I could get an appointment with him. Say it's for some kind of role I'm taking on," Stacie suggested.

Moe thought about the blue collar, low income, ex-industrial area that was Dundalk. "I don't think it will work. No one would believe a Hollywood starlet was slumming it in Dundalk. Especially with this guy. Plus, I don't want you having to get that close to him. We just need to get in and get out. Like we did with Giovani."

"What if we offer him a job?" Stacie asked.

Ami and Moe both waited.

"Like, what if you hire him to beat someone up, but it's actually a trap," Stacie said.

"That could work," Moe said.

"Who's the bait?" Ami asked.

Moe smiled. "My brother Calvin is always up for a fight," Moe said.

"He can handle himself?" Ami asked.

"Oh, he's huge. And cute, in a dark and brooding sort of way," Stacie said.

"None of my brothers are cute," Moe said.

"Tony's clients typically just walk into his gym," Ami said.

"Great. I'll take care of it," Moe said.

"You still got your guy on Santobello?" Ami asked, nodding to the hook-nosed man.

"Yeah, Vinnie's on him. We're going to meet with him for breakfast tomorrow. You make any connection to him and Three-Scar?" Moe asked hopefully.

"No, that guy's a ghost. I can't find him anywhere. I don't think I've ever had this much trouble before," Ami said.

"Thanks for staying on it," Moe said.

"What's going on with your brother? Any way I can help with that?" Ami asked.

"I don't know," Moe said. "He's in town erasing people's memories. The first victim we found was a judge. We need to know why and who else he has hit."

Ami stood and took pictures of the news clipping and a picture of Lance with her phone. "So I take it the nice story about him helping the little Down syndrome girl didn't stick," Ami said.

"Things got dark after that. He didn't choose to help people. In college, he was a mess. Then he joined the military and they turned him into something entirely different," Moe replied with a deep exhale of remorse. Talking about her brother always made her chest feel heavy.

"I'll see what I can get," Ami said, moving to the next column on the wall. "This one is new."

"From this morning," Stacie said.

"Just picked up the case. Wrongful imprisonment. Framed for killing his real estate agent. You up for digging around on him?" Moe asked.

Ami took more pictures with her phone and said, "Yep. That's an easy one. I'll pull all his dirty secrets out." Moving to the last column on the wall, Ami said, "I got nothing on ya boy Bruce. I'm sorry."

"Nothing?" Stacie said with complete shock. "Come on. He's scum. He has to be doing something we can bust him for?"

"Nothing against the law that I've found yet. Just being a scumbag corporate lawyer who drinks too much," Ami said.

"Damn it," Stacie said. "I was sure you'd find something we could get him for."

"It's okay. He'll slip up. And then we'll be there," Moe said. "You mind staying on him?" she asked Ami.

"No worries. I'll keep watching him digitally. Dude-bro like that, it's only a matter of time," Ami said. Looking around the apartment she stretched and asked, "So, what's for dinner?"

Stacie laughed and said, "Orange broccoli chicken. I'll grab you some."

CHAPTER EIGHT

Vinnie was at the diner before them. His beard was as unkempt as always, and his hair was pulled back in a ratty pony-tail. He wasn't wearing his prosthetic left arm today. Rather, a small nub poked out from under his left short sleeve. When Moe entered, Vinnie was reading the newspaper, sipping coffee, and finishing off a huge stack of pancakes. It was clear that only having one arm didn't slow him down any.

Moe and Stacie slid into the booth across from him.

"Ladies," Vinnie said without looking up from his paper. In the few weeks they'd been working together, Moe hadn't learned much about him except that he was fantastic at surveillance. She knew he had been a Lieutenant Colonel in the army serving as an MP. She knew he'd lost his arm in Afghanistan, but even Ami's best hacking couldn't un-redact the documents that told the story about how that had happened. She also knew that her brother Joe trusted him, and that was really all she needed.

"You two gonna be wanting some coffee too?" a

waitress asked.

"Yes, please," Stacie said.

The waitress put two plain white mugs in front of them and filled them both. Moe grinned as Stacie immediately began tearing into sugar packets and pouring them into her mug. She added so much cream, the cup almost overflowed.

"Next time just order a latte, hon," the waitress said. "Y'all gonna want anything to eat?"

"No. Thank you," Moe said with a smile.

As the waitress left, Vinnie put down his fork and took a sip from his coffee. "No matter how much sugar you put in it, you aren't going to make it any better," he said.

"This spot was your pick," Stacie complained.

"I like it. No one in here gives a damn about us. Makes it a safe place to talk," Vinnie said.

"I can think of five safe places to talk, all with better coffee," Stacie complained as she ventured a sip and then winced. "Oh, God. That's terrible," she said, putting the coffee down.

"But I bet none of them are open this early," Vinnie said with a grin.

"That's another thing," Stacie complained, leaning back in the booth. "Is five-thirty really necessary?"

"Vinnie took a bite of his pancakes and said between chews, "Early bird saves nine."

"That's not how that goes," Stacie said, trying her coffee again. She winced a second time and pushed it away.

Moe tried her mug. It was thicker than she was used to and tasted burnt. Not as if the beans had been burnt, but rather like it had been left in the pot too long. She took a second sip. "It grows on you," she said.

Vinnie folded up the newspaper and took another sip of coffee. "The coffee isn't the only bad news I have for you. I haven't seen any sign of your three-scarred-man."

Moe sighed. "Well, maybe soon?" She'd been paying Vinnie for two weeks to follow Damon Santobello, the hook-nosed criminal who'd been part of the gang responsible for killing Sarah's mom and kidnapping her dad. Moe had hope that Santobello would lead her back to the three-scarred man and maybe even the organization he worked for.

"Maybe? I mean, Santobello's been pretty quiet. I've got his normal routine down. Like I told you last week, he goes to work at the casino. Rolls out of his house around nine every morning and is in by ten every night. He always has lunch at one of the casino's restaurants. He puts in seven hours and then hits a bar near his house. He leaves a little after nine-thirty. Then he watches TV until he goes to sleep," Vinnie said.

"He doesn't roll out of bed until nine and you pulled us out here at o-dark-thirty in the morning?" Stacie complained.

"What if he were to leave earlier today? You don't want me to miss him would you?" Vinnie said with a grin.

"What's he watching on TV at night?" Stacie asked suspiciously, as if there were some detail there to discover.

"Lots of baseball. Like all criminals who should be behind bars, he likes the Yankees," Vinnie said with a smirk.

"Any pets?" Stacie challenged.

Entertained by the game, Vinnie replied with smile, "He's got a cat named Captain Fluff that he calls "Captain" and a snake named Boris. His mother is dead and I can't find his dad, but he has a little sister in North Carolina with two kids. Her husband's a doctor, a heart surgeon. From what I can tell, Santobello pretty much raised her. According to his bank account, he likes buying his nephews expensive stuff on Amazon and having it mailed to them. And he really likes playing Clash of Clans on his phone. He does it a lot while he watches baseball, but never at work. Any other personal details you need to know?"

"No. I think that's all for now," Stacie said.

Moe laughed and said, "You're really good at this."

"The army didn't train no chump," Vinnie said with a wink.

"You said you might have something interesting though?" Moe asked.

Vinnie raised his hand and called for the check. "Yeah. Maybe. There was something I noticed this week I thought you might like."

The waitress dropped the check in the middle of the table. Moe picked it up and handed her a credit card.

Vinnie took a sip of his coffee and smiled. "Thanks," he said.

"You were going to tell us something interesting," Moe reminded him.

"Yeah. So, he does this weird thing every morning. After leaving his house, he always stops by this coffee shop. It's downtown, but not necessarily on his way to the casino. He kind of has to go out of the way to get there. He buys a small coffee, and while he is standing in line, he checks out this bulletin board on the wall. Every morning," Vinnie said.

"What's so interesting about that?" Stacie asked.

"He doesn't drink coffee. Two weeks, I haven't seen him take a sip. Sometimes he holds onto it for a while, but he always tosses it," Vinnie said.

"You think someone is passing messages through the bulletin board," Stacie confirmed.

"Bingo. My bet is, he's looking for his next job,"

Vinnie said.

"Has he pulled anything off of it yet?" Moe asked.

"Not yet," Vinnie said.

Moe looked at Stacie. Her friend nodded, reading her mind. "Change of plans," Moe said.

"How do you feel about going full coffee-house-hipster?" Stacie asked.

"I mean, I've got some flannel somewhere, and I wouldn't mind sipping expressos and working on the great American novel," Vinnie said with a grin.

"Great. Watch the board and get photos. I want pics of who's posting on it and who's pulling stuff off," Moe said.

"You got it boss," Vinnie said, as he took another long swig of coffee.

CHAPTER NINE

Dorothy Lumpum was leaning against the hood of her Benz, waiting for them in the parking lot of the Maryland State Correctional Facility. The attorney was wearing a pantsuit so black it shimmered purple. It was a stark contrast to her bright silver hair. The entire ensemble communicated wisdom-filled disapproval.

"I told you that you should have worn another blazer today," Stacie said, as Moe pulled her car into a parking spot next to Dorothy.

Moe, wearing a t-shirt with the words "Get busy living or get busy dying" on the front, smirked at the idea of wearing a blazer two days in a row.

As they stepped from the car, Ms. Lumpum greeted them with a firm, "Let's not keep Malcom waiting." Turning, she led the way to the prison. They followed her through the gates and into the entryway. As they unloaded their pockets into boxes before moving into the visitor room, Stacie asked, "How much did Theo tell you about our methods?"

Dorothy watched with disdain as a guard checked her

briefcase. "Not much. He told me you have unique ways of getting information. The truth is, I don't care. As long as you aren't breaking the law in a way that will blow back on me or my client, I'll take any information you find. If you do break the law, please don't tell me."

Stacie placed her phone in the metal container, closed the lid, and passed it to a guard. "Well, you're probably in for a surprise."

"I don't like surprises," the attorney said.

The visitation room looked like every prison visiting room Moe had ever seen in a prison movie. The walls were cinderblock and seemed dirty, although there were no visible stains on them. The floor was a factory model black tile. Scattered around the room were steel square tables, each with attached benches for people to sit. Moe and Stacie followed Dorothy to a table in the middle of the room. They all three took a seat on one side.

"Any chance you'd let us speak to him alone?" Moe asked.

"No," Dorothy said.

"I need to warn you in advance, what I'm going to ask him to do is going to be a little unorthodox," Moe said.

"Theo trusts you and that's what got you put on my team, but I don't know you and I don't trust you, so you will not sit with my client alone. Are we clear?" Dorothy explained.

"Crystal," Stacie said.

"You want me on that wall. You need me on that wall," Moe said, catching the quote Stacie had dropped from the movie a Few Good Men.

"You can't handle the truth," Stacie laughed.

"I eat breakfast 300 yards from 4,000 Cubans who are trained to kill me, so don't think for one second that you can come down here, flash a badge, and make me nervous," Dorothy said. Before Stacie and Moe could react, the attorney added, "Grow up, ladies. We're here to get an innocent man out of prison."

"I like her," Stacie said.

"She's a keeper," Moe replied.

The doors of the far end of the room opened, and a man in an orange jumpsuit entered. Escorted by a guard, Malcom arrived with his hands and feet chained. He was thin and clean shaven. His curly hair created a halo around his head, and his bright eyes beamed through his glasses. "Hey Dorothy, who are your new friends?" he called with a smile as the guard led him over.

The guard clipped his chains to the table, and the prisoner said, "Thanks for walking me over, Andy," as he took a seat.

"No worries," the guard replied.

Dorothy immediately took charge of the conversation. Using a pen to take notes on the legal pad she had brought in with her, she asked, "How are they treating you? Have you had any problems?" The tone of inquiry indicated it was less out of concern and more a demand for information.

"The food sucks, and I miss the sunlight. And normal clothes. And not being able to leave my room whenever I want. Did I mention the food sucks? But besides that, I've been fine. It seems some of the guys from the program have been putting in a word for me with their buddies in here, so everyone has been really nice. I joined a book club. We're reading a Laura Lippman novel. And a bunch of the guys have a sort of Pokémon game going with cards they've made from napkins. I mean, don't get me wrong. My roommate is a rapist and murderer who is in for life with no hope of parole. It's prison. But I'm surviving," Malcom said.

Moe was impressed by his abilities to keep his spirits up even though he was behind bars. If nothing else, he was resilient.

"How is Katie holding up?" he asked.

"She seems to be doing alright. She asked me to tell you that she has started going back to work again so you can stop worrying," Dorothy said.

"She said that in her last letter. I'm really proud of her. This is so hard on her," Malcom said.

"Hopefully, it won't be for much longer," Dorothy replied.

"Hopefully," Malcom said. Then turning his attention to Stacie and Moe, he said, "Hi, I'm Malcom Sennack. Nice to meet you."

"I'm Moneta Watkins, and this is Stacie Howe," Moe said.

"They are private investigators helping me gather information on your case," Dorothy interrupted.

"Love the shirt. One of my favorites. Perfect attire when visiting a prison," Malcom said.

"I thought so too," Moe replied with a nod.

"So, how can I help you? Do you want me to run through the story? I'm sure Dorothy has given you all the details already," Malcom said.

"You could tell us, but I'd rather you just show me," Moe said.

"Show you? Alright, I'll bite. How do I do that?" Malcom asked.

"I just need you to think about that night and hold my hand. I'll take care of the rest," Moe said.

Malcom held out his hand, closed his eyes, and said, "If this is some kind of weird pick-up line, you should know that I'm a highly desired commodity. I'm engaged on the outside, and several guys in here have laid claim to me if I decide to be a prison wife."

Stacie laughed out loud.

"What's happening now?" Dorothy asked.

"This'll just take a second," Moe said, as she closed her eyes and took his hand.

The air was hot and think. Even with the windows rolled down, it felt like she was sitting in a sauna. She hated this car. Or rather, Malcom hated this car. He wished he had money to get the air conditioner fixed.

Moe pulled the car into a parking spot outside. The lot was mostly empty, not like when he'd come during peak hours on a Saturday afternoon and the office was bustling with real estate agents and their team members and their clients. Then, he'd had to park almost a block away. Today, he could pull right up to the door. He parked next to Charlie's red BMW Z-4 convertible. Malcom had never been one for cars, but that one could make him into a car-guy. It was so sleek. Malcom bet it was fast too. He wondered how much it had set Charlie back.

Before getting out of the car, Moe paused and sat in the heat for a minute. He needed to clear his head. He looked at the text message he'd received from Charlie again. "Get over here. The deal is falling through. Need you to sign some stuff or we lose the sale." He'd been looking for a warehouse he could convert into a dormitory for seven months. The property Charlie had found was perfect. He didn't want to lose it. On the other hand, Malcom knew Charlie might just be exaggerating urgency to get stuff done. For Charlie, everything was urgent.

Moe walked the small path to the front door of Charlie's real estate office. There was a guy in a short-sleeved t-shirt and glasses coming out of the office next door. He had a trash bag in each hand and head phones on. The business's name, "Connections," was frustratingly vague. Malcom thought it was some kind of day care, but he wasn't sure. He smiled and waved, and the guy nodded back.

Moe pulled on the door to the office and stepped into the reception area. Malcom was surprised there wasn't a receptionist on duty. It was unlike Charlie to leave the front door unlocked without someone to welcome potential clients if they happened to wander in. Charlie's real estate agency housed forty-three agents, many of which also had a small support staff. Charlie got a small cut of every sale, and his face was on all the signs. He ran his agency with obsessive precision. No guard at the front gate just wasn't his style.

"Hey, Charlie!" Moe called out in Malcom's voice.

There was a rustling in the back. Moe called again, "Charlie! It's Malcom. You said there was stuff to sign?" There was more rustling in the back, but no one came forward. Moe looked down at her phone. Malcom was supposed to meet Katie for drinks in thirty minutes. He didn't want to just go roaming through the offices, but he also didn't want to stand here and do nothing.

"Charlie! You back there?" he yelled again. He walked past the reception desk, past the rooms used to meet with clients, and into the bullpen. The large room filled with cubicles was empty. "Charlie?" Moe called again.

Moe pressed forward, weaving through the cubicle blocks to get to the far wall where Charlie's private office was located. The shades were drawn, but Moe could hear a strange noise coming from the inside. It sounded like heavy breathing. As he knocked on the door, Malcom worried he might be catching Charlie in the middle of some kind of affair. "Charlie? You in there?" Moe asked.

There was no answer.

Moe pushed open the door slowly. Her mouth fell open. "Charlie!" she yelled. Running into the room, she dropped to her knees next to Charlie. The real estate agent was covered in blood and gasping for air. Moe's heart raced. "Charlie? What happened?"

Charlie's eyes were wide. Groping for air like a fish out of water, he grabbed Moe by the arm. She saw the wound in his neck and placed both hands on it firmly like Malcom had seen people do in the movies. Blood seeped through her fingers.

"Oh, God. Charlie. What happened?" Moe said. She looked around the room frantically for something that might help her. The phone was off the hook. Every surface of the office was filled with unfiled paperwork.

The gasping started to slow. Moe, unsure what else to do, applied more pressure, but the blood just kept coming. Her fingers were sticky with it. Charlie's eyes went wide, he gave a final tug on her arm, and then his fight for air stopped.

"Charlie? Oh, God. Charlie?" Moe whispered with fear. She stood. "Oh, Charlie," she said.

There were sirens. They were faint. But she could hear them. "Someone must have called an ambulance," Malcom thought, not considering the absurdity of that in the moment. He dashed to the front door hoping to guide them back to Charlie. Maybe it wasn't too late. Moe burst out the front door into the waning sun, waving her hands in the air.

Two police cars were there, parked behind her and Charlie's cars. The four officers were already out of their vehicles. Moe waved her hands. "He's back here," she yelled.

Two of the officers pulled their guns. "Sir, stay right where you are!" they demanded.

Moe held her hands up in fear. "No! No! You don't understand! Charlie! He's back there. He needs help!" she tried to explain.

One of the officers removed handcuffs from his belt and held them out. "Keep your hands where I can see

69

them. I need you to lay down on the ground, hands out," he said.

Moe held her hands up high. "No, wait! He needs help!" she exclaimed.

"Sir! We do not want to shoot you! Lay down on the ground!" the officer yelled.

Moe's breath caught in her chest. The danger was setting in. She looked from one gun to the next. An ambulance pulled into the parking lot. Moe took a deep breath and dropped to the ground. She laid down on the sidewalk and put her hands out, like she'd been instructed.

The officer approached. He slapped the cuffs on her right wrist first. Pulling both her arms down, he then slapped them on her left. They were tight. It hurt her shoulders to have them twisted like they were. "He's in the back. Please. Help him," she said, as the officer stood him up.

The three remaining officers entered the building as the first officer pushed Moe toward the police car. Opening the back door, he pushed Moe's head down as he put her in the vehicle. "What's your name, sir?" the officer asked.

"Um. Malcom," Moe said. "Malcom Sennack."

"Well, Mr. Sennack, you have the right to remain silent. Anything you say can and will be used against you in a court of law," the officer said.

Moe's head started to spin. Malcom was just starting to understand what was happening. He caught a glimpse of himself in the rearview mirror. His face was streaked with Charlie's blood. He looked down at his shirt. It too was covered in blood.

"You have the right to an attorney. If you cannot afford an attorney, one will be provided for you," the officer continued.

Malcom's head dropped. Tears formed in his eyes. He thought about Katie waiting at the bar for him. He wished he could call her and tell her what was going on. Tears flowed down his cheeks, mixing with blood. He wondered how long she would sit there before she realized something was wrong. Why did he always have to be late for everything?

"Do you understand these rights as I have read them to you?" the officer asked.

"Yes, sir. I understand," Malcom said.

"Good," the officer said, as he closed the patrol car's door.

Moe opened her eyes and looked at Malcom.

His eyes locked on the table, he pulled his hand away from hers.

"We're going to help you beat this," Moe said.

Malcom bit his lip and stared at the table. "That's, um. That's some trick," Malcom said, not looking up.

"Are you okay? Did she hurt you? If you hurt him, I'll have your ass," Dorothy threatened.

Malcom looked up and gave a weak smile. He seemed smaller. The life had gone from his eyes. "She didn't do anything, Dorothy. Thanks for looking out for me, though," he said.

"We'll catch whoever did this. We're going to get you out of here," Moe said again.

"Thanks," Malcom said with a heavy breath. Shaking his head, he added, "Reliving that was a lot. I, um. I think I need to go and lay down. I'm sure Dorothy can give you any more details you need. I'm, uh. I'm sorry. I just. I didn't expect to see Charlie like that again." He signaled for the guard who came an unlocked him from the table.

"I'm sorry. I should have given you a warning," Moe said.

"Nope. You didn't do anything wrong. There's no

way you could have prepared me for that," Malcom said, as he stood. "Thank you for coming. It was, um. It was nice to meet you," he added in an absentminded way just before turning to leave.

They watched him exit the room in silence.

"That must have been some memory," Stacie said.

"It was rough," Moe said.

"What in the hell just happened?" Dorothy demanded.

CHAPTER TEN

Moe pushed the door open and set the small brown box she'd been carrying on a tall brown leather swivel chair. Judge Marcus' office was surprisingly small. Each wall contained a floor to ceiling bookcase overstuffed with important looking law texts. The furniture was all dark wood. A heavy looking desk with a swivel chair faced the door. In front of the desk were two leather wingback chairs that sat much lower than the desk. Moe wondered what it was like for an attorney to be called into Judge Marcus' chambers and be made to sit in one of the low-to-the-ground chairs. The effect had to be of a child being called to the principal's office.

"So explain this to me," Stacie said, as she followed Moe into the office. "How come Robert comes when we're having cheese, crackers, and a pleasant chat at someone's house, but when it comes time to clean an office out, he's busy with important FBI things?"

"Welcome to my childhood. Shockingly, on days when mom and dad had some major house projects for us to do, Robert always had some kind of practice or something he absolutely couldn't miss," Moe laughed.

Stacie moved to one of the bookcases, pulled a book off the wall, and started thumbing through it. "We aren't actually planning to clean this office, right? Because we didn't bring enough boxes."

Moe moved behind the judge's desk and sat in his chair. "I mean, if you are feeling really generous we could, but my plan was just to search it. Mrs. Marcus said there is a moving crew coming next week that's actually going to clean it out."

"I'll start on this wall I guess," Stacie said, as she pulled a file folder off the shelf and began leafing through it.

Moe began looking through the drawers of the desk. They were filled with random scraps of paper filled with quickly scribbled notes, cold medicine, spare change, and documents once set aside for a purpose long since forgotten.

Hours passed as she and Stacie worked in silence, searching every folder, book, drawer, and nook and cranney, hoping to find something that might explain why Judge Marcus had been singled out. When they'd covered the entire room, they each sat in a wingback chair.

With a single folder in her lap and her hands folded over it as if to keep it from flying away, Stacie asked, "What'd you find?"

Moe, who had a stack of papers in her lap, said, "Nope, you've got a fancy looking folder there, so you have go first."

"First, this is a grungy, normal-looking folder. There's nothing fancy about it. Second, I asked you first. That means you have to go first," Stacie shot back with a playful but stern look.

"Fine," Moe relented. She presented an example of

each item as she talked, laying it on the desk for Stacie to see. "I discovered that Judge Marcus has terrible handwriting. I discovered that his clerk leaves him a lot of notes about calling his wife back. I discovered that he loves Chinese food, or that he is some kind of weird Chinese food menu collector, because I found six different menus in the office."

"I found another five. So many Chinese food menus," Stacie interrupted.

"I also discovered that he has dry-cleaning he hasn't picked up, a half written article for some law journal I'd never heard of, and a ton of unfinished recommendation letters. That's all I got," Moe said.

"Okay. Well. Look at this," Stacie said, as she laid the file folder in her lap on the desk and opened it with an unnecessary amount of pomp and circumstance.

Moe leaned forward. In the folder were promotional materials that said, "William Marcus for Senate." Moe leafed through it while Stacie talked. There was a page of fake promotional materials, a schedule laying out a campaign trial for the spring and fall of 2020."

"So, from what I can tell, Judge Marcus was considering running for Senator," Stacie said with excitement.

"State or national level?" Moe asked, since the promotional materials were generic.

"US Senate. If you look at the campaign trail route, he's planning to cover a large part of the state," Stacie explained.

Moe closed the folder and smiled at her friend. "Well, it's something to chase. Nice work," she said to her friend, as she put everything she'd found in the box.

"Why thank you my dear," Stacie replied with a grin. Grabbing the stack of Chinese food menus, she tossed them in the box as well.

Moe gave her a strange look.

"What? If he loved them that much they're worth looking into," Stacie said with a grin.

CHAPTER ELEVEN

Moe pulled open the door and stepped into Jake's Diner. The poorly lit establishment had its standard small number of patrons scattered around. "Hey Desiree," she called to the hostess.

Stacie stepped in behind her and repeated Moe's, "Hey Desiree."

"Ladies," the hostess said with a glance and smile that communicated affection. Going back to reading her newspaper, she said, "I'll bring your usual back. You know where he is."

"Thanks," Moe and Stacie said in unison as they walked to the back of the restaurant and out the back door to the alley where Baba, Moe's grandfather, held court.

As Moe expected, Baba was sitting at the four-seater table with a smoldering cigar in his hand and a mug of coffee in front of him. Next to him was his ex-partner, Detective Mason. Dressed in a rumpled grey suit with his gold badge hanging around his neck, he was shoveling an overstuffed Rachel sandwich into his mouth. Detective Mason and Baba had been partners for over a decade, until Moe's mother went missing and her father was murdered. Unable to solve the crime, Baba retired from the force and took up residence behind Jake's.

"Baby Girl," Baba said with excitement. "And Ms. Howe. What a treat," he added.

Dropping the sandwich, his mouth stuffed with coleslaw and beef, Detective Mason mumbled, "You old son of a bitch. You ambushed me."

"Baba. Detective. How are we today?" Stacie said, as she and Moe took the remaining seats at the table.

"I'm wonderful. It's a nice day. My friend came to eat lunch with me. And I'm now completely surprised that my wonderful granddaughter and her beautiful partner are going to join us," Baba said.

"Surprised my ass. I feel entrapped. This is entrapment," Detective Mason said, wiping dressing from his mouth with a paper napkin.

"We just asked Baba to get you here so we could pick your brain about something," Moe said with a grin.

"If I wanted to talk to you, I would have answered your calls," Detective Mason grumbled.

"Oh, no. How are we ever going to get out of this pickle?" Baba said, as he took a puff of his cigar. Moe shot him a disapproving glare. She knew he was trying to annoy Stacie with the catch phrase Stacie was famous for declaring on the sitcom she starred in as a child.

"Look, after the whole art thief thing, you two aren't really on the best of terms with the department. If the other guys see me talking to you, they're going to be pissed," Detective Mason complained.

"Why is the department mad at us? We solved it. We caught the bad guys and turned them over to you," Stacie said.

"You brought snipers to a public park," Mason said with a deeply patronizing tone.

"The lady has to bring the right tools to the right job," Baba said with a grin.

"Yeah. Encourage them. See what happens. Private eyes can't survive a week without the department helping them out. You two have pushed on some nerves. You need to lay low for a while. Find some lost cats or something. Stay away from the high profile stuff for a while," Detective Mason pleaded. He seemed genuinely concerned, which didn't surprise Moe. As apathetic as he acted, Moe knew he loved her as if she was his own granddaughter.

"You're in luck. Nothing high profile this time," Moe said.

"In fact, the case is already closed," Stacie said.

Just then, Desiree appeared at the back door with two large burgers, a plate of fries smothered in brown gravy, and two beers. She set them in front of Moe and Stacie. "Here you are ladies. The Moe and Stacie special," she said.

Moe's mouth watered at the sight of the food. "This is amazing. Thank you," she said.

Desiree was already walking back inside as she said, "Don't mention it. Anything for you two."

"Now see, why can't you be more like Desiree?" Stacie teased Detective Mason, who grimaced and sighed in reply.

The detective reached for a fry and Moe smacked his hand. "Nope, info first. Then you can steal our fries."

Detective Mason pulled back his hand slowly. He took another bite of his sandwich and chewed slowly as he considered. Taking a long swig from the beer in front of him, he relented with a nod.

"We need to know about Malcom Sennack," Stacie said.

The detective choked on his beer. "What? I thought

you said you weren't tackling anything high profile?"

"It's not high profile. Not anymore," Moe said, feigning contrition.

"You need to leave that alone. You overturn that case and the department will lose their minds," Mason said.

"So you think it can be overturned?" Moe asked with a sly grin.

"No. That's not what I said. You're putting words in my mouth," the detective protested.

"What do you think about the case?" Stacie asked.

The detective took another swig of his beer. Moe pushed the plate of fries toward him, and he popped one in his mouth. "Look, the kid was on the scene. He was covered in the guy's blood. And we had a call reporting the fight," Mason explained as he chewed. He took a second fry and ate it. And then a third.

"Someone called it in?" Moe asked.

"Yeah. One of the neighbors. Called 9-1-1. Said that this Malcom kid had showed up and was yelling the second he got out of the car. Went running into the building like a mad man. The neighbor said she was 'afraid for people inside,'" Mason explained.

"Which neighbor?" Stacie asked.

"The physical therapy center next door. One of the PT girls was closing up for the evening and saw him come running in," Mason said.

"She said she saw Malcom. Not a man, but specifically Malcom?" Moe asked.

Mason sighed and ate some more fries. "Look. I'll deny this if you tell anyone, but it wasn't the cleanest collar. The guys that were first on the scene, Ambrose and Mitcham, aren't the brightest blubs. But the higher-ups like them because they're young and eager. When your man came bursting out of the office covered in blood, they were sure they had their guy, so they skipped some steps. They brought the witness out and had her identify him on the scene, while he was still bloody and handcuffed in the back of the patrol car."

"I read in the case file that there was a witness that fingered him at the trail. That must have been her. She said he was crazed with rage," Stacie pondered out loud.

"You got it," Mason said.

"Stupid young kids," Baba complained, taking a pull from his cigar and blowing the smoke up.

"Well, if our more experienced detectives didn't retire so early, maybe we'd be able to train the young ones up right," Mason said.

"Fair," Baba replied.

"So the witness was tainted, but Malcom had a crap lawyer who didn't know to look into it. Any chance there's a record of this somewhere?" Moe asked.

"No chance. You look at the paperwork, and it will read letter-to-the-law. Always does. You should know by now that we police never make a mistake," Mason snickered.

"What about the murder weapon? Any leads on it?" Stacie asked.

"Nope. The running theory in the department was that he dropped it in a trashcan we missed, but no one ever found it," Mason said.

"What was it?" Moe asked.

"Nothing fancy. Looked like a kitchen knife to the medical examiner," Mason said.

"Anything else we should know?" Moe asked.

"Yeah. I'm serious about the department. If you overturn this guy's conviction, there are a lot of guys that are going to be pissed. I'd try to keep your name out of it if you can," he said.

"Thanks for the tip," Stacie said, as she took a bite of her burger.

"That means no blogging about it," Baba chided Stacie.

"You're still doing that blog thing?" Moe asked with surprise.

"Only when we close a case," Stacie said, taking a bite from her burger and refusing to make eye contact.

"It's a good read," Baba said.

"Gets lots of hits too," Detective Mason added.

"How do you know that?" Stacie asked with surprise.

"I told you. You're on the department's radar. We all read it," Mason replied with a shrug.

"When do you write it?" Moe asked, stunned. She'd never seen Stacie on a laptop.

"When you're asleep," Stacie said, sheepishly.

"I don't like this," Moe said, leaning back in her chair and folding her arms across her chest.

"Why don't we just go back to pretending like you don't know about it," Stacie quipped with hopeful dismissiveness. It made Moe laugh, which brought a smile to Stacie's face.

"Anyway," Moe changed subjects with a sigh, "we need something else from you besides information."

"I told you. I can't help you," Detective Mason said, eating more fries from the plate, clearly nervous Moe was going to pull it away.

"It's just a phone call. I need you to get us in to see Giovani Corbi," Moe said.

"No more favors. You're going to have to wait until after he is processed and see him in prison like anyone else," Detective Mason said.

Moe weighed whether or not to push. Her hunch was that Giovani didn't know anything, that he was just hired muscle. He certainly wasn't the mastermind. From what she'd seen of the kidnapping of Sarah's dad, Giovani had just taken orders. She looked at Detective Mason and could see in his eyes what a hard position she was putting him in. He wanted to help, but he was also part of the fraternity that was the Baltimore police department. "I get it. Maybe you could talk to him for us?" Moe asked.

"That's more doable, since I made the arrest," Mason relented.

From her back pocket, Moe pulled a picture of Sarah, her mom, and her dad. She slid it across the table to him. "I saw him in a memory kill this woman and kidnap the man. Could you ask him about it? I'm pretty sure he was just hired muscle. But maybe ask him how he got the gig?" Moe asked.

"This is still an open case. I'll tell my captain I got an anonymous tip that he was involved. I'll let you know if I find anything," Mason said, taking the photo.

CHAPTER TWELVE

The building looked exactly like Moe had seen it in Malcom's memory, except the parking lot was full of expensive looking cars. Most of them were red.

"I've never seen so many people compensating for so much in one place before. So many bros wanting us to know how much they're worth," Stacie said, shaking her head.

Moe pulled the door to the office open and advanced into the reception area. A perky blonde with her hair in a ponytail stood behind a tall desk. As Moe and Stacie entered the room, the exuberant woman greeted them with a thick southern twang. "Welcome to Dream Homes Realty. My name's Tiffany. How can I help you on your road to finding your dream home?"

Moe wondered how many times a day she had to say that phrase.

"I love your accent," Stacie said with an authentic grin. "Are you from Mississippi? It sounds like there's a Mississippi pull in there?"

"No. Sorry. Not from Mississippi," Tiffany said with a

smile.

"Alabama?" Stacie asked.

"No. Not from Alabama," Tiffany, flashing an even larger smile.

"Hmm. It's not Texas. Oklahoma?" Stacie tried.

"No," Tiffany laughed.

Stepping in, Moe said, "We're private detectives. We're helping with Charlie's case."

Her smile vanished, and her big blue eyes filled with concern. "Charlie was so special. I just can't believe he's gone."

"We've heard he was loved," Moe lied with a nod.

"Charlie was genuine. You always knew exactly where you stood with him. And, he gave me this job and never made a pass at me. I appreciated that," she said.

"Sounds like you were close," Stacie said.

"Well, I mean. He gave me a shot when I was new to town and no one else would hire me. Even said if I could pass the real estate exam, I'd get to try my hand at selling," Tiffany said.

"He sounds like a nice man," Moe said, hoping Tiffany would share more.

"Charlie was something special," Tiffany said.

"Is that like saying, 'Bless his heart?' You know, one of those Southern phrases that sounds nice but really means he was a total jerk?" Stacie asked with a grin.

"I'm not sure what you mean," Tiffany replied.

"Georgia? Atlanta area," Stacie guessed again.

"No. I'm no peach," Tiffany replied, smiling again. The woman was so polished in her presentation of warmth, Moe couldn't tell if she genuinely enjoyed the game, or if she was irritated and wanted them to leave.

"Like I said, we're private detectives looking into Charlie's case. Can you think of anyone who might want to hurt him?" Moe asked.

"Besides the man that killed him?" Tiffany asked with that same warm smile.

"Besides him," Stacie said.

"You don't make the kind of money Charlie made without upsetting some people, but that's just business. I can't think of anyone who would want to kill him. I mean, besides the man who is in jail for it," Tiffany replied. Moe was impressed by how effectively Tiffany's smile served as a suit of armor.

"South Carolina," Stacie said.

"No. Sorry," Tiffany replied.

"I had to study accents when I was acting. I'm usually really good at this," Stacie complained.

"Bless your heart," Tiffany replied.

Moe laughed.

Stacie glared.

Hoping to stay on track, Moe said, "We're asking everyone this. If you don't mind, could you tell us where you were the night Charlie was murdered?"

"Sure. I was at home. I'd just left work like ten minutes before. Charlie had wanted me to work late. We had some after-hours client meetings. Mr. Malcom – the man that killed Charlie – was the last one. But then, when he was so late, Charlie let me leave. I'm glad too, because if I had still been here, he might have killed me as well. I'm lucky to be alive," Tiffany said with a wistful air, as if she was remembering some special night.

"Would you mind if we went around back and talked to some other people. Maybe they can give us an idea of what exactly happened?" Moe asked.

"I'm not sure what you're investigating. They caught the man that did it red handed. Right? What's left to know?" Tiffany questioned.

"We do the post-conviction investigation. Just to shore up the facts and everything," Stacie said.

"Just double checking everything for the police. Make sure they crossed all their T's and dotted all their I's," Moe added.

"We're pretty busy," Tiffany said.

"Look, you either let us pass, or the cops come back and do it. I'm assuming you have clients back there. I know the last thing I'd want is a bunch of uniformed goons traipsing through the office making a mess in front of my clients," Moe explained, hoping Tiffany would take the bait.

Tiffany cocked her head. Moe could tell she wasn't buying the bluff.

"Kentucky," Stacie said.

"I'm a Petersburg girl. Population six-hundred-twenty. Home of the Creation Museum and the Riverwalk Café. Go Cougars," Tiffany replied with a nod.

"Told you I was good at that," Stacie bragged to Moe.

Moe laughed again.

"Alright. Look, I'll give you a two minute head start. Then I have to call the boss and let her know you're coming back," Tiffany relented.

"Thanks, dear. Won't be but a minute," Stacie said, as she and Moe walked past Tiffany's desk, through the small hallway to the bullpen. The cubicles were filled with energetic people all talking on their phones. They spoke at a soft but rapid pace that created a buzz. It felt like it could break into rage at any minute.

"Pretty people sell houses," Stacie muttered as she looked through the room.

"What?" Moe asked with a smirk.

"That's what they say. Pretty people sell houses," Stacie replied.

"That's not a thing," Moe said.

"Look around the room. Chiseled jaw lines. Toned arms. It's absolutely a thing," Stacie said.

Moe took a second, closer look at the room, and she had to admit that Stacie had a point. Everyone in the room was above average on the looks scale. As her eyes drifted through the bullpen, she noticed the door to Charlie's office was open. Getting Stacie's attention, she said, "Let's see who's in there?"

They walked along the side of the bullpen to the large back office and peered into the room. At the desk was a second blond woman, but, unlike Tiffany, this one had a fierce look in her eye that reminded Moe of a tiger on the hunt. She stood at her computer, checking her email while she also talked to someone through the speaker phone on her cell. When she noticed Moe and Stacie at the door, she put up a single finger, telling them to wait.

The office had been completely transformed since Moe saw it in Malcom's memory. The clutter was gone from the minimalist space. The woman stood at a small standing desk that held a laptop and an extra monitor. Behind her were two leather chairs with a small coffee table in front of them. The walls had works of modern art that were streaks and splotches of paint.

"I just don't know if we can afford that. It feels out of our budget. What if we can't get them to move the property line?" the nervous voice on the call said through the speaker phone.

The woman clicked through her email as she spoke. "Billy. I told you that I would handle the property line. It's not going to be a problem. What I need you worrying about is what your wife wants. Think about making her happy. She wants this house. She's told you it's her dream house. You need to make this happen for her."

"I know. I know. You're right," Billy said through the phone.

The woman held up another finger to Moe and mouthed, "One second." Then, to the phone she said,

"Okay Billy. Let's go through a thought exercise. Walk me through the house and tell me everything your wife loved about it. And don't leave anything out."

"Right now?" Billy asked.

"Right now, Billy. Start at the front door and walk me through it," the woman demanded.

"Okay. Well. She really liked the front door. She liked how it looked out onto the big lawn. And the flower beds. She liked those. And she..."

As Billy droned on, the woman pressed the mute button on her phone, turned to Moe and Stacie, and said, "Can I help you?"

Moe looked at the phone, unsure what to do.

"Well?" the woman said.

"And then in the entry way, there was that really nice tile on the floor..." Billy continued.

Stacie jumped in, "I'm sorry. We're with the Lumpum and Brumtum law firm. We came to follow up with some questions about Charlie Michaels."

"You mean my husband?" the woman said.

"You're Alicia Michaels?" Moe confirmed.

"I am," the woman said. Unmuting the phone, she said, "Yep. That's right Billy. I remember that."

"Yeah. She loved the stove in the kitchen. She said if we had a double range we would be able to entertain more..." Billy continued.

The woman pressed mute again on her phone, turned to her computer, began googling Lumpum and Brumtum, and asked, "What exactly about my husband's murder are you looking into?"

Facts from the case file began running through Moe's mind. There hadn't been any pictures of Alicia Michaels in the file, but there had been a transcript of her testimony. On the stand, Alicia had first delivered the bombshell to the courtroom that Malcom's real estate deal had fallen through and that Malcom had been furious. Then, when Malcom's lawyer had attempted a cross examination, the grieving widow had burst into tears, weeping about how hard real estate was since the housing bubble burst and about how she had always been afraid of Malcom because of the "type of people" he associated with. Seeing the elegant and powerful woman in person, Moe imagined the testimony had been damning.

Realizing the Google search was likely going to end all conversation, Moe quickly asked, "We just have some follow up questions for you about the case. Do you know, besides Malcom Sennack, who might have wanted to harm your husband?" Alicia unmuted the phone and said, "Okay Billy. That's enough of the first floor. Let move to the back yard and then upstairs."

"The back yard. She loved the garden, and she really liked the deck. Plus she thought the way the lawn rolled with that small hill in the back…" Billy said, completely unware that a second conversation was happening.

Alicia peered at her computer screen that displayed news stories that included the phrase "Lumpum and Brumtum." She gave Moe and Stacie knowing doe-eyes and, with a tone of deep sorrow that demanded sympathy, explained, "So, you two are here to try to free my husband's killer. Well, then. Here's a statement for you. Malcom Sennack is an unhinged lunatic who was driven mad when his real estate deal fell through. My poor defenseless husband tried to break the news to Mr. Sennack calmly, knowing that Mr. Sennack had a history with the police, but Mr. Sennack flew into a rage, drove to this very office, and stabbed my poor defenseless husband over and over and over again. I only wish I had been here. Maybe I could have done something to save my wonderful Charlie." Pressing unmute on the phone, in her normal voice, she said, "You can only talk about the bedroom so much, Billy. Move to the bathroom."

"Well, she loved that there were double sinks. And she really liked that the shower heads were those type that completely surround you..." Billy continued.

"You said Mr. Sennack's deal fell through. Would you mind explaining that more to us?" Moe asked.

Alicia turned back to her computer and began checking her email again. "I would mind. I've given you my statement. If you want anything else from me, schedule an appointment through my lawyer," she said.

"We know this is difficult for you to talk about, but if you wouldn't mind explaining to us a little bit more about what other projects your husband was working on, it would be helpful," Stacie pleaded.

Alicia made a few clicks with her mouse and a live shot of Tiffany appeared on her screen. "Yes, Mrs. Michaels?" the receptionist asked nervously.

"Tiffany. These two women are harassing me about Charlie's murder. Call the police and tell them to come immediately," Alicia commanded.

"It was nice to meet you, Mrs. Michaels. We'll be in contact with your lawyer if we have any more questions," Moe said, as she and Stacie backed out of the office.

As Moe left, she heard Alicia click unmute on her phone again and say, "Okay, Billy. Enough visualizing. You understand how sad your wife is going to be if you deny her this amazing home. So let's get down to numbers."

CHAPTER THIRTEEN

Moe and Stacie moved their car to the other side of the parking lot so Tiffany and Alicia Michaels would assume they'd left and not call the cops. While Moe knew they hadn't done anything wrong, there was no telling what Alicia would say when the police showed up. From her performance in court, she clearly didn't have a problem lying to the authorities. Once the car was a safe distance from the real estate agency, Moe and Stacie parked and walked to the physical therapist next door.

AABA Physical Therapy was a chain that stretched across most of the eastern seaboard. Moe assumed all the locations looked pretty much the same. The walls were decorated with black and green patterns that were almost Nike swooshes, but not exactly. On the right side of the room there were exercise bikes, treadmills, and other strength training machines. On the left side of the room, there were padded tables and stations of free weights. Four people worked independently at different stations, while two people in matching green polos and black pants helped clients stretch on the padded tables.

"Be right with you. Go ahead and sign in," one of the green-shirted people said.

Moe walked over to the welcome desk and signed the form, then she went and sat down next to Stacie in the waiting area.

"What was the name of that Chinese food place near here that we found in the judges office? The Sichuan Place?"

Moe grabbed her hand and probed for the memory. An image of Stacie putting the menus in the box appeared in both of their minds.

"The Sichuan House Special. That's right. Thank you," Stacie said, as she punched the keys on her phone with her thumbs.

"What are you doing?" Moe asked.

"Trying to order lunch," Stacie said.

"Hello. I'm Tai Murphy. How can I help you? Do you have an appointment?" one of the women in a green polo asked.

"No. I'm sorry. We don't. We're, um," Moe said, pausing because she didn't want to repeat the mistake they'd made with Mrs. Michaels.

"We work for an insurance company. We're checking on the details of a claim. Is Cher Silverstone here?"

"Hey Cher. They're here for you," Tai called over her shoulder to the other woman who was still helping a client stretch her leg out. "She'll be right with you," Tai said with a smile as she stepped away.

Looking over at the other green shirt, Stacie said, "Another blond? When I blog about this, I'm calling it Too Many Blonds."

"Maybe, Blonds and Blood?" Moe suggested.

"Blonds, Blonds, Blonds, and Blood?" Stacie said with a grin.

"Bloody Blonds Bathed in Murder," Moe said in her

best horror movie sounding voice.

"Blood, Blonds, and Fake Boobs. Putting 'boobs' in the title of the blog always gets a lot of hits," Stacie said.

"How often do you put boobs in the title?" Moe asked with genuine concern.

"Don't worry about it. Almost never," Stacie said.

Saving Stacie from further inquisition, the second green-shirted employee appeared, "I'm Cher. How can I help you?" she asked.

"We're working with the property owner's insurance company following up on some details of the Charlie Michaels case. Would you mind if we asked you a few questions?" Moe asked, picking up on the story Stacie had started.

"Sure. But it was a while ago, and I didn't actually see anything happen," Cher said.

"Would you mind going over for us what you did see?" Stacie said.

"Yeah. It was like I said in court. I was locking up. All the clients were gone, and it was just me. And I saw that man, Sennack, whip into the parking lot. He looked furious. He caught my attention because he was driving so crazy. I thought he was going to slam into the building. Then, he jumped out of the car screaming. It was wild. I'd never seen anything like it. He was terrifying. That's why I called the police," she explained.

"I would have called the police too. Had you ever seen Mr. Sennack before that day?" Moe asked.

"No. That was the first time. He was so wild looking. I would have remembered seeing him before," Cher replied.

"What did you do after you called the police?" Moe asked.

"I came back inside to wait for the police. Right as they showed up, that crazy man came running out into the parking lot covered in blood. I was so scared," Cher replied.

"And then what happened?" Moe asked.

"Well, once the police had him the car, I came out and told them what I'd seen," Cher said.

"Did you go out on your own, or did they come and get you?" Stacie asked.

"I went out to talk to them. I wanted to let them know what I'd seen," Cher said.

"Did you know Charlie Michaels?" Moe asked.

"No. I mean, I'd seen him in the parking lot, but we'd never met before," Cher said.

Moe considered grabbing Cher's arm and just taking the memory from her, but she wasn't sure what the repercussions of that would be. What if Cher called the cops? Then it would be Moe's word against hers, and it would give the killer the chance to cover their tracks.

"Was anyone else here with you?" Stacie asked.

"Sure. Tai was here. She saw it all too," Cher said.

"She didn't speak to the police though," Moe confirmed.

"No. That was just me," Cher said.

"Why didn't she come out into the parking lot too?" Stacie asked.

"She was too scared. I told her that I'd do it. Look, I need to get back to my clients. We've been through all of this with the police already. I even went and testified in court. I really need to get back to work," Cher said.

"We understand," Stacie said.

"Thank you for confirming those details for us. We might be back later if we have more questions for you," Moe said.

"Whatever you need," Cher said.

"Well, she's full of crap," Stacie said, once the door had closed behind them.

"Can you text Ami? We need to know if Charlie Michaels was one of her clients or vice versa," Moe asked.

"I'm on it. Then I'm going to find this stupid Chinese food place, and we're going to lunch," Stacie said, pulling out her phone.

"I'm going to make one more stop. I'll meet you back at the car," Moe said.

Crossing in front of the real estate agency, Moe walked to the offices of Connections. She pushed open the door and stepped inside. The office was arranged like the real estate agency. People coming in the front door were welcomed by a small welcome desk and a hallway that led back to a larger space. Although, this desk was unmanned and, in contrast to the bright colors of Dream Home, these walls were dark and poorly lit. Moe thought about sticking her head down the hallway. Instead she just said loudly, "Hello. Is anyone here?"

There was rustling in the back. A few minutes later a short, unshaven, pale man with thick glasses appeared from the hallway. "I'm sorry. I think you might be in the wrong place," he said. His voice was pinched, and he rocked back and forth on his feet in an uncomfortable motion.

"Actually, I'm looking for someone who works here," Moe said.

"We don't see clients here. You'll need to go to our customer service center," the man said.

"Oh, no. I'm not a client," Moe said.

"We don't see sales reps here either. This is just our tech center," the man said, as he adjusted his glasses.

Moe felt like the only thing he was missing to complete the tech-nerd ethos was a pocket protector. "Let me explain. This is kind of embarrassing. I ran into a guy coming out of this building in the parking lot. He was a little taller than me. He had brown hair and was pretty fit. He was taking the garbage out and listening to headphones? I was kind of hoping I could get his name? Maybe ask him out?"

"Oh god," the man complained as he shook his head. Turning to walk back to the larger space, he yelled, "Josh! She's here for you!"

It was only then that Moe noticed the small camera behind her.

There was more rustling in the back. A minute later, the man Moe had seen in Malcom's memory appeared. He was wearing the same Bose headphones, but now they rested around his neck. "Heeey. How you doin'?" the man said.

"I'm Moneta Watkins, I'm a private investigator looking into the murder of Charlie Michaels. I'd like to ask you a few questions," Moe said.

The man took a step back and cocked his head. "So, you're saying you didn't see me in the parking lot taking out trash and think I was super-hot?"

"Sorry. No. And the other man said your name is Josh?" Moe asked.

"Yeah. Sorry. Josh Rudd. HTML guru, graphic designer, and general tech-nerd at your service," Josh said with a nod.

"Do you remember where you were the night Charlie Michaels was killed?" Moe asked.

"The real estate dude next door? Sure. I was here. We all were. We were pulling an all-nighter," Josh said.

"What do you do here?" Moe asked.

"We're a web-design firm. We're actually just one department that gets contracted out to other departments. There are only five of us in this office. We do mostly government work. Nothing fancy. Just congresspeople's web pages and stuff like that. That night we had to get up a new site for the state's campaign to rebuild schools. It was a rush order, and none of us wanted to work the weekend, so we all voted to stay until it was done," Josh said.

Moe took a deep breath of relief. It was nice to finally talk to someone who was willing to share information with her. "And you're sure that was the night Charlie Michaels was murdered?" she asked.

"Yeah. I remember because nothing ever happens here but then, out of nowhere, there are all these cops in the parking lot. We all came out to see what was going on, and we saw them bring the body out and everything. Then, when we finished around ten in the morning and when we came out, there were all kinds of news trucks and stuff outside. It's usually so quiet here. We get the occasional sports car peeling out of the parking lot or the real estate dude-bros yelling at each other, but never any cops," Josh explained with a smile. He was cute, in a nerdy kind of way. Moe liked how his mop of hair bounced as he spoke.

"You didn't see anyone coming or going before the cops showed up, did you?" Moe asked.

"Yeah. I totally waved to that dude they say said killed that other dude," Josh said.

"Can you describe how he looked when you saw him?" Moe asked.

"I don't know. Normal? He seemed pretty chill. Nothing out of the ordinary?" Josh replied.

Moe did a victory dance in her head. "Would you be willing to testify to that in court?" Moe asked, unable to hide the hopefulness in her voice.

"Sure. No problem. It's what I saw," he said.

"Great. Thank you. Did any of the cops ask you about this?" Moe asked.

"Nah. They were too busy talking to the hot PT girl.

No one ever notices the nerds," he said.

"You didn't happen to see anyone going in before Malcom, the guy that waved to you?" Moe asked. She knew there was no way the case would be that easy, but she thought it couldn't hurt to ask.

"Nah. But we can't see the back door from our windows. Someone could have come and gone out there," Josh said.

"There's a back door?" Moe asked, surprised.

"Yeah. All these offices are basically the same. They all have this little front entryway, offices and a kitchen in the back, and a rear exit," Josh said.

"Good to know. Any chance there is a camera on those back doors?"

"Sorry. No. This place is crazy low tech," Josh said with a laugh.

After Moe had thanked Josh and taken his information, she stepped back out into the parking lot and called Dorothy. She got the attorney's answering service. After the beep, she said, "Hey, Dorothy. It's Moe. I know it's not enough, but I found someone who can discount the eyewitness. He says he saw Malcom go into the building acting normal. And he is willing to testify. Call you back when I've got more."

CHAPTER FOURTEEN

Moe and Stacie shared the bench with Mr. Bear. Moe zipped up her jacket, took her gloves from her pocket, and put them on. The trees, whose orange and yellow leaves were scattered on the ground, had ceased to provide protection from the autumn wind, leaving the occupants of the playground on the plateau exposed.

Federal Hill, a fixture since the founding of Baltimore, overlooked the city. Standing well above its surrounding neighborhood and on the edge of Baltimore's Inner Harbor, it was a prime location for tourists to visit. The location received its name when a parade celebrating the signing of the Constitution of the United States in 1789 ended at its apex. Three cannons pointing at Baltimore's City Hall still stood on the crest of the hill, having famously been positioned there by the Union General Benjamin Butler who, in 1861 following the Baltimore Riots, snuck into the city in the middle of the night and positioned his forces on the hill as a warning to the city that it was to stay in the Union or else. In addition to the monuments, the hill contained a nice playground, a swingset, benches, and a large fenced-in grassy area for events or playing ball.

Moe watched as Sarah flew down the slide, hit the ground running, and bounded up the steps for another round. "So, why do you think the physical therapist is covering for the real killer?" she asked Stacie.

"Sex. Sex or money. How hot are the cops that showed up on the scene? Maybe she wandered out to flirt and found herself caught up in something?" Stacie suggested.

"Why would she testify in court then? And why did one of them stay inside? Feels like a lot of cover-up just to flirt with a cop," Moe said.

"Well, then, maybe she's Charlie's secret mistress, she stabbed him, and then ran out the back to meet the cops?" Stacie suggested.

"And she was so hot, they didn't even notice that she was covered in blood?" Moe challenged.

"Well, maybe she has blood disappearing super-powers that make her and any clothing she is wearing resistant to blood stains," Stacie suggested.

"I mean, I'd like to say that's complete fantasy," Moe started.

"But you relive people's memories, so who are you to say she can't have blood disappearing super-powers?" Stacie finished.

"What do you think, Mr. Bear?" Moe asked the teddy bear between them.

Stacie leaned down, pretending to be listening to the Bear. Sitting back up, she explained, "Mr. Bear said it's super lazy of us to think we could solve the case with one visit to guy's office and that only really crappy detectives would blame a murder on super-powers."

"Screw you, Mr. Bear," Moe joked.

"Right? Who knew? Mr. Bear is kind of an ass,"

Stacie agreed.

"I could see the wife stabbing someone," Moe posed.

"I thought she was going to stab you," Stacie laughed.

"Right? She was fierce," Moe agreed.

Another wind blew across the hill, and Moe shivered. They watched in silence as Sarah went down the slide again. "Okay. We let her slide one more time, then we go in search of hot chocolate," she proposed.

"Agreed," Stacie said.

"It's nice to see her smile," Moe said.

"She felt strong enough to trust us with Mr. Bear. That feels like something good," Stacie added.

"Yeah, even if he is an ass," Moe said with a smirk.

Leaning down again, Stacie said, "Wait. What's that Mr. Bear?" After pretending to listen for a few seconds, she sat back up and said, "Mr. Bear thinks we should investigate the physical therapists. He thinks they're fishy. And Mr. Bear does not like fishy things."

"Agreed," Moe replied.

CHAPTER FIFTEEN

As Moe had followed Antonio Bainchi into the parking lot, Francine had gave her an "I told you so" look. The mercenary-bodyguard had not been as excited about the plan as Stacie, Ami, and Moe had been. She told Moe multiple times that it likely wouldn't go how Moe expected. Now here Moe was, getting into the passenger seat of a Big Tony's 1968 black Dodge Charger, going to pick a fight with her older brother, without having had time to warn him first. She hoped Stacie had called Calvin and let him know they were coming, otherwise this was going to get real weird real fast.

"I had to rebuild the engine because I couldn't afford to just buy one outright, but that was pretty easy because I had two wrecked ones to work from. The hardest part was redoing the interior because I ain't real good with that kind of stuff," Big Tony droned as they turned onto Lexington Street. He'd spent the entire twenty minute drive talking about his car.

Moe glanced in the side mirror and saw that Francine

and Stacie were still two cars back. She looked at her wine colored shoelaces. She watched the silver sparkles dance in the light and told herself everything was going to turn out fine. "You did a good job with it. I like it," Moe yelled for the third time. She had to raise her voice to be heard over the roaring engine.

"I even found floor mats that matched. See, look at those. I had to search a long time for them. But I found them in a wreck that came into the junk yard. Real bad car smashed up, but the floor mats were good," Big Tony said, pointing down to the floorboard with his meaty hands.

Moe looked at the oddly fitting, almost matching floor mat under her feet and said, "Yeah. Good find."

They turned onto Saratoga, and Moe pointed out the blacksmith shop where Calvin worked. "That's it right there," she said.

Big Tony whipped the Charger into a parallel parking spot. "You said this guy is a big guy and that he should have your cash on him?" Tony said, as he killed the engine.

"He always has a ton of cash on him," Moe said nodding.

"Okay. I got this. You just wait here. I'll be back," Tony said, getting out the car.

Moe laughed to herself. She wondered, if she let Tony go on his own, would Tony pocket the money and come back claiming that Calvin didn't have any cash on him after all? Tony might even ask her to pay him for his trouble. She jumped out the car after him and called, "I'm coming. I want to watch you kick his butt."

They crossed the street and entered the front door of the shop. Moe took a deep breath, inhaling the smell of iron and dirt. She loved this shop. It had been building iron gates, railings, and window guards in this same location since the early 1800s. The first floor had two blacksmith stations complete with anvils, welders, raging forges, and racks of various hammers and tongs. Calvin's station was on the second floor next to a large area used for painting finished works. The dirt floor basement was filled with shelves of different sized iron bars. The walls, floors, and even some of the equipment was original to the building. Stepping into the store felt like stepping into history.

Moe noticed the two downstairs blacksmiths were missing. She took that to mean that Stacie had called ahead after all. She peeked her head into the small office to the right of the front door where the designer and receptionist sat. They were both missing as well.

"So, where is this guy?" Big Tony asked, as he cracked his knuckles.

"His station is upstairs," Moe said.

"Alright," Tony said. The old wooden steps creaked under his weight as he ascended.

As they reached the second floor, Calvin came into view. His welder's mask down covering his face, he was hunched over an iron gate, the muscles in his giant arms rippling. Sparks flew around him as he welded two joints together.

"Yo! You Calvin?" Big Tony roared with a low rumble.

Calvin turned off his welder, took his mask off, and set it down on the gate he was working on. Standing up straight, he matched Big Tony in size but outpaced him in muscle mass. "That's me," Calvin said with a look of disdain. He glanced at Moe, and she could feel her older brother's disapproval.

"You owe this little lady some money, and I'm here to collect," Tony said, pounding his fists together as if he were wearing boxing gloves.

"Come get it then," Calvin said with the unenthusiastic tone of a high schooler being forced to read an essay in front of his history class.

Big Tony charged like a boxer at the bell. He clearly hoped to end this with a quick combo. When he came within arm's reach, he shot left jab at Calvin's face, but Calvin was fast and dodged it. Tony tried to follow with a haymaker of a right hook, but Calvin slipped out of its way as well. Catching Big Tony as he followed through, Calvin placed a hand on Tony's arm. The giant boxer crumpled onto the floor and retreated into a fetal position. Following the boxer down, Calvin's eyes sparkled with dark joy as he watched the boxer's nightmare.

Stacie and Francine appeared at the top of the stairs. "What's happening?" Stacie asked.

"The king of darkness is doing his thing," Moe said.

Calvin took his hand from Big Tony and stood over him. Still in the fetal position, Tony was silently weeping. A low moan of agony rolled from him. The joy disappeared from Calvin's face, and his standard stoicism returned. "Can you hear me?" he asked, his voice filled with a dark calm.

Tony sobbed and nodded.

"That was just a small taste. My sister has some questions for you. If you don't answer them, I'm going to touch you again, and I'll bring back some more of your nightmares. Do you understand?" Calvin asked.

Tony sobbed and nodded his head, yes.

Seeing it was her turn, Moe walked over to the giant man that was crippled on the floor. She took the picture of Sarah and her family out of her back pocket. Holding it up to Big Tony's face, she demanded, "You remember this family? You remember what you did to them?"

Big Tony quietly sobbed.

Calvin leaned down again and said softly, "Pull

yourself together, sit up, and answer my sister's questions."

Big Tony flinched at the sound of Calvin's voice. Slowly, he pulled himself to a sitting position. Like a giant baby, he wiped his eyes with the back of his hands.

Moe held the picture up again. "Tell me about them," said demanded.

Through sniffles, Big Tony said, "I didn't know what the job was. Damon just told me to get in the car. I didn't know we were going to hurt the lady."

"Hurt her. You killed her," Moe said.

Big Tony sniffled more and wiped his nose with his hand. He seemed to be regaining his composure. "I didn't do anything to her. That was Damon. He's the one that killed her. I thought it was just another intimidation gig. All I did was drag her downstairs."

"You and Giovani and Damon and another guy. Who was the fourth man?" Moe demanded, still holding the picture in his face.

"I don't know his name," Big Tony said with a pout.

"That's not good enough," Moe said, pushing the picture forward.

"I said I don't know," Big Tony said, pushing Moe's hand away.

Calvin leaned in, and Tony recoiled. "Touch her again and see what happens," he threatened.

"I'm telling you the truth. I don't know his name. We met him at this empty lot and got in his van. He was friends with Damon. Damon called him Jack. That's all I know about him," Big Tony said. His tears had stopped, but he was refusing to make eye contact with anyone.

"You ever work for him before?" Moe asked.

"No. That was the first time. And I told Damon I didn't like hurting women and that I didn't want to do that stuff again. That's not what I do," Tony complained.

"What happened to the man you took from the house?" Moe asked.

"When Giovani and I got him to the van, we duct-taped him up good. Then we went back to that empty lot, and that guy Jack took it from there. I don't know nothing else about it," Big Tony said.

"How did Damon contact you?" Stacie called from the stairs.

"Contact me?" Tony questioned with a laugh. "He does like you did. He just pulled up at the gym and told me to get in the car. You don't say no to a guy like Damon. Not if you want to keep working," Big Tony said.

Moe looked at Stacie and Stacie shrugged, communicating that she didn't have any more questions either.

"I'm done with him," Moe told Calvin.

Calvin leaned down close to Tony again. "Listen closely, because I need you to understand this. You aren't going to tell anyone about this. You aren't going to talk to people about me or my sister, and you aren't going to try and find us to get some kind of revenge, because if you do, I'll come for you, and I'll trap you inside your darkest nightmare forever. You'll live that moment over and over again until you go mad and your mind quits working because it can't take the pain anymore. Am I clear?"

Big Tony nodded.

"Now get. I don't ever want to see your face again," Calvin said.

Big Tony scrambled to his feet and ran down the stairs. It was only a few seconds before they heard his Charger roar to life.

"Thank you," Moe said to Calvin.

Calvin sighed and took off the large leather apron he was wearing. "I don't know why you had to pull me into this. You could have gotten all of that on your own," he complained.

"I'm sorry, but," Moe began to say that she didn't like to steal memories and she knew Big Tony wouldn't just give it up, but was cut short when she thought about what she had done to Giovani Corbi.

"But she didn't want to have to relive seeing Sarah's mom die again," Stacie jumped in.

"I had to clear out the shop and send all the guys to an early lunch. It's just a lot of hassle. Maybe more of a heads up next time?" Calvin said.

"I appreciate you taking care of me," Moe said.

Calvin's face softened. "Anything for my favorite sister," he said.

Francine crossed the room and extended her hand, "I'm Francine," she said.

Calvin shook her hand and said, "Calvin. Nice to meet you."

"If you ever want work, I run a protection business. We could use your skills. I pay well," Francine said.

"Sorry, lady. I only do that for family," Calvin said with a nod. Looking back to Moe, he asked, "You have any more trouble with Lance?"

"Robert and I are tracking him. Trying to figure out what he's doing. I don't think he's been back to visit me again yet. How about you?" she asked.

"No sign yet. I'll tell you if he shows up," Calvin said.

After saying their goodbyes, Moe jumped in the car with Stacie and Francine.

"Whoa. I thought Robert was good looking, but that dark and mysterious thing Calvin's got going on? I mean, damn," Stacie said.

"That's not funny," Moe said.

"I know he said no, but do you think he'd be open to contract work from time to time?" Francine asked.

"Probably not. Something about seeing people's nightmares gives him a weird pleasure, and he hates that," Moe said.

"That's a shame. He has marketable skills," Francine said.

"You think he'd be open to doing some work with me? Of the romantic variety?" Stacie teased.

"Stop it," Moe demanded, pointing her finger in Stacie's face.

Stacie held her hands up defensively and replied, "It's not my fault your brothers are all so hot."

CHAPTER SIXTEEN

"You want to hear my theory?" Stacie asked, as she and Moe waited in Moe's car for Cher and Tai to leave their apartment. It had surprised Moe and Stacie to learn that the two physical therapists who'd claimed to see Malcom entering the real estate agency in a rage were also living together, but it made spying on them easier.

Moe squinted at the front door of the apartment building, trying to see through one of the windows. Like many large three-story row homes in the gentrified neighborhood of Mount Vernon, each floor of this house had been converted into a separate apartment. She took a sip from her coffee, inhaling the steam coming from the cup seconds before she drank. She enjoyed how it warmed her nostrils. "I'd love to hear your theory," she said.

Stacie turned in the car to face Moe. "Okay, here we go. Tai is banging Charlie. After work, thinking all the clients are gone, Tai goes over to see him. Maybe have some risky fun in his office to end the day? But Charlie is angry. Maybe he tells her something like, 'Look. I have a client coming in a few minutes. Plus, this needs to stop. I know I seduced you with my power and money, but I'm married and I can't do this to my wife anymore. I love her. What if she finds out?'"

"Charlie sounds very whiney," Moe interjected, commenting on the voice Stacie used to imitate the real estate mogul.

"Cheating husbands always are," Stacie retorted. Continuing with her story, she said, "So Charlie breaks it off, whining about his marriage, and Tai is enraged. So she runs to the kitchen in the office."

"Was there a kitchen in the office?" Moe asked, trying to remember.

"There's always a kitchen in the office. Where else would they make the coffee? So, she runs to the kitchen, grabs a knife, and stab, stab, stab, stab," Stacie said, making violent stabbing motions. "Then, she realizes what she's done. And she says, 'Oh no! I have to get out of here!' So she exits the back door and runs across the street. She busts into the physical therapy office and her roommate is like, 'What happened? Why are you covered in blood?' and Tai is like, 'I killed Charlie!' and Cher is like, 'Go clean up. I got this.' And she calls the cops telling them an angry man just ran into the building and stabbed the cheating bastard."

"It's a good theory," Moe said, sipping her coffee again.

"Thank you," Stacie said, turning back to face the row home again. They sat for a few moments in silence, and then Stacie asked, "What's your theory?"

"I think it has more to do with the real estate. I think Charlie called Malcom for a legit reason. Maybe the owner of the property was pulling out? Maybe he had cold feet? I think that owner got there first and marched in angry. That's what Cher saw. Charlie confronts the owner. They have a fight. Stab-stab-stab."

"Wait. Where does your knife come from?" Stacie interrupted.

"From the kitchen of course. Offices always have a kitchen," Moe said.

"Agreed. Continue."

"So, owner shows up. Cher sees him. Fight inside. Stab, stab, stab. Malcom shows up. Owner runs out the back. Malcom takes the blame."

"Mine's sexier," Stacie said with a grin.

"And you tell it better," Moe said, tipping her coffee to Stacie.

With dramatic flair, Stacie announced, "Because I'm an Act-tor!"

Moe applauded.

"Oo. Look. Here we go," Stacie said bouncing in her seat and nodding toward the apartment where Tai and Cher were exiting the building. The ladies were dressed for a night out on the town.

They waited for the two women to get a full block away before they exited the car. Quickly crossing the street, they jogged to the thin double doors of the row home. Mount Vernon, one of the city's oldest neighborhoods dating back to the 1830s, used to be the home of the wealthiest of Baltimore. Now it housed the Peabody Institute, the Walters Art Gallery, and the giant Enoch Pratt Free Library. At the center of the neighborhood was a three-story tall monument to George Washington. Designed by the same artist who build the more famous monument in D.C., Baltimore's monument consisted of a tall Doric column with a statue of Washington on top. Surrounding the monument, interspersed between the institutions, were large rowhomes, twice the size of others in the city. They were once lavish single-family homes, but when the population of Baltimore began to decline after the Civil Rights riots of 1968, these buildings were chopped into single floor apartments by developers hoping to maximize profits.

Stacie pushed open the double doors and stepped inside as if she belonged. Through the entry were a small series of mailboxes, an apartment door to the left, and a staircase heading straight up in front of them. Stacie counted the steps and, as Ami had instructed, she stuck a small pinhole camera under the lip of the seventh step.

Admiring her handiwork, Moe said, "That's crazy. You'd never even know it was there unless you were looking for it."

They climbed the steps to the second floor and found a small hallway with a second apartment door. At the end, just over the window seal, Moe placed a second camera. Stacie positioned a third at the other end of the hall, giving them two angles on anyone coming or going from Cher and Tai's apartment.

Finally, Moe stood in front of the door, and at a normal pace, walked back down the stairs to the entrance of the building.

"Nine seconds," Stacie called.

While Moe took out her phone and texted the information to Ami, Stacie positioned the final piece of hardware. Stretching to reach above the door, she put a small sensor. It pointed down to alert the cameras if anyone entered the door, triggering them to start snapping pictures. "Do you think Ami has these all over our office?" Stacie asked, as she finished sticking the sensor to the wall.

"Now that I know they exist, I'm going to say she absolutely is watching everything we do," Moe said.

"Yeah. That's what I was thinking too," Stacie said.

Moe smiled and said, "When we get home, let's play 'find and crush all the tiny cameras.'"

CHAPTER SEVENTEEN

Robert was waiting in front of one of the tallest skyscrapers in Baltimore. Without ornamentation or fanfare, the black glass obelisk rose straight up into the sky, a testament to Baltimore's need to feel like other large metropolitan centers. As they walked toward her brother, Moe looked up at the monstrosity. She disliked buildings like this because they had no character, no passion, and no history. Invaders in Baltimore's charming landscape, they felt like they'd been transplanted from New York and forced into her city.

"Couldn't manage to wear a jacket again today? One day is all I get, huh? Stacie, I thought you had this under control?" Robert complained once Moe and Stacie were in earshot.

Stacie put her arm around Moe and retorted, "There's no improving on perfection."

A small knot formed in Moe's throat, and she glanced down at her wine colored shoelaces. Like most big brothers, Robert's superpower had always been making her feel small. She was thankful she had a friend who would jump to her defense. Gathering her reserves, Moe looked her older brother in the eyes, smiled, and asked, "You come to work or to MC a fashion show?"

Robert shook his head and mumbled, "Let's go."

Robert's badge got them through security with no problem. He briefed them as they traveled up the elevator to the forty-fourth floor. "We got the call a few days ago through back channels. Michelle Dives was working late."

"Michelle Dives the billionaire CEO? The Queen of Retail?" Stacie interrupted.

"That's her," Robert replied.

"What's she doing in Baltimore?" Moe asked.

"Her company has an office here, and she owns a house on the waterfront. She's actually here more than you'd think," Robert said.

"How do you know that?" Stacie asked with a raised eyebrow.

"Because we pay attention when people with mini-armies of security personnel come into town. Plus, it helps that lots of ex-Feds are on her payroll," Robert said.

"That's less fun than the romantic angle I was hoping for," Stacie said with a shrug.

"You two need to get serious. Fast," Robert lectured.

"Continue with your brief," Stacie said.

"Like I was saying, a man walked into the building, made his way to her personal office without being challenged, spent twenty minutes with Ms. Dives, and then left, but no one remembers he was here," Robert said.

"If no one remembers he was here, how did you get called in on this?" Moe asked.

Robert pulled a picture out of his coat pocket and help it up for Moe and Stacie to see. In the picture stood Moe's twin, Lance, in the same elevator they were in. Smiling up a camera, he was holding a sign that read, "Hi, Moe. Hi, Stacie. Robby."

"What kind of sick game is he playing, baby girl?" Robert demanded as the elevator rang, indicating they'd arrived at their floor.

As Moe stepped off the elevator, she replied, "He probably knew he couldn't get all the cameras turned off in a building this big and high tech, so he decided to screw with us instead."

After introducing themselves to the front desk, Robert, Moe, and Stacie were led to a large corner office. Floor to ceiling windows looked out on Baltimore's tourist laden Inner Harbor. The space was shockingly minimal. There was a small circle of uncomfortable looking leather couches and a modern desk with a rolling chair behind it. There were no pictures. No decorations. No unnecessary items of any kind. Even the desk was clear.

"Someone's been watching too much Marie Kondo," Stacie said, as she took a seat on one of the couches.

"Can't question the view though. I bet sunrises are amazing from here," Moe said, as she moved to a window to look out at the city.

A door Moe hadn't noticed opened, and through it stepped three people. They walked at a brisk pace as they chatted in muffled tones. The first was thin woman with short white hair. She strode with confident steps, her heels clicking as she walked. Behind her trailed a younger woman, who was furiously scribbling on an iPad. Moe assumed she was an assistant of some kind. Behind them came an older man with a military haircut. There was a slight bulge in his coat which Moe assumed was a gun in a shoulder holster.

"Please, take a seat," the woman said, as she sat on the couch across from Stacie. The younger woman took up a spot next to her, and the man stood behind her.

Robert moved to the couches. Before sitting, he shook the woman's hand and said, "Thank you for seeing us. I'm Robert Watkins." He then shook the man's hand and said, "Michael."

The bodyguard replied, "Thanks for coming, Robert."

Moe crossed the room and took a seat next to Robert and Stacie. "Ms. Dives. I'm Moneta Watkins. This is my partner, Stacie Howe. Thank you for seeing us."

"You can call me Michelle. I appreciate you coming. Now, what do you know about the visitor we had?" the white haired woman replied.

Moe smiled at how the CEO sought to control the conversation. "He's my brother," Moe said.

"What do you think he wanted with me?" Michelle asked.

"You don't remember your conversation with him?" Stacie asked.

"No. I was honestly surprised when I watched the security cameras. I don't remember him being here at all. Who does he work for? Is he some kind of industrial spy?" Michelle asked.

"We don't know who he is working for yet, ma'am. Does anyone here remember anything?" Robert asked.

"No one. He seemed to be able to walk past my entire security force without being stopped. He was like a ghost. As you can imagine, it's critically important I understand what he and I talked about. I'd like to say that I'm confident I didn't give any vital information over to him, but, at the same time, as you can understand, a man who can walk into this office in that way makes me nervous," Michelle said.

"Should we be concerned for Ms. Dives safety?" her bodyguard asked.

"It's hard to say," Moe said.

"Who is he?" Ms. Dives demanded.

"He's a criminal," Robert said.

"I appreciate that. I'd like to hear from her though, since she was the first one he said hello to with his sign on the security feed," Ms. Dives said, pointing at Moe.

Moe looked down at her shoelaces, trying to decided how much to reveal. Powerful people like this always saw her and her family as assets they could exploit. Moe took a deep breath and decided to keep the conversation minimal. "I'm not going to lie to you, ma'am. He's dangerous. I have no idea who he is working for or what he wants with you. What I can tell you is that he has a special ability. My brother can erase people's memories, and as he erases them, he sees them. He is the thief who traffics in information," Moe said.

Ms. Dives sat back in her seat. Taking off her glasses, she pinched her eyes closed and rubbed her forehead with one hand. "So, he likely took something from my mind? Something I can't remember but he now knows?" she asked.

"That's correct," Moe said.

"Will I ever get it back?" Ms. Dives asked.

"No," Moe said.

"Did he leave you a note by any chance?" Robert asked.

"He did. It was a post-it. It said, 'I had a choice. Forget or die. This was my choice," the bodyguard said.

"Did you write it, or did he write it?" Robert asked.

"It appears to be in Ms. Dives' handwriting," the bodyguard replied.

"It's likely he is done with you then," Robert said.

Leaning forward, Michelle asked, "How could you possibly know that?"

"He doesn't live in Baltimore. He's in town because he is hunting something. If he threatened you like that and you aren't dead, he likely got what he wanted," Moe replied.

Michelle sat back again and took a big breath. "And you can't tell me what he took?" she asked.

"I'm sorry. The best way to figure it out is to explore your memory and look for gaps. It's likely there is a chunk of time missing," Moe said.

"What do you mean?" she asked.

"Well, if he wanted to know what you were doing last Saturday, you'd have no recollection of that day. Look for a blind spot, and you'll know what he was looking for," Moe explained.

"Is this a learned behavior, or was he born this way?" Ms. Dives asked.

"He was born this way," Robert said.

"Well, you must have had a horrible upbringing. With a twin brother like that, it's shocking you aren't a vegetable in a room somewhere," Ms. Dives said.

Moe was unsure how to feel about that comment, so she remained silent.

"Well. I appreciate you coming in. Thank you for your time. You can show yourself out," Michelle said, as she stood.

CHAPTER EIGHTEEN

The Thirsty Horse, Moe and Stacie's favorite place to eat, was packed. All the booths were filled, mostly with parents trying to wrangle their young kids and with baseball enthusiasts watching the O's get destroyed by the Yankees – a routine occurrence. Thankfully, Mike, the tall and attractive manager who routinely asked Moe to go mountain climbing with him, had put a "Reserved" sign on Stacie and Moe's favorite table in the back.

"Wow. Business is booming," Stacie said with disdain, as she made her way back to their table.

"That's a good thing, right? It means this place is going to stay open longer?" Ami asked, as she followed behind.

"Stacie believes this place should exist for her and her alone," Moe teased, as she took a seat at the table.

"For us. It should exist for us and us alone," Stacie said, as she removed the reserved sign from the table.

"Whoa. Wait. What if that sign is for someone else?" Ami asked.

"Who else would it be for?" Stacie replied, as if the question were completely absurd.

From the corner of her eye, Moe saw a petite waitress

with big blue eyes and short brown hair making her way over to them. The glasses on the tray she carried rattled as walked. "This one looks really nervous. What if we did something different tonight and tried being nice," Moe suggested.

"No. Shan't," Stacie said in her best Emily-Blunt-in-The-Devil-Wears-Prada voice.

The waitress arrived at the table and said with a thick southern accent, "Hello, Ladies. Mike told me to bring these over to you." She placed three drinks on the table: a giant beer for Moe, a martini for Stacie, and whiskey for Ami.

"Oh, dear God, there's two of them in town," Stacie mumbled. Then turning to the waitress, she said, "Well, aren't you a Georgia Peach." She took a sip of her martini and grimaced. "Tell Mike less bitters," she said, as she passed it back.

"Okay. I will. And, thanks for noticing. Are you from Georgia? I'm from Alpharetta," the waitress said with a grin.

"No. Not from Georgia. I'm just good at picking out accents," Stacie replied, shooting Moe a nod of triumph.

The waitress reached down to take the martini glass from the table but Stacie pulled it away and said, "No, no. I'll keep this one. You bring me a fresh one."

"My beer is perfect," Moe said with a grin.

"And the whiskey is top shelf," Ami said with a nod.

"Okay, great," the waitress said with a sigh of relief. "So, I'll be right back with that martini."

"Aren't you going to take our orders, Georgia?" Stacie asked.

"I'm sorry. I didn't realize you were ready. My name is Savannah," the waitress said sheepishly.

"I'll have a burger. Mike knows how I like it," Moe said sweetly.

"I'll get the same, and another whiskey," Ami said, holding up an already empty glass.

"I'll have the chef salad with raspberries instead of turkey, cheddar cheese on the side, the mozzarella tossed throughout, dressing lightly drizzled, and the ham chunks not shaved," Stacie said.

"Okay. I'll be right back with that," Savannah replied with a bow.

"Did you just bow?" Stacie asked.

"I'm sorry. I did. This is my first day, and Mike said you were an important table, and I'm really nervous. That was weird. I made it weird," Savannah mumbled.

"No. Actually, I liked it," Stacie said with a smile.

As the waitress left, Stacie chided her friends. "Ladies, we have a responsibility here. You know that Mike entrusts us with putting his new hires through the gauntlet. We have to be mean to them. It's our sacred and solemn responsibility as Mike's favorite patrons."

"She just seems so sweet," Ami said, with a sly grin.

"And nice. She seems very nice," Moe added piling on.

"Enough. Man up, ladies. This is an interview. We have a job to do," Stacie challenged.

"Speaking of jobs, let's talk cases," Moe said, transitioning.

"Where do you want to start?" Ami asked.

Taking a sip of her martini, Stacie said, "I talked to Detective Mason. He said he confronted Giovani Corbi with the picture of Sarah's family, and the guy immediately lawyered up. One point for me."

"One point for you?" Ami asked with bewilderment.

"Yeah. I gave a new piece of information. I get a point," Stacie said with a wink.

"Oh. You've picked the wrong opponent. New information is my only job on this team," Ami said with a grin. "Tai Murphy and Cher Silverstone, the physical therapists. Nothing interesting from the cameras yet, but Charlie Michaels and Alicia Michaels were never their clients. Two points," she added.

"Two points?" Stacie protested.

"One point for Charlie. One point for Alicia. Two points," Ami replied.

"I'll allow it," Moe said.

"Who made you the referee?" Stacie protested again.

"Someone has to be. Would you rather we call Savanah back over?" Moe asked.

"Fine. Vinnie discovered that Damon the hook-nose thug is getting his jobs from a bulletin board at a coffee house. Vinnie is staking out the board for us. We're tied. Two to two," Stacie said.

"I tried to find a way to set him up like we did Corbi, but I'm not getting any traction. He's too careful. Maybe we just grab him like you did with Big Tony?" Ami suggested.

"I'm open to it. I don't think Calvin will help though. Maybe we pull in Francine? Also, on that same note, Big Tony said Three-Scar's first name is Jack. One point for me," Moe said.

"Wait! You can't be both the referee and a player in the game," Stacie complained.

Moe looked in the air as if she were consulting a higher power. "The referee says it is allowed," she declared. "Anything else on Sarah's family?" Moe asked.

"Yeah. We had some face-to-face time with Moe's brother's Calvin, and he is smoking hot in a dark and brooding bad-boy kind of way. One point for me. Three-to-two-to-one," Stacie said.

"That's not relevant to case," Moe protested.

"As the only impartial vote, I say it's allowed," Ami said.

Stacie toasted with her martini and said, "You're my new favorite."

"Okay, ladies. Here is your order," Savanah said, as she appeared with a tray of food. She passed the giant burgers to Moe and Ami. She then began placing the various plates containing Stacie's salad in front of her.

Stacie examined the lettuce of her salad and complained, "I said drizzled dressing. This is clumped."

"I'm sorry. Would you like me to take it back?" Savanah asked.

"It's fine," Stacie said with an annoyed sigh.

"And here is your new martini," Savanah said, passing a fresh glass to Stacie. "Mike told me to tell you that, um. Something like, 'That should solve your pickle?'" Savanah said with uncertainty, messing up Stacie's old television catch phrase.

"Oh, dear god," Stacie complained as she rolled her eyes. Looking across the restaurant, she caught Mike's eye at the bar and pointed angrily at him.

Mike replied by giving her two playful finger guns.

"Did I get it wrong?" Savanah asked.

"Nope. It was perfect," Moe said with a laugh.

"Okay then. Let me know if you need anything else," Savanah said, as she scurried away.

"Back to the game," Ami said, as she jammed a fry in her mouth. "I checked out Tiffany Brown, the receptionist. She moved here a year ago. She had been a junior at the University of Kentucky, but one day she just packed up her stuff and moved to Baltimore. Strange, but not criminal. She's the daughter of Melvin Brown, the Governor of the great state of Kentucky. She's his fifth and the youngest by four years. Governor Brown is in his last term and it looks like he's been putting feelers out about running for a Senate seat that is opening up next election. Point for me. Three-to-three," Ami said.

"That's interesting. I wonder why she just up and left college when she was more than halfway done?" Moe thought out loud. "Any connection between our murder victim and the governor?"

"Not yet. Tiffany has only been on the job for seven months. She also bartends at night, at a place over in Canton called Knife-Wrench. Another fun fact for you though, from the bowels of the realty office. Alicia and Charlie haven't lived together for over a year. She has a house out in Cockeysville. They aren't divorced on paper, but they might as well be. Four points. Ami takes the lead," Ami said.

"We found a new eyewitness. Josh Rudd. He can clarify Malcom's state of mind the day of the murder. Four-to-four," Stacie said.

"We?" Moe asked.

"I was present," Stacie said.

"You were in the car trying to find a Chinese food place to eat at," Moe said.

"Oh. Right. Judge Marcus had Chinese food menus all over his office," Stacie said, as she retrieved the menus from her purse and passed them to Ami. "We need you to look into it. And another point for me. All tied up, except for Moe, who is losing," Stacie said.

Ami inspected the menus. "Doesn't look suspicious," she said.

"Right?" Stacie said, as if that proved some grand point.

"Also, Judge Marcus looked like he was planning to make a run for Senator. Could you look into that too?" Moe asked.

"Which party was he running for?" Ami asked, as she punched in things on her phone.

"Democrat," Moe said.

"That's weird. The current senators are both

democrats and both pretty new. It would be hard to take down an incumbent," Ami commented.

"And to take the lead, Ms. Dives is evidently spooked. She got on a plane yesterday for Paris," Stacie said.

"How do you know that?" Moe ask, impressed.

"She's dating Hugh Jefferson, the action star, and he has an Instagram feed," Stacie bragged.

"You done now?" Ami asked.

"Maybe. I don't know. I might have more," Stacie said guardedly.

"You're done. So, here we go. Bruce Spiniker, your ex-stalker, has been working on a merger and locked up in his office for a whole week. Nothing evil about it thought. Five-to-five," Ami said.

"That's not new information. All you said is you've got nothing," Stacie complained.

"The referee rules that the absence of a clue is point-worthy information if it required leg work," Moe said.

"This is rigged," Stacie complained.

"The game was your idea," Moe said defensively.

"And for the win, the property Malcom was trying to buy was an old brewery on the west side of town. The owner is a guy named Anderson Siltmore. He owns a ton of properties around the city. I emailed you his number and email address. His secretary said he'd be happy to meet with you. And that's the game," Ami said, raising her hands in victory.

"Good game," Stacie said.

"Nicely played, ladies. Now, we've got more work to do," Moe said.

CHAPTER NINETEEN

Anderson Siltmore's office was in a rowhome off Charles Street on the north side of the city. While the rowhome itself, with its tinted windows and lack of personal touches like flowers or curtains, was clearly an office, it was impossible to discern what Mr. Siltmore did from the outside of the building. The small plaque next to the door simply read, "Siltmore Investments," but once Moe and Stacie had stepped through the front, it became clearer.

All around the luxurious lobby were photographs of properties Anderson Siltmore owned. Moe loved how the artistic angles in the photos emphasized specific aspects of each building. There were large pictures of new apartment complexes with plants filling the balconies, pictures of stoic office buildings, even black-and-white pictures of looming parking garages. All the buildings had a "constructed" date and a "repurposed" date recorded on the frame.

To the right side of the room sat a desk with a young looking man behind it. The man wore a black suit and glasses. His desk was clear except for a black phone. Moe wondered how many hours a day he had to sit there in silence. She hoped he had a book or something hidden in one of the drawers.

"May I help you?" the young man asked, as they stepped inside.

"We have an appointment with Mr. Siltmore. I'm Stacie Howe. This is Moneta Watkins," Stacie said.

"One moment please," the young man said, as he picked up the phone. After pressing a button, he said, "Mr. Siltmore. The special private investigators trying to build a wrongful conviction case for Lumpum and Brumtum are here to see you. Yes, sir. I'll tell them." Looking at Stacie, he said, "You may go upstairs."

"Thanks," Stacie said, as she and Moe walked through the lobby to the wide, marble, spiral staircase. As they ascended, Stacie said, "I didn't tell them what law firm we were working with or what the case was when I called."

"And I'm pretty sure Ami didn't either. She's way more secretive than that," Moe said.

"So, this guy does his homework," Stacie said, as they reached the top of the stairs.

The second floor was a large empty room with a long conference table made of dark, rich wood. Around it were fourteen leather chairs. On the walls, where there weren't windows, there were a large flat-screen monitors. It was clear the room was meant to exude power and intimidate adversaries.

Anderson Siltmore descended from the third floor with swagger. His grey suit was tailored to hug every angle. Under his jacket was a pressed white button up but no tie. He was ruggedly unshaven but not bearded. With smoldering eyes and perfectly coiffed hair, he looked like he was preparing for the GQ cover shoot.

"Anderson Siltmore?" Moe asked.

"Moneta Watkins and Stacie Howe. It's a pleasure,"

he said, as he kissed the back of their hands. Stacie shot Moe a disgusted glance and discreetly wiped her hand on her slacks. "And in one of your infamous t-shirts no less," he said taking a step back from Moe. Reading the shirt aloud, he announced, "Time is the best killer." Smiling, he commented cynically, "Cute. What is it? James Bond? Rambo? Or did I hear it in Jackass, maybe?"

"Agatha Christie," Moe said.

"Never got much into her. Jackass though. That's some funny shit." Sitting down at the table, he said, "So, how can I help you two ladies? I suppose you think I had something to do with Charlie's death, which I did not. You can check my alibi. I was giving a TEDx talk in Manhattan that night. "How to Sell Billions While Loving Your Life." Getting my personal philosophy into the world. My speech was one of the last that night. You know what they say about saving the best, so there is no way I could have made it and then gotten back from Manhattan to kill Charlie. Besides, Charlie was one of my best friends. He and I go way back. So I'm clear of this one," he said, raising his hands in the air in surrender.

"We came to ask you about the building you were selling to Malcom Sennack and why the deal fell through," Stacie said, as she and Moe took seats at the table.

Anderson leaned back in his chair and put his hands behind his head. "Is this really as fun as being a movie star? I mean, I know you had some rough years, but you've blossomed. I'm sure you'd have no problem getting back into it."

Stacie looked at Moe and raised an eyebrow.

"Why did you pull out of the deal at the last minute?" Moe asked again.

"I didn't. Charlie did," Anderson said with a smirk.

"What do you mean?" Moe asked.

"Well, I could tell you all the boring details, or, I could show you. I'd love to see that gift of yours in action," he said, holding out his hand.

Moe wondered how he got so many details about them. A good PI could do it, but it would take time. More likely, he knew one of their old clients and grilled them before Moe and Stacie had arrived. Moe looked at Stacie and Stacie shrugged. Moe relented, held out her hand, and said, "To be clear, if you try to put anything inappropriate or sexual in my head, I will fill your mind with so much tragedy, you will weep for a week."

"Feisty. I like that," Anderson said taking Moe's hand and closing his eyes.

Moe closed her eyes and then opened them again. She was in the same room. There was a laptop open in front of her on the table. A cell phone was next to it. She glanced at the computer screen. She'd just opened it up and put in Anderson's password. His stomach rumbled, and Moe realized it was almost dinner. She tried to remember what she'd had to eat today. There was the grapefruit for breakfast. Since then, everything had been liquid.

"Baby. What are you doing? Come back upstairs. I'm not done with you yet." The seductive voice came from behind her. Anderson turned to see Alicia Michaels drifting down the stairs. She was dressed in a white silk robe that hung open to reveal matching lingerie.

It was only then that Moe realized Anderson was only wearing boxers. "Let's get dressed and go get some dinner. I'm starving," he said.

"Only if you promise we can come back after," she said, coming to join him at the table.

Moe closed the laptop and said, "Feed me and then I'm at your service."

The phone rang. They glanced at it at the same time. The screen read, "Charlie."

"What does that worthless sack of shit want?" Alicia asked, the seduction gone from her voice.

"I don't know yet," Anderson said as he picked up the phone. Swiping sideways on the screen to answer, Anderson said, "Charlie. Sitting here with your wife. What's up man?"

"That bitch. Tell her I hope she dies," Charlie said.

"Will do," Anderson said with a laugh.

"I'll wait," Charlie said.

Anderson laughed again. Looking at Alicia, he said, "Charlie said he hopes you die."

"Tell him it's mutual," Alicia replied as she flipped the phone the bird.

"Alright, I'm not your therapist. Leave me out of your fights. What do you want?" Anderson said into the phone.

"Look, I need you to pull out of the brewery deal," Charlie said. He sounded anxious.

Anderson grimaced and leaned back in his chair. "What? No," he protested. "I need that deal. That property needs to go. I need it off my books, and I could use the publicity. You know this."

"You owe me," Charlie said.

"No. I don't," Anderson retorted.

"Come on. I need this. Do it for me," Charlie demanded, his voice cracking with desperation.

Anderson rolled his eyes and said, "This Malcom kid was your idea."

"I'm not saying we kill it totally. I just think we can get more out of him," Charlie said.

"You mean you can get more out of him," Anderson retorted.

"Look, you're giving it to him for a steal. I'm just going squeeze him a little. He's got more. I know it," Charlie said. He was sniffling and his words were strained. Anderson wondered if he was doing cocaine again.

"I'm all for making more, but I don't know. It's a nonprofit. Press could be bad if he starts calling around to pressure me," Anderson said.

"I just think the kid has more, and I want to pull it out of him. Why are you suddenly growing a conscience?" Charlie demanded.

"I need to offload this one. You know it's a piece of crap. No one else is going to take it," Anderson said.

"Remember how I went to bat for you with that Patterson Park property?"

"No. I got that property by leaning on Councilman Black. You just happen to be in the room."

"I won't lose him. The deal will still go through. I just need to string him out a little," Charlie complained.

"Fine. Do it. But if you lose him, I'm not going to be happy. I'll go find someone else, Charlie. And then where will you be?" Anderson threatened.

"I know a hotter blond real estate agent that doesn't screw everything up who would love to work on all kinds of things with you," Alicia said, still not looking up from her phone.

Moe pulled out of the memory and let go of Anderson's hand. She felt sick. His hunger still stuck with her. And she felt dirty, like she needed a shower.

"Wow. That's really something special," Anderson said, smiling at her.

Moe looked down at her wine red laces, steadying herself.

Stacie put her hand on her shoulder and asked, "You okay?"

"Yeah. It wasn't that bad this time. Just have to shake off being in that head space," Moe said. She took a deep breath, looked at her laces again, and then asked Anderson, "Who did Charlie owe money to?"

"I don't know. Everyone. He liked to gamble. He overspent on everything. The guy couldn't keep a dollar," Anderson said.

"We've seen his bank accounts, and they didn't show any of that," Stacie retorted.

"You've seen his accounts?" Anderson said with a grin.

Moe and Stacie didn't react.

"Look, those accounts have his name on them, but they're Alicia's. She does all their books. No one could beat Charlie at wheeling and dealing, but he was stupid with money. She didn't even let him have a credit card. He only dealt in cash," Anderson said.

"How often did he do drugs?" Moe asked.

"Shit. I don't know. We were friends, but I'm not his keeper. Seemed like he kept a steady diet of coke though," Anderson said.

"You know who his dealer was?" Moe asked.

"Sure. Let me write down his name and number for you," Anderson said sarcastic droll.

"We need a name," Stacie said.

Anderson laughed and held his hands up. "Look. I'm clean. I don't do that crap."

"I'm not going to threaten you because you've clearly done your research and you know that if we want to take someone down, we will. So give me something real and tangible," Moe said.

Anderson sat forward and laughed again. "I like you a lot. She was right. Down to the last detail. Maybe we can work together some day. What do you think?"

"I need something to go on," Moe reiterated, refusing to take the "she" bait.

"Alright. Alright. We went to an O's game once and before we got there, he made me stop in Fells. He picked up a bag from a guy named Christoph. He was working as a valet at the Waterford Hotel – charming place if you've never been," Anderson said.

Moe stood, and Stacie followed her lead.

"Thank you for seeing us," Moe said.

"You are fascinating women, and I am an instant fan. Let's find a project to work on together," Anderson said.

"We'll have our people call your people," Stacie retorted cynically, as she and Moe left the room. Once they were clear of the building, Stacie asked Moe, "Did you get anything good?"

"He's sleeping with Alicia Michaels, Charlie is the one who called off the sale hoping to shake Malcom down for more money, the Michaels hate each other, and Charlie does cocaine," Moe said, as she got in the car.

"Damn. That was a productive memory he gave you," Stacie said.

"It felt staged. It was too clean. He'd practiced it before he gave it to me," Moe said.

"People can do that?" Stacie asked.

"Memories are pliable. They change over time. Typically, I get the freshest thing a person has because they don't know I'm coming; but if you wanted to, you could shape a memory to be what you want it to be. That one left him looking too sparkly. He'd even typed his password into his laptop before it started. He was ready for us," Moe explained.

"So, maybe not as productive as we hoped. At least we get to cross off a suspect," Stacie said, as Moe put the car in gear and pulled out into the street.

CHAPTER TWENTY

Moe and Stacie sat in Moe's car watching Christoph, the valet in front of the Waterford Hotel, for a few hours. He'd spent most of his time waiting at the stand in front of the hotel's entrance, playing on his phone.

The Waterford Hotel sat on the water in Baltimore's historic Fells Point. On the corner of a string of row homes, it stood five stories tall. When it had been built in the late 1800s, it was likely the tallest building for miles. Now, there were buildings four and five times its size a few blocks away. The hotel's original intent was to serve sailors coming into port for a night off the boat. As the neighborhood around it had gentrified, it too had lost its bar in favor of a restaurant, beautified its rooms, and become a getaway for tourists looking to avoid the franchise hotel chains that filled every city's downtown.

"This is a waste of time," Stacie said with a sigh.

Moe sighed and nodded. "Christoph isn't exactly hopping with customers, is he?" Moe asked.

"He is not," Stacie replied.

Moe scanned the street for the hundredth time. Couples walked in and out of the boutique shops, carrying small bags, the random jogger passed by, city dwellers walked their dogs with small plastic bags in their hands – there was nothing out of place. "We're going to need to get to his boss. He's just a random corner boy in a strategic location. He's not putting a hit on anyone," Moe mused.

"Let's try something else," Stacie said, as she pushed the car door open and hopped out into the street.

Moe followed behind her.

Stacie caught Christoph's attention halfway across the street. Tucking his phone under the valet stand, he stood up straight and flattened out the red vest he wore. From her sashay, Moe could tell she was turning on all her charms. Christoph wasn't unattractive, but with his scrawny build and mild acne, he wasn't the type of guy to draw a woman of Stacie's caliber. Having someone as beautiful as Stacie Howe pay him any attention must have made his heart want to explode from his chest.

Stacie walked around the stand so she stood next to him and leaned in, letting her breasts come close to his arm. "You're Christoph, right?" she asked.

Christoph took a step back and swallowed. "So, um, what if I am. Who's asking?" he said, his brow filling with sweat, while he crossed his arms across his chest, trying to make himself look tough.

Moe watched in awe as Stacie ran a finger down his chest with one hand and reached under the valet stand with the other to grab his phone. "My friend and I are looking to score and we'd do anything to get our hands on what you've got," Stacie said, as she held the phone behind her back where Christoph couldn't see it.

Catching on, Moe hurried forward. As she pressed up against Stacie and shot a grin at Christoph, she took the phone. Glancing down, she saw the screen hadn't locked yet. She pressed the screen with her thumb to keep it active. Shifting the phone behind her back, she continued to press the screen every few seconds to keep it open.

Christoph swallowed. "I, um, I don't know what you're talking about?" he mumbled.

"Sure you do. Where are those little brown bags you pass out? Like I said, my friend and I will do anything to get some," Stacie said, touching his chest again.

Christoph closed his eyes and laughed. Moe could tell that while he really wanted to give Stacie whatever she wanted, he was more afraid of whoever was in charge of the bags. "I can't. Look. All the bags are spoken for. You have to call ahead. I don't have any extra, and if I give you someone else's order, Benny will kill me. I mean, literally kill me."

Stacie leaned forward, kissed Christoph on the cheek, and whispered, "That's a shame. Maybe next time."

As she and Moe walked away, Christoph yelled with desperation, "I'm sorry. Maybe tomorrow? I'll see what I can get. Come back tomorrow? I'll have some then."

When they got in the car, Stacie and Moe burst into laughter. "That poor boy. He's never going to get over that," Moe said.

"Please, we just gave him a huge gift. He'll dream about that for the rest of his life. Did you keep the screen unlocked?" Stacie asked.

"Of course," Moe said, holding up the phone. Passing it to Stacie, she said, "You call. I'll drive. Let's get some distance before he realizes it's gone."

As Moe pulled out of her parking spot, she saw Christoph searching the valet stand.

Stacie found the contact, press the button to call Benny, and put the phone on speaker phone. As it rang, Moe said, "You or me?"

"I got this," Stacie said.

A deep voice came on the line and said, "Look you little shit. I told you to only call me if this in an emergency, so this better be a damn emergency."

"Hi, Benny. My name is Carla. I'm a private detective. I've spent the last two months documenting your operation. As you can see, I know where all your corner boys are, and I have photos of all the pickups and drop offs. If you don't want this information to go to the police, I'm going to need you to answer a few questions for me," Stacie said in a soothing voice.

"Nice," Moe mouthed to her.

"What the fuck? Bitch. When I find you, I'm going to..." Benny began to yell.

"Now, Benny. Calm down. Nothing's happened yet. I just have a few questions," Carla said.

"I don't know you. How do I know you're not the fucking cops?" Benny demanded.

"Think, Benny. Do the cops make phone calls? If I were the cops and I had Christoph's phone, I'd just come to your house and cuff you. So, either you tell me what I want to know, or those cops you're so scared of will be showing up at your door," Stacie explained.

"I ain't afraid of no cops," Benny declared.

"Stay focused Benny-boy," Stacie said.

"What the fuck do you want?" Benny demanded.

"I want to know about Charlie Michaels," Stacie said.

"Never heard of him," Benny laughed.

"Bullshit," Stacie said, calling his bluff.

Benny laughed.

"Did you kill him?" Stacie asked.

"Kill him? Nah. I don't kill my customers. That's not good business," Benny said, relaxing. His voice was almost a brag.

"How much was he into you for?" Stacie asked.

"Nothing. He was all paid up," Benny said.

"So you were square?" Stacie asked.

"Charlie always paid in cash. He had that real estate

money. He was nice repeat business. I wasn't going to do anything to him. I'm building an empire here. Franchising. I need my paying customers to keep coming."

"You have any idea who killed him?" Stacie asked.

"Yeah. That dude they put in jail for it. And if you know him, tell him he owes me what Charlie was supposed to give me this month," Benny said.

"Benny. This has been a pleasure," Stacie said.

"Fuck you. You better hope I don't find you, Carla the private detective. Because if I do, I'm going to fuck you up," Benny said.

"Have a nice day," Stacie said with a laugh, as she turned off the phone.

She handed it back to Moe and laughed, "We don't know any private detectives named Carla, do we?"

"Nope," Moe said, as she rolled down her window and threw the phone into the street.

"I got skills," Stacie said, leaning back in her seat.

CHAPTER TWENTY-ONE

The one-story, glass building looked out of place in Sandtown. The small front lawn was perfectly manicured and free of trash. On top of the building a large sign read, "Recreate, Rebuild, Resurrect." As Moe parked in front of the building, she couldn't help but notice the two police cars lingering at the end of the street.

"This is great. I thought the entire neighborhood was gone," Stacie said.

Sandtown earned its name from the sand pit that originally employed its residents. At the turn of the century, as wagons picked up sand and carried it back to the ships in the harbor, they would leave trails throughout the neighborhood's streets. Before the war on drugs, the neighborhood was called Baltimore's Harlem, but after decades of unemployment, crime, and neglect, the once proud African American community was mostly abandoned, filled with boarded-up rowhomes, broken windows, and roofs giving way to the tops of young trees.

Moe and Stacie exited the car and walked to the front of the building. The walkway was a steady stream of men coming and going, all with various packs of paperwork in hand. Inside, the building looked more like a department of motor vehicles. There was a large section of seating in the middle of the room. At one end, seven counselors sat at booths helping people one at a time. Above the counselor stations, there was a large counter that ticked off bright red numbers. To the right of the front door stood a picture of Malcom Sennack with his arms around two other men. Under the picture a small sign read, "Pray for Malcom."

Moe watched as the red numbers flipped from 135 to 136 and a large man in sweat pants and a white t-shirt hopped up and went to meet with a free counselor. It was only then that she noticed that Katie Scrasdale, Malcom's fiancée, was working as one of the counselors. Still dressed in all black, Katie was deep in conversation with an older man. They seemed to be trying to decipher a large stack of forms together.

Before Moe could get Katie's attention, a voice from behind her said, "Hello, ladies. How can we help you? Have you gotten a number yet?" Moe turned to see a thin man with a bright smile, red bow tie, and black sweater vest. Moe thought his thick black glasses and crisp goatee gave him a Malcom X vibe.

"We need to speak to Marvin Jacobs? We have an appointment," Stacie replied.

"I thought so. You didn't look like our normal clientele. I'm Marvin. You must be Ms. Watkins and Ms. Howe," he replied.

"It's nice to meet you," Moe said.

"Why don't you come back to my office? It'll be easier to talk there," Marvin said, as he motioned to series of small glass rooms against the back wall.

As they took seats in the small office, Moe asked, "What's with all the glass?"

Marvin laughed. "That was a Malcom thing. He felt like having all glass wall communicated that we had nothing to hide. Full transparency all the time."

"Thank you for taking time to meet with us today," Stacie said.

"No problem. Anything for Malcom. Any luck on his case yet?" Marvin asked.

"We are still just chasing leads, but I think will find something soon," Moe said.

"Even though we just started, it's already become clear that he's innocent," Stacie added.

Marvin took a deep breath, shook his head, and said, "Yeah. He's probably the only guy in here not capable of hurting anybody. Malcom and I grew up together, and I've never even seen him get in a fight. He's about the most peaceful guy I know."

"You've known him for a long time then," Moe remarked hoping Marvin would share more.

"Yeah. I was kind of his first client. When we were in high school, I got locked up for fighting and got sent out to juvie. He sent me a letter every day I was gone. Then he was waiting for me when I got out. Then we started doing the same with every guy we knew that went in. We'd write letters, visit, and then greet them when they got out and get them moving on their new lives. Show them that prison doesn't have to have a revolving door. You can come out, recreate yourself, rebuild your life, and be a resurrection story."

"I love that," Stacie said.

"Yeah. Malcom wrote that in the first letter he sent me. It's been our mantra ever since," Marvin said with a grin.

"So that's what you do here. You help people coming out of prison rebuild?" Moe asked.

"Yep. Coming out you don't get much. So we do job counseling and mentoring. We run free GED classes and get men plugged into community college. We have partnerships with a bunch of trade schools in town too. This is our processing center. They come here to work through legal paperwork and problem solve. Their job coaches meet them wherever they are. We even let parole officers set up in these small offices to meet their charges. Keep it all in one place and in a positive environment, you know? The big piece we are missing is housing. Malcom's dream was to have a dorm for guys coming out. That way we could snatch them up before they fall back in with their old patterns. Most guys coming out don't want to go back, but they come home to family that doesn't have room for them and a job that doesn't pay them anything. Going back to the gang becomes the only option."

"That's amazing work," Moe said.

"Thanks. It was all Malcom's vision. I'm just the right hand man," Marvin replied.

"So, do you know anyone who would want to set him up? Anyone out to get him?" Stacie asked.

"Sure. You probably noticed those black-and-whites parked at either end of the street? They're always watching us," Marvin laughed.

"What's that about?" Moe asked.

"Well, it's not personal. I used to think it was, but it's not. It's just a difference of perspective. See, we think men join gangs, sell drugs, and commit crimes because they have no hope for the future and no other way out of the generational poverty they were born into. They don't see it that way. They think people who do bad things are bad guys, and it's their job to protect the good guys from the bad guys. They don't like us because they think we give the bad guys cover. Which, honestly, is sometimes true. Not everyone wants a new life. Some guys get out and go right back to it, but they take advantage of our services as a smoke screen. We think that's the exception;

the police think it's the rule."

"So the cops that picked up Malcom, they might have known him?" Moe asked.

"Nah. Not at first. They would have just seen a black man coming out of building covered in blood. But once they got him back to the station and started booking him they knew who he was. One of our mentors was there with a guy who was being processed and saw Malcom come in. He called me and a bunch of us went running down to try and get him released," Marvin said.

"Bet that went over well," Moe said.

"Yeah. A bunch of angry ex-cons storming a police station, chanting, 'Let him out! Let him out!' Not my proudest moment," Marvin laughed.

"I'm surprised they didn't lock all of you up," Moe said.

"They let Malcom come out and talk to us. He sent us all home," Marvin paused and sighed and looked out at the crowd of men getting helped by the counselors. "The ship is a little captain-less without him. I'm trying to hold it together, but I'm just not the leader he is. We need him back. I don't know how much longer we can hold it together without him."

"You look like you're keeping things up and running," Moe said.

"Thanks," Marvin replied.

"Is there anything else you can tell us you think might help?" Stacie asked.

"Not really. I really think Malcom just got caught up in all this. Wrong place, wrong time, wrong color. I don't think it has anything to do with him," Marvin said.

Stacie grabbed a post-it note off his desk and started writing her number on it. "If you think of anything, let us know. Okay?" she said, passing it to him.

"Absolutely. We need Malcom out," Marvin replied.

CHAPTER TWENTY-TWO

The house wasn't what Moe had expected. Because of the bravado of his office and the cars in its parking lot, Moe had assumed that Charlie only sold mansions, but this was a simple townhouse on the eastern side of town in a quiet neighborhood. There wasn't anything fancy or expensive about the two-story brick home. Even the brown shag "Welcome" mat seemed ordinary.

"You alright?" Stacie asked, catching Moe staring at the house.

"I just expected more. I guess I thought Charlie only dealt in mansions. You sure this is the right place?" Moe replied.

"Ami said he had seven appointments on his Google calendar, and she was the one right before Malcom. You know, every sale is money in his pocket, and he seems like the kind of guy that would do anything for a buck," Stacie said with a shrug.

"Let's go find out," Moe said, as she led the way up the brick walkway to the front door.

Moe rang the bell. The woman that answered had a comforting smile. Combined with her nerdy, thick, brown-framed glasses and her simply cut long brown hair, she radiated pleasantness. "Are you the two detectives?" she asked.

"We are. Thanks for seeing us," Moe said.

"I'm Jordy McGill. Come in. I was just starting to get my lunch together. Do you want something to eat?" the woman said, as she motioned them inside.

As Stacie began to accept Jordy's offer, Moe cut her off and replied, "No, thank you. We just have a few questions, and then we'll go."

Jordy led them through a small hallway and then to the right, into a charming kitchen. The appliances all seemed in contrast with the linoleum floor that had seen better days. Jordy positioned herself across a small kitchen island on which sat a bowl of spinach leaves. "Are you sure I can't get you something to eat? Or maybe something to drink?" Jordy asked, as she took a bag of raisins from the cabinet behind her and began counting them out and placing them into the salad.

"No. Thank you," Stacie said begrudgingly.

"We wanted to ask you about your realtor, if you don't mind," Moe said.

Looking up from her salad, Jordy said, "I heard that he died. That was so sad."

"We're trying to get a better understanding of what happened on that day. Any info you can give us would be helpful," Stacie said.

"I don't know how much I can help, but I'm happy to talk about what happened. It was all very strange," Jordy confessed. Putting the raisins away, she took out a bag of walnuts and began counting them out and adding them to the salad as well.

"What do you mean, it was strange?" Moe asked.

"Well, for starters, Charlie wasn't my realtor. I was working with a woman in his office named Margret. She was really nice. She's the one that found me this place.

She took me through the whole process. Are you sure I can't make you a salad too?" Jordy said, as she put the walnuts away and took a bag of cheese and an apple from her fridge.

"We're really okay," Stacie said.

Jordy sprinkled the cheese on the salad and said, "Well, like I said, I worked with Margret. She was really nice. We found the house really fast, and it's perfect for me. I live alone, and I was just looking for something small. I don't need a lot of space. Anyway, it only took her about two weeks to find it, which was perfect because my lease was coming up. And she was really helpful when we closed on it too. She walked me through all the paperwork. I'd never have been able to do that on my own."

"So you didn't meet Charlie during the entire purchasing process?" Moe asked.

Jordy took a cutting board from under the island and bright red knife from the drawer. With it, Jordy sliced and cored the apple as she explained, "Well, I met him when I came for the signing. He popped his head in and welcomed me to the 'Dream Homes Realty family.'"

"What did that entail?" Moe asked, trying to puzzle out the words on the knife.

"He took a picture with me for their Facebook page, and Margret gave me a housewarming basket full of goodies. It was nice," Jordy said.

"Was that knife part of the basket?" Stacie asked with a smile.

Jordy passed it to Moe and said, "Yep. There was the knife, this cutting board, a candle, a bag of coffee, a bunch of chocolate, and a thank you card. It was a really nice housing warming gift."

"Do you mind if I take a look at that?" Moe asked. Jordy passed Moe the knife, and she held it so she could read the words "Dream Homes Realty" that were embossed on the handle in white lettering.

"Nice eye," Moe said to Stacie ,as she passed the knife to her.

"When was the next time you saw Charlie?" Moe asked.

"The night he died, I guess? His assistant called me that morning and asked me to come in," Jordy started

"Southern accent?" Stacie asked, as she handed the knife back.

"Yep. Real sweet. She told me there was some paperwork I hadn't signed and that I needed to come into the office. When I got there, it was just the three of them. I went after work. So it was pretty late, but it felt weird that the place was empty. Anyway, she walked me to a conference room and then Charlie came in and he said there'd been a problem with the paperwork and that I owed his firm more money. Which was crazy because they got paid out of the settlement," Jordy said.

"He asked you for more money?" Stacie asked with a raised eyebrow.

"It was wildly inappropriate. He wanted me to pay him like $30,000. I told him I didn't have it. He said that I needed to figure out how to get it. I told him I would need some kind of invoice or something, and he said he would go and print one off," Jordy explained, as she sprinkled the apple slices over the salad.

"What did you do?" Moe asked.

"When he left to get paperwork, I texted Margret, and she told me she didn't even work there anymore. So I got up and I walked out. I never heard from him again. I called a lawyer afterward. I got her name from Margret too, and she told me that what he was doing was illegal, that I didn't owe him money, and that I was right to run out of there," Jordy said.

"You did the right thing. It's good you got out of there. Also, you said there were three of them there?" Stacie asked.

"Yep. Charlie, his assistant, and his wife. I didn't talk to her, and I only know her from the pictures around there, but I saw her there when they walked me back to the conference room. She was working in an office in the back," Jordy explained.

"How did Charlie seem to you that night?" Moe asked.

"Desperate. Almost frantic. He was scary," Jordy said.

"Did you tell any of this to the police?" Stacie asked.

"I went to the station to make a statement, but they said they didn't need it, that they caught the guy red-handed, and that they would follow up with me if they needed any information. But, they never did, so I just figured they had it all sorted out," Jordy said, as she took a bite of her salad.

After thanking Jordy and saying goodbye, Moe and Stacie walked down the brick path in silence, pondering what they'd heard. Once they'd both closed their car doors, Stacie said, "So, Charlie was desperate that night and shaking down old customers."

"Sounds like it. And there are plenty of knives in the office," Moe replied.

"And there were two people there with Charlie between when Jordy left and Malcom arrived," Stacie said.

"Well, this was a productive trip. We've still got a lot of holes in the story though," Moe said, as she started the car.

"Physical Therapy Girls. Wife. Receptionist. Cops. Lots of people lying. Maybe they all stabbed him. Like, one of them held him down and the each took a turn. Some kind of ritual cult thing," Stacie said.

"I'm thinking more romance novel. We've got a desperate husband, his angry almost ex-wife, and his mistress?" Moe guessed.

"Ooo. Juicy. I like that story better than the cult killing," Stacie said with a smile.

CHAPTER TWENTY-THREE

Robert was waiting for Moe and Stacie on the other side of the yellow police tape. Lifting it up, he motioned for them to step under it. "He's escalating," Robert said, as a greeting.

The red and blue police lights reflecting off the windows of the surrounding row homes mixed with the yellow glow of the street lamps and gave the scene an eerie tone. Uniformed officers filled the perimeter, some working and some watching. Robert escorted Moe and Stacie past them to the front door of the grand three-story building.

In contrast to the common red-brick and Formstone three-story Federal rowhome, this house, with its pop-out second floor balcony and triangular attic was part of the Picturesque movement. Built in the late 1800's for wealthy land owners who owned both a city home and a country estate, this fancier style of rowhome was intended to mimic the fashionable styles of London and Paris. They only existed in a few small locations around the city.

Moe and Stacie followed Robert in silence through the front door, past the lavish living room, through the ornate dining room, and into a sleek modern kitchen. The white cabinets, silver-blue slate floor, and stainless steel appliances were all overshadowed by the dead body lying in a pool of drying blood. The man on the floor had a single bullet hole in his forehead. Two police officers buzzed around him snapping pictures and collecting evidence from his body.

"Who is he?" Stacie asked.

"Jensen Beauchamp. The CEO of the Beauchamp Group. They're an international engineering and design firm," Robert said.

Moe scanned the corpse lying next to the kitchen island. Mr. Beauchamp was dressed in black and purple running gear. Air Pods were still in his ears and his pristine white sneakers were laced tight. Moe would put the man in his mid-sixties. There was no sign of dirt in the treads of his shoes, which led Moe to assume there was an exercise room somewhere in the house. On the floor, next to Mr. Beauchamp's right hand, was a Smith and Wesson Governor, a sub-nosed single-action revolver often used for home protection. A drawer to the kitchen island was partially open, so Moe assumed that was where the gun came from.

"Do you think you can pull a memory from him?" Robert asked.

Moe reached down and touched the dead man's hand. It was hard and stiff. Standing, she explained, "I think he's been gone for too long. Plus, I'd need to electrocute him and I don't think you want me compromising all your evidence by hooking him up to a car battery."

"I don't think my office would be okay with that," Robert agreed.

"There isn't any sign of a struggle," Moe remarked.

"There also isn't any sign of a break-in," Robert said.

"How do we know it was Lance?" Stacie asked.

Robert got the attention of one of techs photographing the body and asked, "Can we take a look at the note?"

Reaching into a black case, the officer produced a Post-It note sealed in a plastic bag and passed it to Robert. Robert handed it to Moe and Stacie. The note read simply, "I gave him a choice. He chose to die."

"He's nothing if not consistent," Moe said, handing the note back to Robert.

"Were there any witnesses?" Stacie asked.

"No. He appears to have been home alone. He was recently divorced. His wife is living in one of their other houses out in the county," Robert said.

"How long ago did this happen?" Moe asked.

"The gunshots triggered the house's security system, which alerted the police. That was about two hours ago," Robert explained.

"Shots?" Moe asked.

Robert turned and pointed at the wall behind them where a bullet hole marked the wall next to a small kitchen table. "It appears that Mr. Beauchamp got a shot off. I figure Lance was sitting there," Robert said pointing at the small kitchen table, "and Beauchamp was standing here. He pulled the gun from the drawer and fired once before Lance took him out."

"Look, I've met all your other brothers, and I can't see any of them doing something like this. Are we sure this is Lance?" Stacie protested.

"Lance isn't like the rest of us. He's a trained killer," Robert said.

"What do you mean?" Stacie asked.

"After mom disappeared, we all had our mini-rebellions. I dropped out of school. Joseph became Catholic," Moe began.

"I left my law practice and went into law enforcement," Robert added.

"And Calvin disappeared for a while," Moe continued. "Lance went to war."

"What did he do?" Stacie asked.

"He started as a Marine," Moe said.

Robert interrupted. "But he moved into classified black-ops crap that even I can't get clearance to access. And then he went into the private sector. Paramilitary stuff. Security force for hire."

"I knew Lance had a body count from his time within the service, but I've never seen one of his victims face-to-face," Moe remarked. She couldn't put a finger on how she was feeling. It wasn't shock. She'd seen dead bodies before. The sensation in her chest felt like indifference, but that wasn't it either. She finally decided, it was confirmation. A small part of her had hoped that Lance wasn't the sociopath they all believed him to be, that they'd had misjudged him all these years, but her hopes were now lying dead on a slate kitchen floor. She wasn't sad or angry. She was resigned. Her family's fears were true. He twin brother was a monster. Wanting to push these thoughts away, Moe asked, "So, there's a body now. How does this change things for the case?"

"It's moving from a B and E, intellectual property theft to a murder investigation. There's going to be more resources devoted to the manhunt and more oversight. Which means we're going to have less freedom to operate," Robert said.

"What do you need from us?" Stacie asked."

"Just keep working the case. It's going to get a lot harder to bring you in on stuff like this, but I'll keep you posted when I can," Robert replied.

"If we get anything, we'll let you know," Moe said.

After saying their goodbyes, Moe and Stacie walked themselves out. As she passed through the house, Moe found herself cursing Lance under her breath for the chaos he was bringing into her world.

CHAPTER TWENTY-FOUR

Moe looked at the clock on her phone. Any second, Damon Santobello was due to come out of his rowhome. All of the details of the mission raced through her mind. She glanced at Francine's van and saw two of Francine's team waiting in the front seats, their black sunglasses radiating indifference and focus. She looked at the empty storefront across the street that had once been a men's clothing store. She looked at the red-light camera perched at the corner to catch speeders and hoped Ami had been able to turn off all the digital eyes on the block. Moe's eyes drifted down to her shoes. The red wine laces looked almost brown in the shade of the bus stop pavilion. She took a deep breath and exhaled it slowly.

There was so much that could go wrong with her plan. She was crossing a line. She could feel it. Tricking Giovani into thinking about drugs was one thing, but outright stealing memories? She was supposed to be above this. At the same time, Sarah's dad was still out there, and maybe he was with Moe's mom? If there was the smallest chance, shouldn't she do everything within her power to find them?

"You alright?" Stacie asked.

"Why do you ask?" Moe replied.

"You're looking at your laces again," Stacie said.

"I didn't know you knew about that," Moe replied with a grin.

"Of course I know. What's up?" she asked.

"I'm nervous about breaking the rules," Moe said.

"We stole Giovani's memory, and that went well," Stacie offered.

"That felt different. We knew he had taken the drugs, you made him think about the drugs, I just stepped in at the right time. I don't know what I'm looking for. Not really. I'm just going in to poke around," Moe said.

Stacie faced her, took both her hands, squeezed them softly, and said, "Relax. Your plan is good. This is going to work. Today we are going to get one step closer to bringing down the guys that killed Sarah's mom and kidnapped her dad."

Moe wished she had her friend's confidence. She watched her laces sparkle in the light and said, "I'm nervous I'm leading us across a line."

"Would you rather I try to seduce him like poor Christoph the valet?" Stacie said with a smirk.

"Poor Christoph the valet," Moe reflected with a laugh.

Changing her tone from playful to encouraging, Stacie said, "Hey. Look. Desperate times. Desperate measures. You and Francine have walked through this over and over. It's a simple plan. I'd even say elegant in a brute-force kind of way. Plus, there's no law against stealing someone's memories. I don't care what Robert says. So, relax. We're going to get this guy."

Moe looked up to see hook-nose Damon Santobello stepping from his front door into the morning sun. He was whistling and playing on his phone as he walked. Moe felt like they should have some kind of ear-based communication device like in the movies so she could touch it and say, "The package is in position," or something spy-ish like that. Instead, she and Stacie stood in silence, trying to look like they were waiting for a bus. Moe had chosen the spot because it allowed her to see the entire range of Damon's movement while hiding in plain sight amongst the daily commuters.

She watched out of the corner of her eye as Damon walked down the front steps of his house to his car. Damon cocked his head and pulled the note Moe had left for him off his windshield. It read, "Santobello. Across the street. Anderson's Big and Tall. 300k payout."

Damon turned and looked up and down the sidewalk. Unsatisfied, he walked out into the street and searched left and right for something out of the ordinary. If he knew what Moe looked like, he didn't let on. He looked across the street at the abandoned store. Stuffing the note in his pocket, he crossed the street.

Moe held her breath as he pulled open the door and gazed into the building.

"Take the bait. Take the bait," Stacie whispered.

The table with a briefcase opened revealing three-hundred-thousand dollars was, in the end, too much for Damon. He stepped inside and the door closed behind him.

"Got him!" Stacie declared with a celebratory whisper and first pump.

Moe started the timer on her phone. Francine had told her she needed two minutes. It would take thirty seconds for the remifentanil/carfentanil gas to work, another minute to clear the air, and then an additional thirty seconds for safety.

Francine's women stepped from the van and moved to stand guard in front of the door.

As Moe and Stacie watched the seconds tick away,

Stacie asked, "You know what you are going to look for?"

"Yeah. I think so. I'm going to start with an image of that guy Jack. If that doesn't get us what we need, I'll focus on Sarah's dad and work backwards," Moe said.

"You sure you don't want to hold my hand and take me in with you?" Stacie asked.

"It's harder that way. I need to just get in and out," Moe said.

The timer on the clock hit zero and Stacie said, "Showtime." She and Moe jogged across the street. Francine's guards opened the door for them.

The room was dark, and it took a moment for their eyes to adjust, but once things had come clear, Moe saw Francine packing up the money. In front of the table was Damon, fast asleep, seated, his arms and legs tied to a steel chair, his eyes covered with a blindfold. The smell of rubbing alcohol tainted the air, and Moe assumed it was what was left of the knockout gas Francine had used.

Francine put a finger to her mouth, reminding Moe and Stacie that no one was allowed to speak in front of him. With the briefcase in hand, she walked over to Damon, took two vials of ammonium carbonate from her pocket, crushed them in her hand, and waved them under Damon's nose.

Santobello gasped for air and came to life. Rocking the chair, he fought against his restraints. "What the fuck!" he screamed over and over, as he wrestled to escape.

Stacie nodded encouragingly at Moe. Francine stepped back and did the same.

Moe took a deep breath and moved around the chair until she was behind Damon. Closing her eyes, she pictured the three-scarred face of Jack. Touching the top of Damon Santobello's head, she invaded his memories.

Moe opened her eyes. In front of her was a small television playing a static-filled cartoon of Mickey Mouse driving a steamboat. The cartoon made Damon uncomfortable. He wasn't sure if he was supposed to laugh at it or be impressed by it. It made him feel nothing. His eyes drifted to the top of the television where a host of small, framed pictures were set up. Moe's eyes locked on a portrait of the three-scarred man sat. Like the cartoon, it too was confusing. It felt out of place.

There was yelling in the kitchen behind him. Moe turned around as Damon's mother smashed another plate in the kitchen. She screamed, "I'm so sick of you!" Another man was about to be kicked out of their house. Her pain made him sad. He wished she were happy with how things were. He didn't understand why she kept bringing these men home with her. He thought about getting up to fight with the man, but he decided that he would let this one go because he couldn't even remember his name. He'd fight with the next one.

Moe pulled out of the memory. Opening her eyes, she stepped back from Damon and looked at him. The glow of the static-filled television was a ghost in her vision. She shook it off. Looking up, she met Stacie's eyes.

Stacie raised her eyebrows, asking for confirmation.

Moe shook her head no.

Stacie gave her a curious look.

Moe shrugged. Taking a deep breath, she stepped forward again and closed her eyes. This time she thought about Sarah's parents, visualizing them both in her mind. Hoping to jump into the moment of their death, she placed her hand back on Damon Santobello's head and dove back into his memories.

Moe opened her eyes. Again, in front of her was a small television playing a static-filled cartoon of Mickey Mouse driving a steamboat. Again, she felt Damon's uncomfortableness with the cartoon. She looked to the top of the television. Panic rushed through her as her eyes locked on two pictures. Next to the picture of the three-scarred man there was a picture of Sarah and her parents.

There was yelling in the kitchen behind him. Moe turned around as Damon's mother smashed another plate in the kitchen. She screamed, "I'm so sick of you!" The man in the kitchen replied, "I'm sick of you too, bitch. There was a loud smack, a yelp of pain, and a crash. Damon jumped to his feet. He moved toward the open door. The man was growling in a low and dangerous voice, "Look what you made me do! You bitch! Look at what you made me do!"

Damon waited outside the doorway, waiting for his mom to reply. Waiting for her to cry. Waiting for anything. But the only sound that came was the man leaving the house through the back door.

Moe pulled out of the memory. Opening her eyes, she stumbled back from Damon. Grabbing the table behind her, she used it to balance herself. Young Damon's fear for his mother still raced through his chest. The glow of the static-filled television was stronger in her vision. She shook it off again. Looking up, she met Stacie's eyes for a second time.

"Are you okay?" Stacie mouthed.

Moe's heart began to race. She felt sick to her stomach. "I don't know," she mouthed back.

Francine mouthed, "Stop?"

Moe took a deep breath and looked down at her laces. She'd never experienced this before. She was always able to find what she wanted in a person's memories. Was this some kind of performance anxiety? She didn't feel sick. She bit her bottom lip and looked back up at Stacie and Francine. She held up a finger and mouthed, "One more."

Stacie nodded, concern filling her eyes.

Stepping forward and closing her eyes, Moe brought a clear image of Sarah's parents into her mind. She saw Sarah's mom bleeding out on the floor of Sarah's house. She watched in her mind as Damon talked with the three-scarred man. She saw Sarah's dad being dragged into the street and thrown into the black van. She could smell the room. She could feel the terror of the moment. She focused on Damon's voice and put the sound of him and three-scarred Jack arguing. With the powerful memories fresh in her mind, she put her hand on Damon's head again.

Moe opened her eyes. Again, in front of her was a small television playing a static-filled cartoon of Mickey Mouse driving a steamboat. Again, she felt Damon's uncomfortableness with the cartoon. She looked to the top of the television and felt a wave of defeat. Next to the picture of the three-scarred man and the picture of Sarah and her parents, there was a blood filled picture of Sarah's mom and a picture of Sarah's dad being thrown in the van. Moe felt tears in her eyes. A pit formed in her stomach.

There was yelling in the kitchen.

Quickly, knowing the memory was going to move to the kitchen, Moe began searching the other pictures on the television. With each photo, she could feel Damon's anxiety grow, demanding that he go into the kitchen to see his mother. Skipping from the picture of Three-Scar, through Sarah and her parents, past Sarah's mom, Moe discovered pictures of Big Tony and Giovani Corbi, a photo of the inside of a casino, a picture of Damon's house, a photo of the coffeehouse Vinnie had been staking out, a picture of a flyer for a lost dog, a photo of a self-storage place, and finally a picture of Damon giving the camera the middle finger.

Moe pulled out of the memory. Opening her eyes, she

fell backward onto the floor. Tears were streaming down her cheeks. Her head pounded with the sound of Damon's mom yelling. Her eyes burned from the static-filled glow of the television.

Stacie ran to her side and wrapped her arms around her. "Are you okay? What happened?" she whispered.

"Do it again," Damon said.

Moe looked up in shock. Her heart stopped.

"Do it again. Do it as many times as you want. I'm ready for you, bitch," he declared with a sneer.

Moe shook her head in disbelief. Her mind raced for an explanation.

Damon continued, defiant and proud. "What?" he challenged, "You thought Big Tony wouldn't come to me? You thought I wouldn't go and talk to Giovani? You thought I wouldn't research you? That I wouldn't ask about how your little superpower works. You can't keep what you do a secret. I know who you are, Ms. Watkins. I know what you can do. I know what your brothers can do. And I'm ready for you, bitch. All of you. You're not getting in my head. So keep trying. Keep coming. I'll show you my mom's murder all day. We can play this game as long as you want. As long as you want, bitch."

The tears flowed uncontrollably. Moe lost her breath. She gasped for air. Her heart felt as though it would erupt from her chest. She felt out of control.

"Take her out," Francine said, breaking the silence.

Moe felt Stacie helping her to her feet and supporting her weight. As Stacie walked forward, Moe followed. She looked at Francine and tried to say she was sorry, but all that came out were sobs.

"It's okay," Francine replied right before pulling a gas mask over her face.

"Don't leave! Come back! Let's play some more!" Damon yelled, as Stacie led Moe out of the store.

The sun blasted Moe in the face. She couldn't see anything but its brightness. Stacie guided her to the van, pulled the side door open, and helped Moe inside. Hugging Moe, she said, "It's okay. It's okay."

"I couldn't. I couldn't do it. I couldn't see it," Moe said between sobs, her senses slowly coming back to her.

"You're okay. It's okay," Stacie said.

Moe worked to slow her breathing. She could feel herself coming down. She concentrated on settling her heart.

"Are you okay?" Stacie asked, her voice filled with concern.

Moe wiped the tears from her eyes. She took more deep breaths. "I'm okay. I think. I think I may have just had a panic attack. I've never, um. I've never felt anything like that before. I was. I was so powerless."

The side door to the van opened, and Francine got in. At the same time, her two team members climbed into the front seats. The engine of the van roared to life, and they started to move. "Are you okay?" Francine asked.

"Yeah. I think so," Moe said.

"What happened?" Stacie asked, bewildered.

"He had a memory waiting for me. It was strong, something he could force me into no matter what emotion I looked for. And he had filled the memory with pictures of everything I might know about him. He built a trap for me," Moe said.

"So he knew we were coming," Stacie said.

"He's smart. He was ready. Good for him," said Francine.

"I shouldn't have broken the rules. I don't steal memories. I know that. I shouldn't have broken the rules," Moe said, more to herself than to Stacie and Francine.

Francine touched her leg to get her attention. "Hey,"

she said, "cut yourself some slack. You tried something. He outsmarted you. Now you have to decide if this is a setback or a defeat."

Moe's adrenaline was fading. She could feel exhaustion coming on. She bit her lip and closed her eyes. "We'll get him another way," she said.

"We can talk about it later. Right now, you need to get some sleep," Stacie said.

Moe heard her voice as if someone else was speaking. She could feel herself drifting off to sleep. "We need to get him the right way. We need to figure something else out," she said, as she fell asleep.

CHAPTER TWENTY-FIVE

Moe held her coffee cup in both hands and watched the steam rise above the lip of the mug. It spun in the air as if it were a dancer dangling from an invisible rope in the sky. She blew on it. It vanished, and then, just as quickly, reemerged. She blew again and again, watching it go and come back. The improvised chaos of Mingus's II B.S. played softly in the background. Moe pulled her knees to her chest and tucked them in her t-shirt. The white lettered words printed on the black fabric stretched. She bit her lip and pondered the Fitzgerald quote, "Never confuse a single defeat with a final one." She sighed and looked back at the steam coming off of her coffee.

Her daze was interrupted by the sound of the door being unlocked. Moe looked up as Stacie came into their office/apartment. In one hand, she balanced a Styrofoam tray with two fresh coffees. In the other, she carried a plastic bag from the Wawa down the street. "Oh good, you're up," Stacie said, as she crossed the room and placed things on the table. Taking the mug from Moe, Stacie said, "Where did you get this?"

"It was in the pot," Moe said, collapsing on the couch.

"That's from yesterday. Gross," Stacie said, as she

poured it in the sink. Putting the fresh coffee in Moe's hand, Stacie said, "Drink."

Moe took a sip. It was strong but not bitter and carried a hint of cinnamon. She held it in her mouth before swallowing. She could feel the warmth travel down her chest.

Stacie marched back to the table, took a small box out of the Wawa bag, and walked it over to Moe. "Best morning after food in the world. Sausage, egg, and cheese croissant from Wawa. Eat."

Moe look at the sandwich in the box. "Is that even real sausage?"

"Why would you ask that? Of course it is," Stacie said, sitting down next to her friend on the couch.

"It's from a gas station," Moe complained.

"Eat," Stacie demanded as she took a sip of her coffee.

"I don't feel like eating," Moe said.

"Look. Every time I found out I didn't get a part, I would go into this massive funk. And the only thing that would bring me out of it was a sausage, egg, and cheese croissant from Wawa, coffee from Zeke's, and a new script to read. So drink. Eat. And let's get back to work," Stacie insisted.

Moe looked down at the stretched letters on her shirt again and said in a wounded voice, "No one's ever done that to me before. It was like I was lost in some sick world that kept replaying. I dreamt about it all night."

"I'm really sorry," Stacie said, rubbing her friend's back.

"I shouldn't have tried to steal his memories. I don't do that. It was wrong," Moe said, still looking down at her shirt.

"Yesterday was a hard day. We went too far. So what? Hasn't the great Moe Watkins ever failed before? Look, if you keep hanging with me you better get used to it because I'm an expert in failure. I do it all the time. So now, eat your damn sandwich, drink your damn coffee, and let's get back to work," Stacie demanded.

Moe smelled the sandwich. It smelled good, and it was warm.

"I said eat it," Stacie demanded.

Moe took a bite. Like the coffee, it was rich and sparked something in her mouth. The croissant was surprisingly flakey and the sausage was salty. She chased it with a second mouthful of coffee. She could feel herself coming back awake. Looking up at Stacie she said, "So, where are we going today?"

"We're meeting Robert downtown because Lance struck again," Stacie began.

"He's escalating. It hasn't even been forty-eight hours," Moe reflected.

"See? Working feels good, right?"

Moe sipped her coffee and said, "Thank you."

"That's what I'm here for. So, after we see the continued carnage of your brother, this afternoon I got us an appointment with the second to last person Charlie saw before he died," Stacie said.

"Big day," Moe said.

"Big day," Stacie agreed. "You want me to pick out an outfit for you? I've got a really great pantsuit that you would look amazing in?" she added hopefully.

Moe groaned as she stood. "No. I can dress myself," she said with a yawn.

"Can you though?" Stacie teased.

After pulling her hair back, Moe selected jeans and a black t-shirt with a purple Edgar Allan Poe silhouette. She took her Converse and undid the red-wine laces. "Time for a fresh start," she told herself, as she took a purple set from her dresser and ran them through the holes in her shoes. Picking through Stacie's closet, she took a deep purple blazer and tossed it on. She'd never admit it to Stacie, but the suit coat made her feel more adult in some weird way. When she walked back into the living room ready to go, Stacie smiled but said nothing.

The bar where they met Robert had once been a bank. The white marble-tiled floors, the stained-glass skylight, and the dark colored leather chairs were all holdovers, but the most prominent feature was the huge vault. The giant gear-filled door stood open to reveal the walls of brass security boxes and a single table that sat six. Rumor was that mayors used to come to the vault to drink in private and be able to speak their minds without being overheard by a reporter hiding among the bar's patrons.

Robert was waiting for them next to the bar. He wasn't standing at it like someone who might order a drink, but rather adjacent to it as if it were a complete coincidence that he and the bar were in the same space at the same time. "He'll be here in a few minutes," he said with a nod.

"Who is it we are meeting with?" Stacie asked.

"Commissioner Davis," Robert said with a hush tone.

"The Chief of Police, Commissioner Davis?" Moe asked.

"That's the one. Lance hit him last night," Robert said.

"Bold," Stacie said.

The door to the bar opened, and an older gentleman dressed in police blues entered. His breast pocket was filled with decorative ribbons of rank. A younger cop followed behind him. The man nodded to Robert and motioned to the vault before walking into it and taking a seat.

It was odd sitting in a room whose walls were brass. It gave the room a strange glow and filled it with a metallic smell. Moe and Stacie pulled up chairs across from the commissioner, forcing Robert to sit at the head of the table. The young cop stood at the entrance to the vault with his back to them, which struck Moe as strange.

"Before we begin, would you mind if I saw some credentials?" the Commissioner asked.

Robert removed his badge and passed it to the older man. "I'm Robert Watkins with the Baltimore office. This is Moneta Watkins and Stacie Howe. They are private contractors providing additional support with the case," Robert said.

The Commissioner examined Robert's ID and then passed it back. "Well, your chief said you were the one closest to this, so thank you for meeting me today," the Commissioner stated.

"Not a problem, sir. The Bureau is always happy to help," Robert replied.

"Well, I appreciate your discretion with this. I know this isn't a traditional meeting place. I needed a room I knew was secure," the Commissioner apologized.

"It's not a problem, sir. We understand," Robert said.

"So, I was told you might be able to explain something to me," the commissioner continued.

"We'll try, sir," Robert said.

"Last night, I woke up with this note on my chest. I had one of our techs run it. The only finger prints on it are mine. The handwriting appears to me mine too," he said, as he pulled a clear plastic evidence bag from his breast pocket and passed it to Robert. Inside the bag was a small post-it note that read, "You chose to forget." Robert examined it and then passed it to Moe and Stacie.

"You woke up with the note? You don't remember how you got it?" Moe said.

"When I found it, I was in my bed. In my house. With my wife next to me. Is this someone's idea of some kind of sick joke?" the Commissioner growled.

"It's not a joke," Stacie said, passing the note back to

171

the Commissioner.

"It's likely you had a conversation you don't remember, sir," Robert said.

"Explain," the Commissioner demanded.

"There is a criminal currently operating in Baltimore who is capable of stealing people's memories. He takes information from your mind," Moe explain.

The Commissioner looked at her through slit eyes and asked, "How?"

"It's difficult to explain," Robert said.

"Try," the Commissioner said.

"The perp has been isolating high powered individuals and holding them at gun point. After a brief conversation, the individuals are given a choice. They either give him access to their memories or he shoots them," Robert explained.

"But how does he steal memories?" the Commissioner demanded.

"Truth is, we don't completely understand it. We just know he can," Stacie said with a comforting smile.

The Commissioner leaned back in his seat. "What did he take?" he asked.

"Do you have any holes in your memory? Any blank spots?" Moe asked.

The Commissioner thought for a moment, pursed his lips, and said, "Not that I can remember."

"Are you missing any days? Is there any time you can't account for?" Stacie asked.

"I don't think so," the Commissioner said. His gaze began to drift down and Moe could tell defeat was starting to set in.

"And you don't remember anything about last night? Does your house have a security system? Maybe a camera caught him?" Moe asked.

The Commissioner laughed to himself and replied,

"Never thought I needed a security system. Who would be brazen enough to break into the Chief of Police's house?"

"The good news is, sir, it sounds like the perp got what he wanted. You will likely never see him again," Robert said.

"Who were the other targets?" the Commissioner asked, shifting back to a more commanding tone.

"Judge Marcus was the first we've found. He was attacked in his office. He hit Michelle Dives the CEO in her office a few days ago. We also believe this perp is behind the murder of Jensen Beauchamp, the CEO of the Beauchamp Group." Robert said.

The Commissioner thought and nodded.

"Can you think of any connection you have to those individuals?" Moe asked.

The Commissioner thought and then replied, "Can't say that I've ever met them. Is there anything else you can give me?"

"Unfortunately, no," Robert replied.

"I'll expect you to keep my office in the loop," the Commissioner ordered.

"The Bureau is happy to help however we can, sir," Robert said.

As the Commissioner stood to leave, Stacie leaped up and asked, "One more quick question. You didn't happen to notice any Chinese food menus sitting around did you?"

The Commissioner paused, looked at her, and smiled. Reaching into his back pocket, he pulled out a folded menu from The Sichuan Palace. Passing it to Stacie, he said, "It was on my end table. I thought maybe I had just left it there and forgotten about it. I brought it, in case it meant something. What's its connection?"

Stacie took the menu from him and looked at it. While

it looked similar to the ones they'd seen in the judge's office, the menu items were all different. "We're not sure. Can we keep it?" Stacie asked.

The Commissioner thought for a moment and then said, "I want a full report on how it's connected."

"Deal," Moe said.

"Then it's yours. Thank you for your time today," he said, as he marched out of the vault.

CHAPTER TWENTY-SIX

Knife-Wrench was poorly lit and packed with college-aged patrons longing for a connection. Most gathered around the long bar. Others filled the small tables around the outskirts of the room. The energy of alcohol-induced-optimism mixed with the smell of desperation and hung like wet clothes on the bar. Twenty-somethings tried to lock eyes with potential companions and occasionally made ventures to other tables. A local band that was set up in a corner played '90s hits with an acoustic White Stripes flare that occasionally caused the crowd to burst into song.

During the two hours that Moe and Stacie had been positioned at the back table, no less than five men had approached Stacie, offered to buy her a drink, and floated a terrible pick up line. The drinks she always accepted, while also demanding one for Moe as well. The lines, however, were always rejected.

"Is it always like this for you at these places?" Moe asked, as two more college guys slunk off, trying to regain their dignity.

"At college bars, pretty much. College guys have a weird thing for me. I think it's a sexy-enough-to-be-fun, not-old-enough-to-be-their-mom, but old-enough-to-teach-them-something vibe," Stacie said with disdain.

"I mostly just get ignored in places like this," Moe said with a grin.

"That's not a bad thing. No one is finding the love of their life tonight. At best, you vaguely remember having a good time," Stacie said.

"You spend a lot of time in places like this?" Moe asked.

"In another life," Stacie said, taking a sip from her martini.

Moe looked back at the bar and caught the eye of Tiffany Brown for the twentieth time. Tiffany immediately looked away, which Moe understood. Being spied on is nerve racking, which was the point.

Moe and Stacie had discussed trying to hide their presence from the receptionist/daughter of the Governor of Kentucky, but once they were in the bar it was clear there was nowhere to hide, so they took up a table that they believed would give them clear line of sight. Moe wasn't sure what she hoped to discover tonight. If anything, she just wanted to shake Tiffany's tree and see if anything fell out that would help them untangle the puzzle of that night.

"So far, this is a bust," Moe said.

"What do you mean, we're getting all kinds of free drinks," Stacie replied with a grin.

"I don't know. I'm not sure what I hoped would happen."

"The night is still young. Give it time. At any second, Alicia Michaels is going to storm in here to discuss their grand conspiracy, and then we'll catch them both in the act. Just like that old weird detective in the trench coat used to do."

"Colombo?"

"No. The one who squinted with his eye."

"Colombo."

"No. No. The one that was in The Princess Bride."

"That's Colombo."

"Agree to disagree."

Moe laughed and decided to change the subject. "Why do you think the daughter of a Governor is working a college bar in Baltimore? Her daddy's got money. What's she doing slumming it as a receptionist and bartender?"

They watched as Tiffany flirted with a customer to upsell a drink. After a moment of thought, Stacie asked, "Is her daddy a Republican or Democrat?"

"Republican," Moe said.

"Well, there are only two things that would cause the daughter of a Republican to be cast out and run to Baltimore with no plan. Either, she got an abortion, or she's gay. Or she murdered someone in Kentucky."

More took a deep breath. "So, let's play this out. She gets to town with no job. Where does she stay? Why Baltimore?"

"Someone else in this picture is from Kentucky," Stacie confirmed.

Moe took out her phone and texted Ami, "Could you figure out who else in this picture is from Kentucky besides Tiffany?"

"On it," Ami replied.

A new crowd of co-eds came flooding into the bar. Already buzzing, they'd clearly come from a different bar. "Must be some kind of bar crawl," Stacie remarked.

With the increase of patrons, Moe lost Tiffany in the crowd. "I can't see her anymore," she said.

"Don't worry. She's going to be stuck back there for a while," Stacie replied as she finished her martini.

Moe jumped at the stern Southern voice behind her. "You can't do this. You have to leave," Tiffany demand.

Moe turned to see her standing directly behind her.

"We're just having drinks. We're paying customers," Stacie said with a smile.

"Bullshit," Tiffany retorted.

"What would the Governor say about that mouth?" Stacie snapped back.

"I wouldn't know. I don't speak to him anymore. If you talk to him, feel free to ask," Tiffany quipped.

"Look," Moe said, holding up her hands defensively, playing good cop to Stacie's bad. "We're not here to fight. We just want to know what happened that night. We know you and Alicia Michaels were both there, and we know that Charlie had you calling in clients to shake down for more money. We came here to give you a chance to change your story before we go to Alicia Michaels and ask her who left first – you or her."

Tiffany glared.

"Look, our client is behind bars right now unjustly because of some shit that went down, and you stink of it. So what do you say you get your hands clean and tell us the truth?" Stacie said.

"It happened just like I told you. I was at the office working with Charlie. It was a hard day. Mr. Sennack was late, so Charlie sent me home," Tiffany said.

"Can you prove that?" Moe said.

"No. And I don't have to because I didn't do anything wrong and you aren't cops. You're just two nosey people trying to make a buck," Tiffany said.

"Why did you leave Kentucky? Why did you drop out of school?" Stacie demanded.

"That's none of your business," Tiffany retorted.

"We're just trying to help. Malcom has a fiancée. They had to push their engagement aside. He helps a lot of people. His nonprofit is turning a section of the city around, but he can't be there to help if he's in jail. Give us something," Moe urged.

"Your client is a stone-cold murderer who stabbed my boss to death in a rage when he found out he didn't have enough money to pay for his building. I thank God every day that I wasn't there to see it happen, or I'd be dead too. That's what happened, that's what Cher saw, that's what the cops saw, that's why your perfect client is in jail, because he killed my boss. Now, my five minute break is over. I have to get back to work. I have nothing else to say to you. Get the hell out of my bar," Tiffany said, as she turned to walk away.

Moe and Stacie sat in silence for a second. After taking a sip of her beer, Moe said, "Nice bad cop."

"Why thank you," Stacie said with a grin. Then she added, "So, Tiffany is on a first name basis with our physical therapists?"

As she stood to leave, Moe said, "Maybe this trip wasn't so unproductive after all."

The air outside was chillier than Moe expected. She crossed her arms over her chest to fight it back. Parking had been hard to find, so they'd had to settle for a spot five blocks away. They'd had to hike through several blocks of rowhomes and old factory buildings before making it to Tiffany's spot. Moe wasn't looking forward to the hike down the dark streets. She wished she'd Uberred to the bar. In hindsight, that would have been smarter.

They were only a block away from the Knife-Wrench when Moe started to feel like something was wrong. She glanced over her shoulder and noticed two men walking slowly behind them.

"You checking out our tail?" Stacie said casually without looking back.

"Yep," Moe said.

"Let's take a few turns to see if they keep on us,"

Stacie said, as she picked up the pace.

They turned left down a small block and then took a quick right. Moe looked back and felt a wave of release because the two men seemed to be gone. "I don't see them. I think we're okay," she said.

"No. We are not," Stacie said, stopping in her tracks.

Moe looked up to see one of the two men at the end of the block. He was young and fit with broad shoulders and a tight haircut. He looked like he could have been pulled off an army recruitment poster. "Come on," she said, taking Stacie by the arm and turning to go back the other way, but in the middle of the street, at the end of the block was the other man. He too looked like a GI Joe action figure come to life.

"This is bad," Stacie said.

Moe's heart started to pound, and she clenched her fists. She knew she couldn't beat either of these men in a fight, but if they wanted to get physical, they were going to regret it. "Stay next to me and aim for their balls," Moe said.

"I'm not going to let them hurt you," Stacie replied.

Moe felt a knot in her throat and a tear form in her eye.

The men moved forward slowly. Moe looked up and down the street for signs of life, but the block was silent. She thought about screaming, but she knew there wasn't anyone in the large factory buildings around them. The places had closed up at 5:00, and everyone had gone home.

The man in front of them reached into his pocket and pulled out a badge. Holding it high in the air, he loudly declared, "Stop! Police! Put your hands above your head and face the wall!"

"I'm not sure if this just got better or worse," Stacie quipped.

"Worse," Moe said, glancing behind her. The other man had his gun drawn on them. "Do what they say or they're going to shoot us," Moe told Stacie as she put her hands up.

"I'm not facing any damn wall," Stacie said.

"POLICE! GET YOUR HANDS UP!" the first cop screamed.

Moe faced the wall and demanded, "There aren't any cameras here, and there aren't any witnesses. They will kill us. We're not getting shot tonight. Face the damn wall."

"Fine," Stacie said, mimicking Moe's actions.

The two officers closed, the one behind them keeping his weapon drawn. As the first one moved forward, he said, "Do either of you have a weapon on you?"

"What is this about, officer?" Moe asked.

"Answer the question, ma'am," the first officer said.

"We haven't done anything wrong," Moe said.

"Do you have a fucking weapon?" the one with his gun drawn demanded.

"No," Moe yelled.

"I have a gun in my ankle holster and a permit in my back pocket," Stacie confessed.

"You got'em?" the first officer asked his partner.

"You move an inch, and I'll put you both down. Now put your fucking hands against the wall," the second officer said.

Moe stretched her arms out and touched the wall. She felt the first officer's hands on her. They were rough and unwelcome. Moving up her leg, she refused to flinch when they neared her crotch. She could feel his breathing increase as he patted down her stomach and lingered under her breasts.

"Having fun, asshole?" she said.

"Watch your mouth or this is just the beginning," he

whispered.

"Leave her the fuck alone," Stacie demanded.

"Keep it together. I'm fine," Moe said.

"No. You're not," the cop said, as he grabbed her hands, forced them behind her back, and zip tied them together. Using the zip tie as a leash, he backed her up and forced her to her knees.

Moe's tears had been replaced with a hatred that burned like a furnace in her chest. "If you're going to shoot us, get it over with," she demanded.

"Shut your bitch mouth," the cop said, pushing her head down.

He then moved to Stacie. Taking the gun from her ankle, he tucked it in his back pocket. Moe watched in disgust as his hands moved up her friend's leg. Stacie gritted her teeth as he moved to her crotch.

Moe's hatred turned to rage and she screamed, "Leave her the fuck alone!"

The first cop turned to her, pointed his finger in her face, and yelled, "Shut your mouth, bitch!" Returning to Stacie, he felt around her waist and, like with Moe, lingered around her breasts.

"I said, get the fuck off of her," Moe screamed at the top of her lungs.

"Finish it up," the second cop said.

The first cop pulled Stacie's hands down, zip tied her, and forced her to her knees as he had Moe. "You're lucky we're gentlemen, ladies. Otherwise, this could have gone horribly wrong," the first cop said.

"You dumb fucks. I'm going to have your badges," Moe declared.

The first cop laughed. "You really think you're something special, don't you?"

"Which one are you? Are you Mitcham or Ambrose?" Moe demanded.

"Officer Philip Mitcham at your service, bitch," the first cop said.

"You need to understand your place," the second cop said.

Moe gritted her teeth and barked, "I don't need to understand anything! You know your buddy here just assaulted us, and you've pulled your weapon for no reason. At best, you're going to be a goddamn janitor when I'm done with you. I'm not just going to take your badge, I'm going to take your whole life."

"See, that's your problem," Mitcham said. Moe could hear his smile it was so big. "You think you're in charge. You think you can go and dig through our cases. You think you can do whatever you want. But you're not in charge here. We're in charge. You hear that, bitch. We're in charge."

Moe laughed. "You honestly have no idea who you are fucking with," she said.

Mitcham moved so that he was between them. Speaking in soft, angry, measured tones, he said, "I know who you are. I know every fucking thing about you. I know where you live and where you hang out. I even know where you walk your damn dog every morning. What you need to know is that any time I want, I can find you and have you in cuffs on the side of the road just like this. You keep fucking with our cases, and I'll put your bitch-ass behind bars. You get me? And you'll never see me coming. I can snatch you off the street whenever I want, and there's nothing you can do about it. Remember this moment. Kneeling on the ground. Powerless to do anything. Because this is your new life if you keep poking around our cases. Got it, bitch?"

"Fuck you," Moe said.

There was a snipping sound, and her hands were freed. She immediately stood to face him as he clipped Stacie free.

Stepping back, Mitcham said, "This was a nice chat, ladies. We'll see you again."

Ambrose holstered his weapon and the two men walked away. Moe looked down at her friend who seemed frozen in time. Dropping to her knees, she wrapped her arms around Stacie. Her friend did not respond. She remained ridged and unmoving.

"Are you okay? I'm so sorry. Are you okay?" Moe whispered in her friend's ear.

Stacie began to cry. Tears streamed from her eyes as she grabbed Moe with both hands. The first sound from her mouth was a scream of pain.

Moe held her close. "I'm so sorry. I'm so sorry," she said.

"I said... I said... I said..." Stacie tried to say through her tears.

"I'm so sorry," Moe said again.

"I said... No one... No one would make me feel that way again. Never... Never again," Stacie sobbed.

"I'm so sorry. I'm so sorry," Moe said, her eyes filling with tears.

"I want them dead. I them both fucking dead," Stacie demanded, squeezing Moe as she cried.

"I'm so sorry. We'll get them. We'll make them pay," Moe said, stroking her friend's hair. "We'll make them pay."

CHAPTER TWNETY-SEVEN

"How are you?" Moe asked, as she sat on the bed next to her friend and brushed some hair from her face.

Stacie stared into the distance.

Stroking her hair, Moe said, "How did you sleep?"

Stacie took a deep breath and let it out slowly. Her eyes were still puffy from the tears she'd shed last night and she rubbed them with both hands. "I don't know," she said. "It's all kind of a blur."

"That was hard last night," Moe said.

Stacie closed her eyes, took another deep breath, and again released it slowly.

"I'm going to call off our meetings today. Let's just take a day to recover," Moe said, still stroking her friend's hair.

Stacie opened her eyes and looked at Moe. She reached up, touched Moe's cheek, and said, "Thank you, but I don't want to do that. I need to keep moving. Dwelling on it won't help."

"I think we should take some time to recover," Moe pushed back.

Stacie closed her eyes, inhaled, and then exhaled slowly again. "We have cases to solve," she said.

"Screw the cases. The only thing I care about right now is you," Moe said.

Stacie smile. "I'm going to be okay," she said.

"I want you to take care of yourself. Let's do what you need today," Moe said.

Stacie stretched. "I need to work. I need to get out of bed. I'm not going to let a couple of douche bags slow me down." She sat up and stretched again.

"Are you sure you're okay?" Moe asked, rubbing her back.

"It just brought back some old feelings. Things I thought I had buried," Stacie explained.

"Bruce Spiniker?" Moe asked.

"Yep," she said with a final stretch.

"I love you, and I hate seeing you in pain. I'm here when you're ready to talk," Moe assured her.

Stacie smiled. "Maybe someday. Today, I'm going to bury it deep, deep down and pretend like it never happened."

Moe continued to rub her back as she said, "I don't think that's healthy."

"That's the Howe way," Stacie said with a grin.

"I'm serious. I'm here when you want to talk about it." She paused, looked down, and added, "I'm sorry I made you stand against the wall. I shouldn't have told you to do that. I wasn't thinking that…"

Stacie interrupted by touched her face. Stacie smiled and said, "You have nothing to be sorry for. You didn't do anything. You were right. He was looking for a reason to shoot us. The only thing we could do in that moment was survive. So, thank you for keeping your head on your shoulders. Now, is that coffee I smell?"

Moe reached over to Stacie's end table and grabbed a Zekes' coffee and a bag from Wawa. "I got you the Stacie Special," she said.

Stacie snatched the coffee and took a sip. "Oh. That's so good," she said.

"Are you sure you don't want me to cancel the day? We can stay in and watch old movies. I'll even cook for you for a change," Moe offered.

"Oh-God-no," Stacie said. Digging through the bag, she found the Wawa sandwich and added, "You know me so well."

Moe laughed.

"What's up first for today? Hit me with the schedule," Stacie said.

"Ami is coming over in an hour. I figured at a minimum we needed to regroup," Moe said.

"Then I'm going to get up and get dressed," Stacie said, throwing her covers off.

"You're sure?" Moe asked.

"I'm sure. Let's get to work," Stacie affirmed.

An hour later, when the trumpet blasts of Panic at the Disco's "High Hopes" began blaring through the speakers in their apartment, Stacie and Moe jumped.

"We need a different tech friend. One who doesn't take pleasure in scaring the crap out of us," Stacie complained as she cleaned up the coffee that she'd spilt.

Moe smiled and went to unlock the door. "You love her. You know you do," she teased.

"What did you say? Ami's the worst? Yes. I agree. That's what I'm saying too," Stacie yelled pretending she couldn't hear over the inappropriately loud music.

Moe opened the door to find Ami standing there with her camera around her neck, laptop bag on her back, and a brown envelope in her hands. "I come bearing gifts from the angry man downstairs," Ami said with a grin.

"What? I can't hear you over that insanely loud music," Stacie yelled.

"Some people's arrival demands fanfare," Moe said,

as she took the envelope from Ami.

"Moe gets me," Ami said, as she took a seat on the couch facing their case wall and used her phone to lower the music. Bosley jumped up on the couch next to her and put his head in her lap.

Moe opened the envelope and asked, "Did Mr. Hudson say anything when he gave this to you?"

"He said that it was delivered by FedEx. No sender was listed," Ami said.

Moe pulled a single glossy photo from the envelope. It was a picture of a distinguished looking elderly man in a trench coat and sunglasses walking across the street. On the photo was a post-it note that read, "Your brother's next target. Be ready." Moe took a thumb tack from the coffee table and pinned the picture to the Lance section of the wall next to pictures of Judge Marcus, Ms. Dives, the police commissioner, and the Chinese food menus.

Stacie laid three coffees on the table in front of the couch and took a seat next to Ami. "Who is it?" Stacie asked.

Ami, already banging away on her laptop, said, "It looks like Ezra Bonito. He's the owner of the casino downtown, among other businesses."

"The casino where Hooknose works?" Stacie asked.

"That's the one," Ami said.

Moe took a piece of string and ran it from the picture of Hooknose to the new picture. "Who do you think sent it?" she asked.

"Your brother?" Ami posed.

"Not his style. If he wanted to show us something, he'd take us to it and then make us forget how we got there or some kind of nonsense like that," Moe said.

"Maybe someone who is connected to his victims?" Stacie suggested.

"Do we even trust it?" Ami asked.

"Do we have a choice? It's our first real lead. Right now we're just waiting for him to take someone else's memories," Moe said. She took a picture of the photo and texted it to Robert.

Moe let her eyes drift to the photos Vinnie had taken of the bulletin board at Hooknose's coffeehouse. Nothing seemed out of place. There were advertisements for a local gym, an announcement from a guy looking for potential band members, flyers advertising apartments for rent, and a page with a picture of a lost cat in the middle and a number to call if the cat was found. "You find anything weird about the bulletin board yet?" Moe asked.

"Nope. I checked out all the flyers, and they're all legit," Ami said.

"We're missing something," Stacie said.

"Yep. There's something with the lost cat. Something I saw in his memory. I can't put my finger on it though," Moe agreed.

"I looked into the menus. They're both different. Some similarities, but mostly different. What's weird is that the special numbers are all off. On a typical menu, they start at 1 and go to whatever. Around number 10, these numbers start jumping all over the place. It seems like some kind of code. Maybe a cipher for something else? I couldn't crack it though. We need more examples," Ami said.

"Nice work," Moe said.

"I aim to please," Ami said.

"I called the attorney Jordy gave us this morning," Stacie said. "She said that Jordy was the fourth of Margret's clients to be contacted that day about the same thing. 'Missing money. You need to come here and pay me right now.' She said no one paid him and that Jordy was the only one that went to the office after getting the call."

"We knew Charlie needed cash. Looks like he was more desperate than we thought," Moe said.

"Why is Tiffany helping though? Sweet innocent Kentucky girl doesn't seem like the type to jump in on a cash grab," Ami said.

"Speaking of," Ami declared, "Ami delivers again. But before I get into it, I want to be clear that this wasn't easy. Tiffany isn't on social media, which makes cyber stalking infinitely harder."

"That's weird for a happening bartender in her twenties," Stacie remarked.

"Right? That's what I thought. So I did some digging through people who lived in Petersburg Kentucky that went to her high school, and I found this," Ami championed, passing her phone to Moe who looked and then passed it to Stacie.

On the phone was a picture of Tiffany with her arms wrapped around a young woman with the words, "Happy Pride Day!" underneath.

"Damn it. I really didn't want to feel bad for her," Stacie said.

"Yeah. When I first found it, I felt really bad. LGBTQ pride, you know? We have to watch each other's backs. But, then I looked closer. She's gay, but that's not why she left town. She'd been out for years before she ran," Ami said.

"I appreciate you looking into that. I'm sorry if it put you in an uncomfortable place," Moe said, putting her arm around Ami and giving her a side-hug.

"Please, you're my girls. I had a moment of advocate brain, but I was going to tell you," Ami said, leaning her head on Moe's shoulder. "So, as I was saying," she continued, "Once I found a trail, things got easier to follow. From what I could dig up, Tiffany was in the closet until her junior year of high school. At the

University of Kentucky, she started up a relationship with an older woman named Jemma Flemming and joined an advocacy organization," Ami said.

"So, she had a community around her. Even if her father didn't like it, he'd been living with it. Why drop everything and come to Baltimore?" Moe asked.

"Still working that one out," Ami said.

"When you say older, how much older?" Stacie asked.

"Jemma looks like she is in her 40's. So, fifteen? Twenty years?" Ami said.

"To each their own I guess. I'm not going to judge," Stacie said holding her hands up.

"What happened to Ms. Flemming?" Moe asked.

"That's the weird one and the real prize from all my hunting. Drum roll please," Ami said.

Stacie started beating on her legs.

"Jemma's social media accounts get frozen in time right around when Tiffany left. So I scraped the local newspaper pages in Lexington, and I found a short article about a bar fight. Jemma was working as a bartender. A fight broke out. Two men were shot. Jemma went to jail for murder. Seems like intense stuff. Tiffany left town right after that," Ami explained.

"Were they stabbed?" Stacie asked.

"Nope. Shot with the shotgun behind the bar," Ami said.

"So, Tiffany's partner kills two guys in a bar fight, and she goes away for it. Then Tiffany runs away to Baltimore. Out of grief?" Stacie clarified.

"Hard to know," Ami said.

"And why Baltimore? If you're looking for the big city escape, most go to New York," Moe added.

They all let the question hang in the air, pondering it together.

"I've got another one for you. Ambrose and

Mitcham," Stacie said, breaking the silence.

"The two cops?" Ami asked.

"They grabbed us last night, frisked us, and zip tied us to let us know that they were in charge," Moe said.

"Are you okay?" Ami said with shock.

"We're good," Stacie said. "But what I was thinking about was, how did they know where to find us last night?"

"That's a good question. You think Tiffany called them?" Moe asked.

"It makes sense. That's not a place we usually go, and we didn't see them follow us there. They had to have picked us up when we came out. Either they do an amazing job of tailing people, because you and I are both pretty good at spotting a tail, or they got tipped off that we were there," Stacie explained.

"Let's assume the latter. They got tipped off by Tiffany. So she is somehow connected to the cops that showed up," Moe said.

"Doesn't mean she killed Charlie though. Maybe she called them to cover for Alicia," Stacie added.

"Maybe," Moe thought out loud.

"It's thin. Not holding up in court," Ami said.

"True," Stacie replied.

"Anything good from the camera in at the PT girls' place?" Stacie asked.

"Nothing yet. Just them coming and going and every once in a while a food order gets delivered," Ami said. "Also, I'm sending you the next ten people to close on houses after the murder," added as she punched on her phone.

"Time to knock on some doors and check some knives," Stacie said.

"More power to ya. Feels like a waste of time to me," Ami said.

"Maybe we get lucky. And even if we do, we still have Cher and Tai's eyewitness testimony to deal with," Moe noted.

Stacie pointed at the emptiest column on the wall, where a picture of Bruce Spiniker hung. "Anything on our boy Bruce?" she asked.

"Nope. Nothing. I'm sorry," Ami apologized.

"It's fine. It's just a matter of time," Stacie said.

"What about our friend Damon Santobello?" Moe asked.

"Nothing there either. The man is keeping himself squeaky clean," Ami said.

"No way. Guys like that, there's always some kind of con running," Stacie quipped.

"He's not leaving a digital trail if he is," Ami replied.

Moe took a sip of her coffee and thought about Sarah. She mused, "Maybe that's the problem. Santobello isn't like Big Tony or Giovani. He's not muscle. He's a boss. To get to where he is, he's been careful and smart. Always ready to pin it on someone else."

"Vinnie said the guy only ever went three places – that coffee shop to look at the bulletin board, the casino, and his house," Stacie said.

"To catch a boss, we need another boss to roll over on him," Moe said.

"You're thinking about offering a trade?" Stacie asked.

"I'm thinking that package on our windshield came at the perfect time. Want to go to a casino and gamble?" Moe asked Stacie.

"Let's do it," Stacie said with a smile.

CHAPTER TWENTY-EIGHT

As Moe and Stacie were led past the aisles of buzzing slot machines, Moe was reminded of how much she disliked casinos. The constant noise and the flashing lights made her uneasy, and the absence of windows and clocks made her uncomfortable. She felt like she was in a sensory deprivation tank designed to suck money from her pockets. There were only a few people at the slots and even fewer at the gaming tables. This early in the morning, the only gamblers were the hard-core addicts wanting to get an early start or those who were still finishing their night.

"These places are a lot more fun when you're drunk," Stacie mused.

Moe laughed.

Their guide, a muscular man in black slacks and a red vest, led them to a small door in a corner of the room. The door was designed to look like the wall. Moe never would have found it if she didn't already know where it was. Through the door was a different world. The lavish carpets, ornate chandeliers, and dark colored walls were replaced by plain white walls, beige tiling, and fluorescent lighting. Along the hall were occasional grey doors, all simply marked with a black number.

"A girl could get lost in here and never be seen again," Stacie quipped.

"Perfect setting for a horror movie," Moe added.

That made their stoic guide chuckle. He led them through a maze of turns, each hallway looking exactly like the last until finally they reached a door that said, "Office 3."

Through the door, the world changed again. The hunter green walls of Office 3 were warmly lit by multiple lamps. The carpet was soft beneath Moe's feet. There were black leather couches along the walls and a large mahogany desk in the middle of the room. The desk was clear. There were no computers or phones in sight. In the corner of the room was a small bar filled with crystal glasses and various liquors. In front of the desk were four black leather armchairs, and behind it was a large black chair. In the chair sat a heavy man in a grey suit. His skin was olive in complexion, and his thinning grey hair was greased back. Moe thought the only thing he needed to complete the Godfather look was a cat in his lap.

"Mr. Bonito, this is Ms. Watkins and Ms. Howe," the guide said.

"Thank you, Sammy. You can wait outside," Ezra Bonito said. There was a low mumble and a slur to his voice that made him sound like he'd been drinking, but Moe could tell from the spark in his eyes that he wasn't impaired in any way. "Please. Sit," he said, motioning to the chairs in front of them.

Moe and Stacie took seats across from him. Mr. Bonito's chair was elevated just enough to ensure that he was looking down on them.

"Thank you for seeing us. I'm sure you are extremely busy," Moe said.

"Well, when someone with your reputation tells me

there is a threat on my life..." Ezra said, leaning back in his chair.

"Our reputation? You've heard of us?" Stacie asked with surprise.

"I have," Ezra replied, giving nothing away.

"As we said in our message, we have urgent information we think might interest you. Since you know of our reputation, then you know that it is credible," Moe said.

"I'm all ears," Mr. Bonito said, as he leaned back in his chair.

"But first, we would like some information from you," Stacie said.

"You want to make a trade?" Mr. Bonito said with a grin. It was the kind of smile a parent gave a child when the child asks for something they aren't old enough to understand.

"We want information on Damon Santobello," Moe said, ignoring the patronizing expression.

"Now, who would that be?" Mr. Bonito asked.

"He's one of your floor managers," Stacie said.

"I have a lot of floor managers. This is a big operation. I employ hundreds of people," Mr. Bonito replied.

Moe realized this wasn't going anywhere, and she decided to take a risk. "You know him because he does extra work for you on the side," she said.

Mr. Bonito studied Moe's face for a second, smiled again, and then quipped, "Don't try to bluff a professional gambler, Sweetie." Leaning forward, he placed his arms on the desk. With a far more sinister tone, he said, "You could always just grab my hand and try and pull the information you want out of my head. I'd love to see what that feels like."

For a brief moment, Moe was tempted. She understood the trick Hooknose had used on her, and she was sure she could get around it if she ran into it again. How hard would it be to grab the man's hand and take what she needed?

Sensing her friend's hesitation, Stacie jumped in, "We're not here to play games, Mr. Bonito."

"Are you sure? Last chance," he said to Moe.

Moe leaned back in her chair and said, "Michelle Dives. Commissioner Davis. Judge Marcus. Jensen Beauchamp. You're right. We don't know how you are connected, but we do know that your little group is being hunted. And we know that you are next."

Ezra Bonito leaned back in his chair again. "And what exactly can you do about it?"

"What we should do is let the hunter get you," Stacie said.

"And he will get you. No amount of security will stop him. You can't hide from him. He is coming for you, and he will get to you," Moe added.

"He got to Michelle Dives, and she is in a fortress," Stacie said.

"He got to the Judge in a federal courthouse," Moe continued.

"Hell, he took down Baltimore's top cop. Walked right into his house," Stacie tacked on.

"So, it doesn't matter how many Sammys you have roaming these halls," Moe said motioning to the door from which their escort had exited, "If this hunter wants to get to you, he will get to you."

"And you think I'm next?" Ezra Bonito said.

"We know you are," Stacie replied.

"What are you offering?" Ezra asked.

"You let us become your personal bodyguards. We'll also call in the Feds. We can stop him," Moe said.

"Because he's your brother?" Mr. Bonito replied.

"That's right," Moe said.

197

"And in return, you want information on Damon?" Mr. Bonito restated.

"He hurt someone we care about," Moe said.

Ezra took a deep breath and looked at the ceiling. Moe thought she saw a crackle of fear in his eyes, but it was difficult to tell. "I tell you what you want to know after I survive the attack," he said.

"No. Now. Or we walk and let him take you," Moe countered.

"We don't actually care what happens to you," Stacie said.

"She's not bluffing," Moe added.

"Oh, I can tell," Ezra replied. He thought again for a second and then said, "You got a deal. Damon has been overstepping recently anyway. Getting too big for himself. I was going to bring him down a notch and put him in his place. I'll kill two birds with one stone this way. What you don't know about Damon is that his work in the casino is only part time. His real job is running guns. I don't know much about the operation on purpose, only that guns are delivered once a year from a supplier I hooked him up with in New York."

"That's all you can give us," Stacie said.

"I can also tell you that things have been pretty quiet lately. He hasn't made a sale for a couple months," Ezra replied.

"How would you know that?" Stacie asked.

"I get a ten-percent cut of every sale because I let him do it. You catch him though, and I'll make sure the next guy gives me twenty. Win-win," Ezra smiled.

"With as many shootings as Baltimore has, feels like guns would sell faster than every few months,' Moe questioned.

"Damon isn't selling handguns to your local gang bangers. He sells in bulk only. He's the middle man. He fills three to four orders a year to guys that sell them off one or two at a time. Sometimes he gets a huge order, but that's rare. See, the thing about Damon – he's not greedy, and he is patient. It's not about getting rich for him. It's about winning. Which is going make it hard for you to get anything on him. He's playing a game, and you are losing. Now, how are you going to keep me safe from this hunter-brother of yours?" Ezra asked.

"We have a plan. First, tell us about the Chinese food menus," Moe demanded.

"I have no idea what you're talking about," Ezra said with a grin. "I paid my fee. Now, your plan for your brother."

"We need to change locations. We have to get you someplace with stairs," Moe said.

CHAPTER TWENTY-NINE

The closet was dark and cramped, and Moe was tired of waiting. She wished Lance would hurry up. She picked up the walkie-talkie and pushed the button. "Any sign yet?" she asked.

"Nothing yet. You doing alright down there?" Stacie replied.

Moe shifted her weight and tried to change her leg position, but there wasn't much she could do in the small space. "Just feeling a little claustrophobic," she said.

"Stay off the line," Robert's voice demanded through the walkie-talkie.

"Sorry you got stuck in the closet. You want me to come and join you?" Stacie asked.

"It's tight enough in here already," Moe said.

"These aren't toys. Stay off the line," Robert demanded.

Moe could tell from the irritation in his voice that he was also frustrated about being in a tight space. The linen closet was a bigger than the coat closet she was in though, so she didn't care.

"Ezra wants to know how we know this is going to work," Stacie said. Moe could hear the smile in her voice and how much joy she got from irritating Robert.

"It'll work. We've done it before," Robert said through the walkie-talkie.

"If you've done it before, don't you think he'll be expecting it?" Stacie asked.

"He doesn't even know we're here. Now stay off the line," Robert complained.

"You're assuming that. What if he's the one that left the picture for us at our office?" Stacie questioned.

"Not his style," Moe replied again with a laugh. She loved that Stacie was asking questions she knew the answer to just to bother her brother.

"Look. This is a simple plan. He has to come up those stairs to get to Mr. Bonito. When he does, we'll have him trapped, and Moe and I will take him down. Now stay off the line. If he figures out we're here, then this whole thing is blown, and I've been sitting in this damn closet for an hour for nothing," Robert ranted.

Moe put the walkie-talkie down and looked at her phone. It had been an hour. No wonder her back was so sore. She tried to stretch, but there wasn't much space. Slowly and as quietly as she could, Moe stood up. She stretched her hands to the ceiling and pressed against it. It felt good to change positions.

"Okay, team," Stacie said over the walkie-talkie.

"I said stay off the line," Robert interrupted.

"He's here," Stacie said. "He's coming in the front door now."

Moe put down the walkie-talkie and picked up the baton stun gun Robert had given her. She heard the front door lock being picked, and her heart started to race. The door swung open. Moe could feel sweat building on her brow. She wished it hadn't come to this. She squeezed the baton tight in her hand and tried to slow her breathing, but it didn't help.

She listened as Lance slowly walked through the front two rooms of the rowhouse. She wondered if he were always this careful. His footsteps were as light as a cat's. He'd been the clumsier of the two of them in college. She wondered where he learned to walk like that.

She heard him pass the closet and move into the kitchen past the stairs. He checked the back bathroom and the back door. Moe wondered if he'd bought their story that Ezra had gone home sick and was laid up in bed with the flu. Probably not. Moe wouldn't have. She'd have expected a trap, but she knew it didn't matter. Lance was always so cocky. She knew he'd walk right into a trap no matter how obvious it was, confident that he would come out the other side.

Moe listened as Lance came back to the stairs. He began moving up them slowly. She could tell he was listening for noises on the second floor, but the house was silent. There were fourteen steps in the stairway, and like all good old rowhomes, the stairway was a cave with a rounded plaster ceiling. To escape, he'd have to come through them.

When Lance hit the fifth stair, Moe sprang from the closet. She spun to face him, depressing the taser button on her baton. The stick buzzed menacingly with energy. She made eye contact with Robert, who was doing the same thing at the top of the stairs.

Lance looked good. Stronger than Moe remembered. His black suit was perfectly tailored, and his shoes were newly shined. The trench coat he wore made him look like a character from the Matrix. He turned and smiled at her. There was warmth in his eyes. Her heart fluttered, and a knot formed in her throat. Standing face to face with him brought to the surface feelings of loss and love she thought were gone.

"Hey, sis," he said with a gentle nod.

"Hey," she said back. It was how they had greeted each other their entire lives. Nothing fancy. Every day after school. "Hey, sis." And, "Hey." But those three simple words communicated volumes. They were words of support and togetherness and love. No one understood her like her twin. They were two halves of the same whole.

"I've missed you," he said.

Moe took a deep breath. "You too," she replied.

"Enough, Lance!" Robert barked from the top of the stairs.

Lance turned to face Robert and the tone of his voice became more playful. "If it isn't Big Brother Bobby. You're looking good, dog. Working out more? You pumping that iron? How's that woman you've been seeing? Silvia? The pictures of her in your apartment were hot. Nice bag, bro," Lance teased.

Moe giggled. She couldn't help it. Teasing their oldest brother used to be their favorite game.

Robert tossed handcuffs down the stairs. They clanged at Lance's feet. "This is over, Lance. Put those on, and we'll all go sit down and talk this out."

Lance looked down at the handcuffs and then back at Moe. "Really? This is your plan?" he laughed.

"It worked before," Moe replied.

"You mean that time you were mad at me because I borrowed that kid's bike," Lance said.

"Don't try to rewrite history. We remember. You stole seven bikes and were selling them," Robert corrected angrily.

"Oh, really? Whose bikes? You asked the whole neighborhood, and no one said I stole their bikes. No one even remembered the bike I was on. Maybe I magicked the bike from the air? You don't know. No victim, no crime, Big Bro," Lance challenged.

"That's not how the law works," Robert pushed back.

"I'm pretty sure it is," Lance laughed.

"There's a victim this time. We saw the body. Put the cuffs on," Robert demanded.

"Or what? You're going to take me down like you did back then? Taser me until I pass out?" Lance asked with a grin.

"Something like that," Robert replied.

"You know I'm not that same fourteen-year-old kid anymore, right?" Lance asked.

"You might have been working out, but I'm still your big brother, and I can still whip your ass," Robert declared as he charged down the stairs. With lightning speed, he stabbed at Lance with the baton. Following his lead, Moe charged up the stairs and did the same.

When they were fourteen, Moe had felt horrible about shocking her twin. She remembered how it felt when the stun gun had connected with him. She remembered how his body quivered and then his legs collapsed. She'd been so afraid that they'd hurt him. She remembered Robert carrying him upstairs and tying him to a chair. She remembered how drool had slipped from the right side of his mouth. She remembered how angry mom and dad were when they found out. Moe had been grounded for a month from any electronics. But, Lance stopped stealing bikes, and the goal today was the same. She didn't like hurting him, but she couldn't let him continue to hurt others.

Except, unlike last time, Moe's baton didn't connect with Lance's back. Rather, with surprising agility, Lance dodged Robert's attack and pinned his baton against the wall with his left hand as he simultaneously grabbed Moe's the baton with his right hand. Ripping it from Moe's grip, he then turned it on the descending Robert.

To Moe's surprise, Robert gritted his teeth and

powered through the jolt of electricity. Using the momentum provided by the higher ground, he swung his fist hard at Lance's head, but Moe's twin slid out of the way and countered by slamming his left elbow into Robert's ribs, stopping the older brother's descent down the stairs. In a smooth motion, Lance finished their older brother off with an uppercut to his jaw. Moe watch Robert's eyes roll back in his head as his legs lost their strength. But Lance didn't let Robert fall. Instead, he struggled to catch the weight of their older sibling and eased him down onto the stairs.

As Robert blacked out, his baton slipped from his grip and fell toward Moe. She reached for it but stopped when she heard Lance say, "Don't do it."

Moe looked up and met his eyes.

"Look, sis. Decking big bro is fun, and he's had it coming. But I don't want to hurt you," Lance said.

Moe took a step back and held her hands up in the air.

"Thanks," he said with another smile.

"I know when I'm beat," Moe said.

"So, Ezra Bonito? He's upstairs? With Stacie I assume," Lance said.

Moe nodded.

"She isn't going to try and shoot me or anything is she?" he asked.

"I told her that if you get to her just to get out of your way," Moe said.

"Good. I like her. She's good for you," Lance said.

A sudden wave of protective rage hit Moe, and she grabbed Robert's baton. "You leave her alone," Moe threatened.

Lance held his hands up and began backing up the stairs. "Look. I've changed. I don't take advantage of people anymore like that," he said.

"No. Now you just kill them in their kitchens," Moe

said.

"That wasn't my fault. He didn't have to die," Lance retorted as he took another step up the stairs.

Moe quickly counted. Three more steps. She needed to keep him focused on her. She moved up two more steps and let the electricity crackle from the baton. "This needs to stop, Lance," she demanded.

He took another step up and replied, "Don't worry. This is the second to last one left in Baltimore. I'm going to Boston tomorrow, and I'll be out of your hair."

Moe took another step forward and picked up the second baton. She let both of them crackle and declared, "No. You're not going anywhere. This ends now."

Lance took a final step up and said, "I'm sorry, sis. You can't stop this."

Moe smiled and said, "You're right, I can't."

"But I can," Calvin said, his voice booming from the top of the stairs as he clamped both his giant hands around Lance's head.

Fear flowed through Lance's eyes, and he tried to fight, throwing a blow to Calvin's chest, but their giant brother just absorbed the blow with a grunt. Pushing down, Calvin sent Lance to his knees. Lance grabbed at his brother's arms and screamed in horror. Calvin pushed downward again and sent Lance to the floor.

Moe watched as, like Robert, Lance's eyes rolled back in his head. "That's enough!" she screamed.

Calvin let go and stumbled back.

Moe ran to the top of the stairs. As she placed the cuffs on Lance, she looked up to check on Calvin. Her giant brother was bracing himself against the wall. "You okay?" Moe asked.

Calvin looked up at her. It was the first time Moe had ever seen fear in his eyes. It scared her. "You okay?" she repeated.

Calvin took a breath. Tears welled in his eyes, and he replied, "Our brother has seen some dark stuff. He's messed up, Moe. He's really messed up."

CHAPTER THIRTY

The first thing Robert did after they woke him up was call Commissioner Davis and get an interrogation room set up. The second thing he did was call his commanding officers and let them know what he was doing. The way Robert explained it, it sounded like he had taken Lance down single-handedly. While Moe didn't want her and Calvin's names in some FBI report, she also didn't want Robert getting all the credit. Moe knew it was childish to let something small like that get to her, but she couldn't help it. She wished she were more like Calvin. Once they'd gotten the cuffs on Lance, Calvin went home.

The police station was buzzing when they showed up. Everyone wanted to get a look at the mysterious killer who could erase people's minds. Lance played the role beautifully, smiling and nodding as Robert marched him to the interrogation room as if he were walking some kind of red carpet. After locking him to the interrogation table, Robert took a seat across from him, leaving Moe and Stacie to stand in the back of the room.

"Alright little brother, we have about fifteen minutes before my superiors get here and cart you off to some hole," Robert began.

Lance flashed a teasing smile and joked, "From what I see, your superiors are already here. Am I right, ladies?"

Stacie snickered, but Moe just sighed.

"Look. We don't have time for games. We aren't kids anymore. I've only got you for a few minutes before I have to give you up. If you don't tell me anything, then I can't help you when they get here," Robert lectured.

"How's your jaw? I could have sworn I broke it. Your head is still as hard as a rock. It felt like punching a brick. A big, stupid brick," Lance laughed.

"Stop playing around, Lance. This is serious," Moe said. To her own surprise, her voice betrayed some sadness.

The defensive grin disappeared from Lance's face when he made eye contact with her. He sighed and said, "I'm sorry to drag you into this, sis."

She believed him.

"Dives, Bonito, Davis, Beauchamp, Judge Marcus. What do all of these people have in common?" Robert demanded.

Lance locked eyes with Robert and said, "I know all you see is the troubled kid who was selfish with his powers. I understand. I did a lot of terrible stuff. But you need to understand, I'm not that kid anymore. I haven't been him for a long time."

"As much as I'd like to sit around and chat about where you've been for the past four years, we don't have that kind of time. I'm trying to help you, here. Lance, they are going to put you in a hole so deep no one will ever find you. Give me something I can use to help you. Some reason for all of this chaos," Robert pleaded.

The smile returned, but there was a sadness that lingered in his eyes. "Come on, big bro. You're smarter than that. You know they don't put people like us in holes. They put people like us to work."

"We're running out of time," Robert said.

Lance laughed and said, "You have no idea."

"Lance. Please," Moe said.

Lance sighed. He looked at the camera on the wall and then back at Moe. "I'll show you," he said.

Moe swallowed and looked down at her purple laces and then back at Lance. He gave a knowing and loving smile. She wanted to accept and take whatever memories he had, but she'd seen Calvin's face. Her brother has demons. What if he passed them on to her?

"No. Not that way. Just tell us now. Dives, Bonito, Davis, Beauchamp, Marcus. What's the connection?" Robert demanded again.

"You can trust me, sis. I'd never give you anything that would hurt you," Lance said.

"You aren't in charge here. You don't get to set the terms. If you don't tell us right now, I won't be able to help you," Robert threatened.

There was a commotion in the hallway and a series of small crashes.

"Sis, my people are coming for me, and I can't promise you'll remember any of this in a few minutes. Let me explain it to you so you won't forget. Last chance to understand," Lance said holding out his hand.

"Your people? What people? You don't have people," Robert laughed, but Moe ignored him. Gathering her courage, she crossed the small room, took Lance's hand, and closed her eyes.

It was hot. And gritty. She felt dirty. Moe opened her eyes and the room started to take shape. Two rows of cots and footlockers, but they were all empty. And it wasn't a room, it was a tent. She was alone. She felt alone. She looked down at her uniform. Where was she? Syria. This was Syria.

She sat down on her footlocker. Her BDU was

streaked with blood, but she knew it wasn't hers. She started to remember the screams of terror. She could feel the weight of the knife in her hand. She remembered creeping down a hall. Her heart started to race.

"Not that way, sis. Stay in the moment," Lance's voice whispered in her head.

Moe centered herself and looked around the room again. She missed having a unit. She missed the silent fraternity that turned into laughter once the mission was down. Lance hated being the lone wolf. She needed a shower and new clothes. She rubbed her bald head. Every part of her was covered in sand. Lance hated the desert.

Moe bent down and started unlacing her boots, but before she could get the first one done, there was motion at the entrance to the tent. She glanced up and saw two men entering the tent. The first was Lance's commanding officer. The second, a lean gentleman with silver hair who was dressed in civilian clothes and black sunglasses. Lance had never seen him before. Lance stood and snapped to attention.

"Gunny Sergeant Watkins, welcome back," the man in uniform said.

"Thanks, Colonel Matthews, sir," Moe barked back.

"At ease, Gunny," the Colonel replied.

Moe relaxed, but not completely.

"That was a hell of a thing you did, Gunny. We didn't think you were going to make it out of that one. Nice work, Marine," Colonel Matthews said, extending his hand.

Moe shook her commanding officer's hand and said, "Thank you, Sir." The Colonel's handshake was filled with strength. Lance liked this one. He was one of the good ones.

"I've got some good news and some bad news for you, Watkins," the Colonel continued. "The good news is, you're getting out of this wasteland."

"What's the bad news, sir?" Moe asked with Lance's voice.

"You're also being transferred. If you accept your next mission, when I leave this tent, you'll no longer be a Marine. Your service to your country has been exemplary, and while I'd never surrender a Marine of your caliber, these orders are coming from as high up as they come. So, I'm going to step out, and my friend here is going to stay. It was a pleasure serving with you, Watkins," the Colonel said with a smile.

"Semper Fi, sir," Lance replied.

"It has been a pleasure," the Colonel said.

Moe snapped back to attention and saluted as the Colonel left the room.

Once he was gone, the man in sunglasses spoke. His voice carried the sharp-gruff tones on of a heavy smoker. "Lance. My name's Erik Wagner. I run a small intelligence agency called NAGI, and I think you would be an excellent addition to our team."

"I've never heard of the NAGI, sir," Lance said.

"The National Agency of Gifted Individuals isn't something we advertise," Wagner said, as he removed his glasses to reveal silvery eyes that matched his hair.

The memory faded, and the tent disappeared.

Suddenly, Moe was chilly. She was wearing in a button down and slacks. The sleeves of her shirt were rolled up to her elbows. The light from the window forced her to squint. She was in an office. There were windows on the east wall. She could see the Capital Building. She was in D.C.

The room was void of any furniture, except for a table and a single chair. In the chair sat a man with a black bag on his head. There were two other people with Lance. An Asian woman stood in the corner. Moe knew her name was Kyosin, and Wagner was there.

"Go ahead," Wagner said.

Lance stepped forward and pulled the bag off the man's head. Underneath was Jensen Beauchamp. "Are the theatrics really necessary? Hooding me. Dragging me here. Why not just make an appointment with my secretary and meet me in my office," Beauchamp complained.

"They can't know you're working with us, or they'll kill you. Kidnapping you gives you plausible deniability. It's for your protection," Wagner said.

"My protection? It's insulting is what it is. I come to you with valuable information about an organization you didn't even know existed, and this is how you treat me?" Beauchamp protested.

Lance hated his entitled whining. Of all their informants, this was his least favorite.

"Do you have the location of the farm or not?" Wagner barked back, cutting off any negotiation Beauchamp was likely hoping for.

"No. I have something else. There's a new member in the Chinese Food club. Michelle Dives. The Michelle Dives. This is big news. A player like her, someone already so successful. Imagine what she can do with the knowledge the club provides. And I can get you closer to her. Maybe bring her onto our side," Beauchamp said, leaning back in the chair.

"There is no 'our' side," Wagner said.

"Don't be an ass. You know what I mean. I'll just need a little capital to show her that I'm legit, and I can flip her. So you drop me a couple hundred grand, I'll get close to her, then I'll flip her for you," Beauchamp offered with the confidence of someone who'd watched too many spy movies.

"We bought your way into the club, you've made

millions off of this relationship, and now you want more money?" Wagner laughed.

"Look. If I'm going to get close to an international powerhouse like Michelle Dives, I'm going to need more resources than I currently have," Beauchamp reasoned.

"Do you have the location of the farm or not?" Wagner demanded.

"It's not like they share that with us. They aren't giving tours. But, I'll get it. I just need more time. Getting close to a club member like Michelle Dives will help me get in better with the mangers. I'm doing this for us," Beauchamp reasoned.

"If you waste our time again, you'll be sorry. I'll make it so you wake up one morning in Bangkok thinking you're a homeless pig farmer with an intestinal worm. Do you understand what I'm saying? Is this getting through to you? You have one goddamn job. You're only fucking job is to get us the location of the goddamn farm. Don't fucking call us again without the goddamn location to the goddamn farm you fucking moron," Wagner said with a threatening glare. Turning to Kyosin he said, "Put this asshole to sleep."

Kyosin motioned gently with her hand, and Beauchamp's body went limp, his eyes closed, and he began to snore.

"Lights up," Wagner said.

Suddenly, the room began to change. The empty space with a view of the capital disappeared and was replaced by a control room buzzing with people. At a conference table, four other members of the team sat watching the interrogation. Beauchamp still sat sleeping in the chair with the same table in front of them, but all around them, people worked computer terminals. The walls were covered with screens on which technicians were surveilling various targets and running analysis. Lance glanced over and gave a nod of appreciation to a tall, gangly man with short red hair named Cletus. Lance had huge respect for his abilities. He loved how Cletus could manipulate a room.

Cletus, Wagner, Kyosin, Lance, and the four others at the conference table all moved across the room to one of the larger screens. "Bring up the Chinese Food club," Wagner said.

The technician seated in front of them gave a few key strokes, and the data on the screen was replaced by a map of the United States. Five cities were highlighted. Next to each city there was a list of people. "That confirms that Dives was added to the Baltimore club," Wagner said.

Lances eyes went to Baltimore's list that contained small pictures of Michelle Dives, Ezra Bonito, Commissioner Davis, Judge Marcus, Jensen Beauchamp, and Anderson Siltmore.

Lance's voice entered Moe's head. "Bottom right," he whispered.

Moe let Lance's eyes drift to the bottom right of the screen. The list there was not attached to a city. Its heading was "Known Captured Assets." There were ten people on it. The seventh name down was Sarah's father. The third name on the list was Rashida Watkins, Moe and Lance's mom.

The memory changed again. Moe was at a front door. It was a door she knew. She had the key to it. She unlocked it and stepped in. The room came into focus. It was Jensen Beauchamp's house. "Agent Watkins, is that you?" Beauchamp called from the kitchen, "Come on back."

Lance closed the door behind himself and walked through the front rooms to the kitchen. Beauchamp was cutting an apple at the kitchen island. "Can I get you some coffee? Take a seat," Beauchamp said, motioning to the kitchen table.

"No, thank you," Moe said with Lance's voice as she sat down at the kitchen table.

"I appreciate you coming down to meet me. This is much nicer than you putting a bag over my head and throwing me in a van," Beauchamp said.

"Do you have the location of the farm?" Moe demanded.

"No. I don't," Beauchamp said with a smile.

"Then why am I here?" Moe demanded.

"You're here because we need to talk," Beauchamp said, setting down the knife and reaching into the open drawer in front of him.

"Agent Wagner was clear. Your only job is to get the location of the farm," Moe said.

Beauchamp smiled, and from the drawer he drew a gun. Pointing it at Moe, he said, "I'm changing the plans. I'm done. You're here because I want out. So, you're going to go back and tell your boss that I'm out. I'm not giving you any more information."

"That's not how this works," Moe said with Lance's voice. She wasn't concerned by the gun drawn on her. So many guns had been drawn on Lance that the experience had lost its thrill. At the same time, Moe was suddenly hyper aware of the pistol in her ankle holster.

"That's how this is going to work. I'm not having my mind wiped like the others. This isn't what I signed up for. You can't just go from powerful person to powerful person removing everything they know. It's not right, and you're not doing it to me. We're done. I'm out. That's the end of it," Beauchamp declared.

"Put the gun away, Jensen," Moe said.

"No. No. I won't. You're going to listen to me, because if you don't, I'm going to go to the papers. I'm going to tell them all about your little organization of freaks. I'll bet they'd love to hear about a secret government organization that is stealing peoples' memories. Hell, I bet this story gets me on Good Morning America. So, unless you want your face plastered across every TV in America, you're taking orders from me now," Beauchamp said with a smile so big it looked like it hurt his cheeks.

"I have a counter offer. You're going to put that gun back in that drawer, I'm going to pretend like this didn't happen today, you're going to keep doing whatever we tell you to do, and if we decide to take your memories, you'll be eternally grateful for whatever we've allow you to keep. Now put the gun away before something happens that you can't take back," Lance said.

"See, here is how I see it. From what I've gathered, you're the only one capable of erasing memories. So if I get rid of you, then your little team can't take anything from me," Beauchamp said with a grin. He held the gun out straight. It shook slightly in his hand.

Lance watched the man's trigger finger. He knew Beauchamp would likely go for a headshot. They always did. Lance took a slow breath. "It doesn't have to go down like this," he said.

"I'm afraid it does," Beauchamp said. Lance saw the man's finger start to move. He rolled to the left as the gun shot went off. Grabbing the pistol at his ankle, he put a single bullet between Beauchamp's eyes. The informant fell with a thud to the ground.

Moe stood and removed a phone from Lance's pocket. Pressing the call button, she said, "I've got an issue. Informant 15 is down."

Wagner's voice answered, "Make it look like the others and evac."

Moe opened her eyes. She was back in the interrogation room across from Lance. Tears streamed

217

down her cheeks. "Mom?" she whispered.

Lance smiled. His eyes began to water. "I'm so close," he said.

"What did you see? What did he show you? What about mom? I need to know!" Robert demanded.

There was more yelling in the hallway. More crashes. Moe understood now. The department was falling asleep.

"I'm sorry to leave like this. You'll have to fill them in. Don't look for me. I'll come and find you," Lance said.

Robert jumped to his feet, his eyes wide with panic. "You're not going anywhere!" he screamed. "Tell me! Tell me what you saw!" he ordered.

"Moe?" Stacie asked, as her legs gave out, and she slipped to floor.

Moe began to feel sleepy. She had a deep urge to lay down on the floor. She fought it off, battling back with all her might.

"What's happening?" Robert said, as he sat back down. He laid his head down on the table. "I don't... What's happening?" he said softly, as his eyes closed.

The door behind Moe opened and Kyosin stepped into the room. Wagner walked in behind her and motioned toward Moe. Kyosin moved her hand. Moe fought to keep her eyes open, but it was hopeless. Everything went dark.

When Moe awoke, Robert was sitting at the table rubbing his head. Stacie was still fast asleep on the floor. Moe looked at her brother and asked, "How much do you remember?"

"We were at the casino," Robert said in a haze. "We caught him? Didn't we? I think we had him. Did the stair trick work? I remember waiting at the top of the stairs."

Moe smiled. "It worked great. Just like we planned," she said. Laughing to herself, she realized that Lance hadn't taken anything from her. She remembered it all.

CHAPTER THIRTY-ONE

As they walked up the street to the next house, Stacie repeated her summary for the fourth time. "I'm sorry. It's just too much. You're telling me that Robert didn't shock Lance on the stairs, but instead, Lance beat Robert's ass and it was Calvin that put him down, and that Lance is actually working for a secret government agency, and that I was right about the Chinese food menus and they are the key to everything."

"I didn't say that they're the key to everything," Moe interrupted.

"Wait. Don't change the facts now. You'll confuse me, and I'm trying to get it all straight," Stacie replied. "So, let's start again. What I hear you saying is that Anderson Siltmore is wrapped up in all of this, that he is one of the people that took your mom, that she is on some kind of farm working for some kind of weird billionaires club, and that the Chinese Food menus were the most important part of cracking the case; and that, most importantly, I was right."

"Yes. I guess that's what I'm saying," Moe said with a smile.

"I knew it. I knew the Chinese food menus were the key," Stacie said.

They arrived at the two-story Colonial home in the Cockeysville neighborhood of Springdale. It was the sixth home sold after the death of Charlie Michaels. They had already visited the first five that morning.

Despite the first five trips being a complete waste of time, Moe was optimistic. She'd woken up with renewed joy this morning. Everything felt lighter and more possible. Knowing her twin brother wasn't a monster had lifted a weight off of her she didn't fully realize she was carrying.

They walked up the concrete path through the nicely manicured lawn to the front door, and Stacie rang the bell. A petite woman in exercise clothes answered. "Can I help you?" she asked with caution.

"Yes, ma'am. We're sorry to bother you. We need to inspect some of your knives. Specifically, we need to check the knife you received from Dream Homes Realty when you purchased your home. We're worried it has some defects," Stacie said with mundane confidence.

"What kind of defects?" the woman said, skeptically.

"They've been killing people, ma'am. Stabbing them to be specific," Stacie said.

"I'm sorry. Excuse my partner," Moe said, shaking her head at Stacie's antics. "We're private investigators looking into the death of Charlie Michaels. We think one of the knives given away by the company might have been used in his murder. If you'd let us check the knife you received from them, we'll be out of your hair."

"Oh. Um. Can I just go and get it for you?" the woman asked.

"Absolutely. We can check it here on the porch," Moe said.

"Okay. I'll be right back," the woman said, closing the

front door.

"You should have let me keep running with it. The whole knife company thing was working this time," Stacie said.

"It was not," Moe said.

"Well, will never know now," Stacie said with a smirk.

The woman returned to the front door with the large carving knife. The red words "Dream Homes Realty" engraved on the red handle. "Here you go. I haven't really used it yet. We don't have a lot of use for a knife this big," she said.

"Thanks," Moe said, as she took the knife. Removing a spray bottle from her backpack, she placed the knife inside the bag and then squirted it with luminol. Like the five other knives before it, there was no trace of blood. Handing the knife back to the petite woman, Moe said, "Thank you. You'll be happy to know that this knife didn't kill anyone," Moe said.

"Keep an eye on it though. You never know when it will start acting up," Stacie added.

"Thank you?" the woman said, as she closed and locked her door.

"Where's the next house?" Moe asked Stacie as they walked back toward the street.

"They sold one more in this neighborhood. It's about a two blocks that way. You want to hoof it or drive?" Stacie asked.

"Let's walk it. It's a nice day," Moe replied.

As they strolled, she took in the trees and neatly arranged flower beds. The lawns were manicured, and the streets were quiet. It seemed like a nice place to live.

After a few houses, Stacie broke the silence. "So, you said this Chinese Food club has a buy in?"

"Yep," Moe replied as she admired a particularly full

patch of Black Eyed Susans.

"And we know Charlie was shaking people down for money, and that he was Anderson's friend. Maybe he was trying to get that buy-in cash?" Stacie deduced.

"Makes sense," Moe said with a nod.

"So if we want to find the killer, we just need to figure out which of the people he shook down would want to kill him for it," Stacie said.

"I mean, that's going to be super easy. This thing is as good as closed," Moe joked.

"And Malcom is as good as free. We should just go tell him. Yo, Malcom. No worries. We totally cracked this," Stacie teased.

"Dorothy would love that," Moe laughed.

"Side note. How have we not discussed in great detail the name Lumpum and Brumtum?"

"I know, right. I mean, those were two last names that were made for each other," Moe replied.

"I bet Brumtum's last name was actually something like Baker but Dorothy was like, 'If we're going to be partners, then your name needs to rhyme with mine.'"

"Oh. You think Brumtum exists? I thought Dorothy maybe had split personalities and Brumtum was just her in a different suit and a wig. Like BD Wong in Mr. Robot," Moe joked.

Stacie retorted in her best posh British accent, "By jove, good man. I do believe you've cracked the case. Ms. Brumtum was Mr. Lumpum all along."

"Flip that," Moe replied with a laugh."

"Ms. Lumpum was Mr. Brumtum all along," Stacie corrected.

"We are, simply, the greatest detectives of all time," Moe said.

"I think I'll keep the accent for a bit," Stacie continued. "Learned it for a part in which I was hoping to play a highborn lady of society who fell in love with a lowly carriage driver who had a young daughter and had been recently widowed by some tragic accident."

"Ooo. Like Downton Abby?" Moe asked with genuine curiosity.

"No. Not exactly. A little less of a production budget. It was a Hallmark Christmas movie. The whole thing was going to shoot in a week. It was called, 'The Christmas Carriage Wheel.'"

"I think I saw that one. The carriage driver was really good looking. And your character was promised to the real jerk of a guy. And the daughter was super cute. And in the end, your father said he just wanted you to be happy and your character kissed the carriage driver," Moe remembered.

"That's the one. Sadly, they gave the role to a country music singer instead of me. They said I didn't have enough 'pizazz,'" Stacie said.

"Because that's what I'm looking for in an early-nineteenth century period piece. Pizazz," Moe laughed.

"In their defense, I was drinking a lot back then. I can't promise I didn't show up to the audition a little drunk," Stacie said, returning to her normal voice.

Moe took Stacie's hand and squeezed it. "It's hard for me to imagine you like that," she assured her friend.

Finally, giving up on the accent, Stacie said with a shrug, "It was a different life. I had different friends."

They walked holding hands for another half-a-block, enjoying the quiet suburban day. As they passed a blue house with a perfectly groomed lawn, a tricycle on the front porch, and a green minivan in the driveway, Moe asked, "You think you'd ever want to live this life?"

"I don't know. I've met some shockingly stunning men recently. One of them is a blacksmith. His arms? Dear, God," Stacie teased.

Moe stabbed her in the side with two fingers, and Stacie yelped. "Seriously," she said.

"And give up saving the world with you. Not a chance," Stacie said, as she squeezed Moe's hand in return. "You?"

"I'd go crazy and spend all my time spying on my neighbors," Moe said.

"You would be the absolute best neighborhood gossip. You'd have all the juicy details," Stacie laughed.

"You know it," Moe replied, with a nod. "And Lord help the teacher that tries to lie to me about what my kid did in school. You know I'm coming for that memory."

"Oh, God. That poor teacher," Stacie laughed.

Moe came to a stop in front of a white wood-sided house with blue shutters. There was a small child's swing hanging from the branch of a tree, the flowers in the front bed were perfectly mulched, and grass still hadn't reclaimed the square of dirt where the "For Sale" sign had been. "I think this is our stop," she said.

Marching up the front path, Stacie returned to her British accent and declared, "I've got a good feeling about this one."

"You had a good feeling about the last six," Moe muttered trailing behind her.

To Moe's surprise, it was an elderly man with a walker who answered the door. Dressed in sweatpants and a white t-shirt, he adjusted his glasses, smiled, and asked, "How can I help you?"

"Hello, sir. We've come to inspect your knives," Stacie said with a smile.

"No. I'm sorry, Sir," Moe corrected as she elbowed Stacie. "We're private investigators. We heard you recently bought this home using the services of Dream Homes Realty. We were wondering if we could ask you a few questions?"

"Come on in. You want some coffee?" the man said, as he turned and walked slowly toward the kitchen.

Moe closed the door behind them and took the house in. The floors seemed freshly swept, and there was no dust in sight. There was a child lock on the inside door handle, and the wall sockets were all blocked with white child-safety outlet covers. The kitchen was straight out of a catalog with its brown and beige tile, stainless steel appliances, and a rack of pots hanging over the kitchen island.

The man retrieved two mugs from a cabinet, put them on the counter, and asked, "Cream or sugar?"

"Yes, please," Stacie replied with a smile.

"Just black," Moe said, taking the mug.

A voice called from a room behind them, "Dad? Was that the front door?"

The old man passed a sugar bowl and a small container of coffee creamer to Stacie and asked, "Now, what did you lovely ladies say you were here for?"

"Dad? Who are these people?" a woman asked from behind them. She had short hair and couldn't have been a few inches over five feet tall. Her expression was a mix of confusion and fear.

"We're sorry. We didn't mean to intrude," Moe said.

"Dad. We talked about this. You can't just let people into the house," the woman chided.

"You said I couldn't let salesmen into the house. These are not salesmen. These are two beautiful women. And when beautiful women show up at your door, you don't ask questions. You thank Jesus and let them in," the old man said, pouring his daughter a mug of coffee.

With her arms crossed across her chest, the woman turned to Moe and Stacie and said, "Whatever you're selling, we aren't buying."

"We aren't selling anything," Stacie said, holding her

hands up defensively.

"We're private investigators. We came to talk to you about Dream Homes Realty," Moe explained.

"I told you I didn't trust that shifty little man," the older man said to his daughter. Then turning to Moe and Stacie, he explained, "I told her he was too eager. All he wanted was the commission. He didn't care what kind of house we landed in, as long as he got paid."

"Cut it out, Dad. You're in enough trouble already," the woman said.

"I told her we didn't need to buy this place. My house was perfectly fine. We could all have just move in there. It had been a good enough for her when she was a child. I don't know why it's suddenly not good enough now," the father continued.

"We moved because he needed a bedroom on the first floor. He can't take stairs anymore," the woman explained.

"Don't listen to her. I take stairs just fine. I'm in my prime," old man said to Stacie.

"Dad. Enough," the woman demanded.

"I'm sorry. Let's start over. My name is Moneta Watkins. This is Stacie Howe. We're following up with all the recent clients of Dream Homes Realty in conjunction with a case," Moe said.

"Stacie Howe? From the TV show?" the woman asked.

Stacie smiled. "That's me," she said.

"Oh my, gosh. I loved your show. I was completely addicted. I watched it every day," the woman gushed, her mood taking a shocking turn.

"She couldn't get enough of it," the old man said.

"Dad. Don't pretend like you know what we're talking about," the woman scolded with irritation.

"I know what I'm talking about. She was the sidekick.

The one with the line about the pickle," he said.

"He's right," Stacie laughed with surprise.

"Of course I'm right. Don't believe a word she says. I'm as smart as a tack," the father replied.

"You forgot to put on pants this morning, Dad," the woman snipped back.

"Don't worry. I've got them on now," the dad reassured Stacie with a mischievous grin.

The woman sighed and said, "As amazing as it is to have the Stacie Howe in my kitchen, my two-year-old is going to wake up at any minute. I don't mean to be rude, but why are you here again?"

"We'd like to take a look at the knife Dream Homes Realty gave you when you closed on your home. We think it might have been used in a crime," Stacie said.

"The knife they gave us?" the woman said putting her hands on her head.

"When you closed, they would have given it to you as a housewarming present. It probably came with a big basket of stuff," Moe replied.

"Wow. I don't know. Everything has been so crazy. I'm not sure we got one," the woman said.

"Of course we did," her father answered as he maneuvered his walker to the corner of the kitchen. Opening a cabinet, he reached as high as he could and pulled a long red box from the top shelf.

The woman shook her head, sighed, and muttered, "I'd totally forgotten about that thing."

Moe sat the box on the counter and opened it. "You've never used this?" Moe asked.

"Never. I forgot we even had it," the woman said.

"Would you mind turning out the lights?" Moe asked, as she removed the spray bottle from her backpack.

The woman flicked the switch to kill the lights while Moe sprayed the knife with the luminol. The knife lit up in a fluorescent purple hue.

"We got it," Stacie celebrated under her breath.

"Would you mind if we took this with us? It's going to help free an innocent man from prison." Moe said to the woman.

"It's all yours," the woman said.

"Well, this has turned into quite an interesting day," her father said, as he sipped his coffee.

They walked back to the car with new pep in their step. "It feels really good when we get a break. I think this is my favorite part of the job," Stacie said.

"Yeah. Things are starting to come together. We've got the knife for Malcom, and we are starting to understand Lance. All we need now is to figure out how to get Damon," Moe said.

"We're still missing something. There has to be a way to get him to sell us some guns. We just need to know how he is doing it," Stacie said.

They walked in silence as Moe started running everything they knew through her mind. She thought about the night at Sarah's house. She thought about catching Damon's muscle. She thought about her failed attempt to still his memories, and she pondered what Ezra had said, and then a huge smile surged across Moe's face.

"What are you grinning about?" Stacie asked.

"I just got an idea. You still have that number from angry Benny the drug dealer?" she said.

"Nope," Stacie said, holding out her hand.

Moe grabbed it and together they visualized the number on the valet's phone they had stolen. Stacie pulled out her phone and dialed the number. As it started to ring, she handed it to Moe.

"Who the hell is this?" an angry voice barked on the other end of the line.

In a stern voice, Moe replied, "Benny. This is Carla.

The Private Eye you want to kill."

"Yo. You got a lot of nerve calling me again. I'm gonna kill you, bitch," the voice ranted.

"Yeah, yeah. I know. You're big and tough and I'm a dead woman. When you're done, let's talk money," Moe said.

"I'll talk money. But it better be a lot," Benny said.

"I need a favor. I have a new client, and he'll pay top dollar for guns. A lot of guns. He's got a huge job coming up. I need you to set up the deal," Moe said.

"I don't know anything about that kind of stuff," Benny declared.

"5k to step it up. Use the lost dog guy," Moe said.

There was silence for a second. Then, Benny said, "I'm not saying I know what you're talking about. But I can ask around. I'm gonna need that 5k up front though."

"Text me how to get you the cash. My client has 1.7 million to drop on the deal. He wants to see everything," Moe said.

There was silence again, and Moe's heart skipped a beat. She knew the number had to be big enough to indicate the cops weren't involved, but she hoped she hadn't shot too high.

"This phone number good to use for the 'lost dog?'" Benny asked.

"This one's great. Text me where to put your cut. You get the cash. Set it up the deal. And don't cross me. I know I don't scare you, but my client should. You don't want him coming to look for you," Moe said.

"Okay, Carla. You got a deal," Benny agreed.

Moe handed Stacie her phone back and flashed her friend a smile of victory.

"You're a genius," Stacie laughed.

"I love it when a plan comes together," Moe said with a laugh.

CHAPTER THIRTY-TWO

They stood outside the Knife-Wrench, watching the bar from across the street, the engine of their Uber humming behind them. "If you want to wait in the car, I completely understand," Moe said.

"Please. Do you even know me?" Stacie replied.

"I'm just saying. I know about painful memories. If what happened before is too fresh, I can go in there alone. I get it."

"I'm not giving those assholes any power over me. If they can keep me in the Uber, then they win. Fuck them," Stacie said.

"Right. Fuck them," Moe replied, admiring the determination in her friend's voice.

The bar seemed far less crowded today. There wasn't any foot traffic on the street. While there was clearly activity inside, no one was coming in or out.

"So how do you want to play it?" Stacie asked.

"I want to walk in, sit down at the bar, and tell her we found the knife," Moe said.

"Just hit her with it?" Stacie confirmed.

"Yep. Just come right at her with it. I think her reaction might reveal something," Moe said.

"Sounds like a plan," Stacie said. Turning back to the car where the Uber driver sat with her window rolled down, Stacie took a hundred dollar bill from her back pocket, ripped it in half, passed half to the driver, and said, "Circle the block. We'll be out in a few minutes. If you're here when we need you, you get the other half. Deal?"

"You got it," the excited woman said.

They crossed the street in silence and walked to the door. The last thing Moe wanted was another encounter with Mitcham and Ambrose. She didn't want to see their faces again until she was putting them behind bars. Coming back to this bar felt like a risk. Moe knew it was magical thinking. She knew there were a billion reasons why the two cops grabbed them at that moment, and most of them had nothing to do with the bar. At the same time, since one came after the other, it was hard not to connect the two things.

"Oh, shit," Stacie exclaimed as she stepped in the bar. Taking her phone out, she immediately began snapping pictures.

At first, Moe didn't understand what was causing the uproar, but as her eyes adjusted to the light, it became clear. Standing behind the bar in her Knife-Wrench black t-shirt was Tiffany. Across from her, holding her hands, was Tai Murphy, the Physical Therapist.

"Oh shit is right," Moe said.

The two women were leaning close, completely oblivious to the world, whispering to one another in a way that looked like it might become a kiss at any second.

"You get good shots?" Moe asked.

"Of course," Stacie said.

"Good," Moe said, as she walked over the bar. When she took the stool next to Tai, both of the women at the bar jumped. "Don't stop on my account," Moe said with a grin.

"Hey Ladies," Stacie said, taking up the stool on the other side of Tai.

Tiffany dropped Tai's hands and took a step back. Tai stood, her eyes wide with panic and her mouth hanging open. "I thought you said this was safe," she said.

"Shut up, T," Tiffany snapped.

"Alright, lovebirds. Spill it. How long has this been going on?" Stacie asked.

"That's none of your business," Tiffany snapped.

"You know she may have killed her boss?" Moe asked Tai, but before Tai could answer, Moe added, "Oh, right. Of course you know. You were a part of the scheme to set up an innocent man."

"I didn't. I don't know what you're talking about," Tai stammered.

"Get out of here, or I'll call the cops. This is harassment," Tiffany declared.

Moe laughed. "Call 'em. Let's get all the conspirators in one place. Line you all up and see if you can give me the same story. How do you know Mitcham and Ambrose by the way? You dating them too?"

"I don't know who that is," Tiffany said.

"What about you, hon? You know who that is?" Stacie asked Tai.

"I'm not sure what you're talking about," Tai mumbled.

"That's how we're going to play this then? Fine," Moe said. Smiling wide, she locked eyes with Tiffany and said, "We found the knife. Went and got it from that house in Springdale and everything. It's with our law firm right now."

If Tiffany was nervous, she didn't show it. "Look. I don't know what you are talking about. It's like I said. I was there with Alicia Michaels and her husband. I left. She left right after me," she explained.

"Yeah. Yeah. I can testify to that. She left with me," Tai said, perking up.

"I'm so sorry, dear. You aren't really a reliable witness right now," Stacie said.

"Last chance," Moe said. "Give us the truth."

"That is the truth," Tai said.

"We've been telling the truth the entire time. So, you can leave," Tiffany said.

"Bless your heart," Stacie said with a grin.

Moe stood and said, "We're going. But, I'd suggest both of you seriously consider calling us with the real story. At some point, this is going to get out of our hands. Once all of this gets to the cops, there isn't anything we can do for you."

"Here's our card. One for each of you," Stacie said, as she put two business cards on the bar.

CHAPTER THIRTY-THREE

Moe held up a one-hundred dollar bill for the old man to see. "Do it, and it's all yours," she said.

"And all I have to do is give this bag to that guy over there?" the old man said, pointing to the panhandler who was walking from car to car at the intersection of Howard and Conway holding a sign that read, "Hungry. Need Food."

"Just give the guy the bag and walk away," Stacie said.

The old man hesitated and watched the guy at the intersection for a few minutes. "He's not going to jump me or anything, is he?"

"Nope," Moe said.

"Why don't you take him the bag?" the old man asked.

"It's complicated," Stacie said.

"What's in here? Is it a bomb or something?" the old man asked, patting the bag.

"It's a ton of money," Stacie said.

The old man unzipped the bag and exclaimed, "Hot damn!"

"So, you'll go and hand it to the guy over there?" Moe

clarified.

"How do you know I won't just get out of this car and run for it?" the old man asked.

Moe looked in the rear view mirror and raised her eyebrow at the octogenarian whose walker was parked next to the car.

"You don't know me, lady." Motioning up and down his body, he added, "Maybe this is all just an elaborate hoax to get you to give me this bag of money? You don't know."

"We'll take our chances. Are you going to do it or not?" Stacie asked.

"Alright. I'll do it," the old man said.

Moe passed him the hundred. He jammed it in his coat pocket and got out of the car. Moe and Stacie watched in irritation as he slowly walked from where they were parked in the Camden Yards parking lot to the young man hustling cars out of their cash. When the old man arrived, the young one took the bag. Dropping the sign, the young man pulled a phone from the back pocket of his jeans and made a call. As he talked on the phone, he walked away from the intersection. Before they started the car, Moe made sure the old man was clear of the traffic.

As Moe revved the engine, Stacie's phone pinged with a text. "Vinnie says a little kid just hung a lost dog flyer in the coffee house. I love this cloak and dagger stuff," she said.

"Text him back and tell him that he's back on tailing Hooknose today. At some point, he's going to check that stash, and we need to know where it is," Moe said.

CHAPTER THIRTY-FOUR

Conference room number four at Lumpum and Brumtum Attorneys at Law was intimidating. On the fortieth floor of the building, the room's windows gave a spectacular view of Baltimore's inner harbor. Besides a small cart in the corner that held a pitcher of water and drinking glasses, the only furniture in the room was a long mahogany table with sixteen chairs around it. At one end of the table, on a small tripod, a hand-sized camera was mounted. Moe was shocked at how comfortable the chairs were. She felt like she could spend all day playing with the seven different adjustment knobs on the chair.

She smiled at Stacie who returned the look with a playful eyebrow raise of impatience. Across from them sat Alicia Michaels and a very expensive looking lawyer who had introduced herself as "Tabitha Halibut, Ms. Michaels' attorney." Since the initial exchange of names, six minutes ago, they'd been sitting in silence, waiting. Alicia had remained focused on her phone while her attorney pretended to read through a file, leaving Stacie and Moe to gaze out the window at the city and occasionally pass a look to one another.

Finally, Dorothy Lumpum arrived. With two

associates in tow, she entered the room like a wrecking ball, throwing the glass door open and storming to a chair. "Good morning everyone. Thank you for coming. No need for introductions. Let's keep this brief," she said, as she took her seat. The entrance was one of the most baller power moves Moe had ever seen.

As Dorothy spoke, one of her two associates gave a folder with summary documents to each person at the table. "I don't have a lot of time for this today, so let's get straight to the point.

While Alicia put her phone down and rolled her eyes, her attorney began casually paging through the documentation.

Continuing, Dorothy lectured, "I just got off the phone with Judge Hotten, and with the new evidence that has come to light thanks to our firm's private investigators, whom you have met, she has agreed to grant my client, Malcom Sennack, an appeal. Because of the egregious nature of the police's original case and the poor representation my client initially received, this appeal will be expedited to next week."

Tabitha the attorney closed the file and leaned back in her chair.

Dorothy continued, "As you will see by the summary documents I have provided, not only have we found the murder weapon in a place only an employee of Dream Homes Realty would know where to hide it, we also have a new eyewitness that will contradict the testimonies of the original witnesses. Under my scrutiny in court, I have no doubt the original eyewitness to my client's arrival will crumble."

On cue, one of the associates stood and turned on the camera.

Dorothy's words continued to pound the room like a barrage from a Gatling gun. "Not that it will impact the outcome of my client's case, who I am certain will be released from prison with a full apology from the court concerning his wrongful incarceration, but, for the sake of full disclosure and to aid the state prosecutor's office in bringing the true guilty parties to justice, we will be providing the court with a complete picture of the evening in question by calling witnesses who will place two other suspects at the scene shortly before the crime. It should be noted that neither of the suspects have yet provided alibis for the murder of Charlie Michaels. This meeting is simply a courtesy to inform you that your false testimony about my client and the night in question will be called to account in court and that you will be made to answer for your role in wrongfully imprisoning an innocent man, costing him months of his life, and forcing him to postpone his wedding. And, in addition to being held accountable for your false testimony concerning my client, you will also be listed as one of the two prime suspects in your estranged husband's murder."

Tabitha smiled and replied in an unshaken voice, "Dorothy. It's a pleasure as always. I like your suit today. The dark blue is a nice change from your typical black, and that was a mighty nice presentation. Now, let's cut the crap and get to the point. You and I both know that nothing you throw at my client is going to stick because she is completely innocent of these libelous charges, and I know you wouldn't have asked us here if you didn't need something from my client. So, what exactly is it you want?"

"I don't need anything from your client. This is simply a courtesy," Dorothy replied.

"It seems to me that your case would be stronger for your client if there were one clear suspect rather than two," Tabitha suggested.

"Either way, my client will walk. This is just a

courtesy," Dorothy said again.

"Are you planning on seeking damages then? Are you looking to settle before the case goes to court, because settling a civil suit with us before your client is even released is putting the cart before the horse, and while I admire that ambition, it makes me worry about you. Are you hard up for cash, Dorothy?" Tabitha asked with a grin.

"While my client would be entitled to compensation for his pain and suffering, we have no plans for further litigation at this time. Again, just a courtesy today," Dorothy said for the fourth time.

"Cut the courtesy crap, Dorothy. Why did you drag us down here? My client is exceptionally busy. If this was just about wasting our time, then I'm extremely disappointed in you," Tabitha barked.

Alicia sighed, put down her phone, held out her hand to Moe, and said, "It's fine. I'll show her."

Moe smiled.

"You don't need to give them anything. They have nothing on you. This is all just a ridiculous charade," Tabitha said.

Alicia locked eyes with Moe and said, "This is why I'm here, right? You don't know if it's me or the Southern belle? I could tell you, but not with the camera rolling. Besides, I'm sure you'll trust your own eyes more. So, let's get this done. I've got things to do today."

Moe looked at Dorothy.

Dorothy leaned back in her chair and nodded, and the associate turned off the camera.

Moe leaned forward, took Alicia's hand, and closed her eyes.

Moe opened her eyes. She was standing in front of a computer screen reading through emails. Her inbox was down to a cool 97 unanswered. Considering she'd started the day at over two hundred, she considered this a huge victory.

She looked around the office. It was filthy. Charlie had left papers and used cups everywhere, and the to-go box with the remnant of his lunch was still open on the floor. Alicia wondered how she'd ever been in love with him.

The volume of his shrieking rose again, meaning he'd lost another one and was coming back to the bullpen to regroup.

"Damn it!" he yelled at the top of his lungs.

Moe glanced out into the empty bullpen to see what was happening. Tiffany was walking quickly across the room with Charlie nipping at her heals.

"That was a complete shit show! Damn it, Tiffany! I thought you were supposed to be smart! But that was just plain stupid!" Charlie yelled as he chased behind her.

Tiffany didn't reply. She walked faster, made it to the safety of the bathroom, and closed the door.

Charlie stood next to it and continued to yell at her. With each beat of each sentence, he pounded his fists on the door as hard as he could. "I told you! We! Need! Money! You had one job! One goddamn job!"

Charlie turned and began kicking the wall and shaking the cubicles as he screamed. "I said, 'Get people with money!' But you get garbage! Garb-age! You get in the poorest assholes on our roster! You stupid bitch!

Returning to the bathroom door, he began pounding on it again. "Get out here, bitch! Get out here and give me my money! You hear me? I'm getting paid! I'm! Getting! Paid!"

His hair was frazzled, and his shirt was untucked. Veins were popping from his neck and a wheeze had started in his breathing. Alicia hated Charlie's manic states. She decided she didn't want to engage. When he was like this, it wasn't worth it. She went back to her email and tried to ignore him.

Charlie stepped back from the door and screamed at it as if it could here him. "You can't hide in there forever, bitch! You have to come out! Sooner or later! And I'm still sixty-fucking-thousand short!"

He grabbed a trash can and threw it across the office. It crashed into a desk on the other side of the room. "The next client better pay! Because I'm getting paid! Them or you!" he screamed again.

Alicia could hear the receptionist sobbing in the bathroom. Alicia only felt a tiny twinge of compassion for the receptionist. She was sure Charlie had hired her in hopes of sleeping with her, but when it became clear that wasn't going to happen, he'd become obsessed with "getting something out of her." Alicia had demanded several times that he back off, but when Charlie discovered that Tiffany had been in a bar fight and a man had died, there was nothing she could do anymore. It only took a few calls to Kentucky for him to get enough information to deduce that Tiffany had actually been the bartender that pulled the trigger that night. From that moment on, she had been under his thumb, and there was nothing anyone could do about it. Not that Alicia wanted to do anything anyway. The girl should be in jail. As far as Alicia was concerned, having to put up with Charlie was the prison sentence the girl deserved. At the same time, Alicia had cried in small places while Charlie raged so many times wishing that someone would come to her aide. She remembered how that felt. She couldn't just pretend like it wasn't happening again. "Leave her alone, asshole," she yelled from the office without looking back into the bullpen, knowing it would draw him away from the door.

"Shut your face, whore! You dirty, disgusting whore!

I'm not talking to you! I'd rather pour hot coffee in my eyes than talk to you. Then I wouldn't have to see your ugly whore face!" Charlie yelled back.

Alicia snorted a laugh. He'd reached the nonsense level where his insults stopped making sense. She was so sick of him. Peeking into the bullpen, she snapped back, "Does picking on that little girl make you feel like more of a man? Grow up, asshole!" Asshole was her favorite name for him because it's what his father called him, so she knew it stung.

"You don't get to call me that anymore!" he screamed.

"I'll call you whatever I want, asshole!" she yelled back, punctuating the insult.

Shaking a cubicle wall again, he screamed, "I'm doing this for us! This is for us! I'm just trying to take all of this to the next level!"

Alicia laughed and then shot back, "Is that's what you're doing? Screaming at the receptionist is taking this to the next level? I should have listened to your dad. He was so right about you."

His face went red and spit formed in the corners of his mouth as he screamed. Slamming another plastic trashcan on the ground, he began stomping on it like a child having a tantrum. "You'll see! I'm going to get into that club! And I'm going to make more money than you can even count! And then! And then, I'm going to walk out of this hellhole! And I'm going to leave you! I'll leave you here with the scraps! The goddamn scraps! You'll be sorry then!"

Alicia laughed again and retorted, "I'm sorry now. I don't have to do anything else. I'm sorry right now!"

He clenched fists and began knocking stacks of papers from desks and throwing file folders around the room, he screamed, "You don't even know what sorry means! I'll show you sorry! I'll make you sorry!"

Alicia put her hands to her mouth in mocking fear. "Oh, no. Is little Charlie going to make me sorry. I'm so scared." Grabbing his food off the floor of their office, she marched back to the bullpen and threw it as hard as she could. The lettuce, tomatoes, ham slices, and cheese from the sub sandwich went in all directions, but the bread actually came close to hitting him, which made her proud of the effort.

Marching back to her office, she tried to return to her email, but she couldn't focus. She stared at the screen as she listened to him continue to pitch a fit.

He began banging on the bathroom door again, yelling "Get out here! Get out here right now!"

Moe listened as the bathroom door opened. She could hear Tiffany quietly sobbing.

"You're crying? Why are you crying? I should be the one crying. I'm the one not making any money!" he screamed. Moe glanced back out into the bullpen to see him standing dangerously close to the receptionist.

"Dry your eyes, suck it up, and charm some fucking money out of the next client to walk in here, or I'm going to make a call to Daddy," he threatened.

Tiffany met his gaze, her mouth open with shock.

Charlie smiled and continued, "That's right. I'll call your Daddy. Because I'm getting my money. I bet there's a whole bunch of journalists at the Lexington Herald who would love to run with the headline, 'Lesbian Daughter Let's Her Lover Take the Fall.' Do you understand what I'm saying? You get what is happening here?"

Tiffany looked down and said through tears, "I understand."

The buzzer sounded indicating that someone was coming in the front door.

Charlie took a step back and said, "Good. Now go and get my money."

Tiffany wiped her eyes and smoothed her dress. Composed, she walked across the bullpen to greet the next potential victim.

Charlie licked his hand and tried to smooth his hair, but he couldn't get it to fully lay down.

Moe stepped out of her doorway to see who Tiffany was escorting to the conference room. Alicia didn't recognize the woman and was happy it wasn't one of her clients.

Charlie took a deep breath. He shook his head back and forth and his cheeks rattled as air escaped them. He jumped up and down several times, shaking his hands as he did. Feeling confident, he marched to the conference room, declaring in a pleasant tone, "Hey, Jordy! Thanks for coming in! I'm so sorry for the inconvenience." His words rattled out a beat too fast, making him sound like he was on speed.

Moe leaned against the wall and watched as Tiffany closed the door to the conference room and stepped into the bullpen. Staring into space, her shoulders were slumped and her eyes were puffy.

"You look like hell," Alicia said.

Tiffany looked up and flashed desperate eyes at Alicia. "I can't get him to stop," she said.

Alicia knew that withered tone in her voice. She'd had it once too. It was the sound of a woman at the breaking point with Charlie. She sighed and shook her head. "Look, sweetie, he's going to blackmail your dad. There's no stopping that. If not today, then tomorrow, or the next day. When Charlie gets a hold of a chip like that, he's not letting it go. So, this goes down one of two ways. You either walk out of here right now and never come back, or you ask him for a cut. Those are the only plays you have left."

"But, dad will be ruined. I can't... I can't let him do

that," Tiffany said quietly to herself.

Alicia stepped back into her office and hit the power button to put her computer to sleep. Walking into the bullpen, she looked at the damage. Surprisingly, it wasn't all that bad. She laughed at the realization that Charlie couldn't even destroy a room right.

Not wanting to be sucked into Charlie's conversation with the client, Alicia turned and moved to the back door. As she left, she met Tiffany's desperate eyes and said, "It's time to grow a pair, honey. The second that Charlie found out you killed that guy in the bar, your daddy was going to pay. Accept it and move on."

"Can you help me? Please. I need help," Tiffany said, her quiet voice cracking with the request.

Alicia sneered and replied, "I could. But I'm not going to. You really should have thought about all this before you killed that poor man in that bar."

Alicia took a refreshing breath as she stepped into the night air. It felt good to be able to walk away from Charlie. She liked not having to deal with his nonsense anymore. She got in her Mustang, revved the engine, and tried to decide what she wanted for dinner.

Moe let go of Alicia's hand and opened her eyes. She looked at Dorothy and shook her head no.

"We're done here then?" Alicia said, standing to leave.

"We're done for now. Don't leave town," Dorothy said.

Moe watched in silence as Alicia and her lawyer thanked Dorothy, left the room, and walked to the elevator. Moe was going to let the women leave without another word, but she could still hear Charlie screaming and she could Tiffany's tears. She couldn't let it lie. Jumping to her feet, Moe ran into the hall and said, "Wait!"

"I think my client has provided you with all the answers you need," Tabitha replied, stepping between Moe and Alicia.

"I just need to know. Why'd you lie? Why not just tell the court the truth?" Moe asked.

"Off the record?" Alicia asked with a grin.

"I just need to know," Moe said.

Alicia laughed and stepped close enough to Moe so only she could hear. In a hushed tone soaked in pleasure, she said, "Because. It's better for business if we have a crazy client than if we have a crazy receptionist. Plus, the daughter of the governor killed a man in a bar? That's information that's worth something, as long as you control when it comes out."

CHAPTER THIRTY-FIVE

Moe turned her lights off a block before they arrived to the parking lot that Vinnie had texted to them. She spotted him parked in the corner of the empty lot and pulled her car into the spot next to his Hyundai hatchback. At two in the morning, the streets of Towson were silent.

Stacie rolled down her window and said to Vinnie, "Funny meeting you here."

Vinnie laughed. His left arm rested on the car window sill. Covered by the flannel shirt he was wearing, if you didn't know it was a prosthetic, you wouldn't be able to tell at first glance. Nodding with his head across the street, he said, "They're in there."

Moe squinted her eyes. She could barely make a tall chain-link fence. A man stood at the entrance, but everything that lay behind it was shrouded in darkness.

"They drove in with a U-Haul. I think it's one of those old storage places, you know, where all the doors face out," Vinnie said.

"Who's they?" Stacie asked, peering into the darkness.

"Well, your boy Damon picked up the truck and then swung by a gym and grabbed a big ugly dude. That's who's standing at the gate. Damon is somewhere inside," Vinnie said.

"Any chance Big Tony will just let us by if we ask nicely?" Stacie asked.

"You've met the giant?" Vinnie said, with a grin of amusement.

"We've met. And my bet is he'll be looking for payback. We need to figure out how to get by him," Moe said.

"So, wait. Let me get this straight. Your plan is to get past the humongous killer who already wants to get his hands on you, go into the terrifying and pitch black storage lot from hell, and sneak up on a criminal mastermind who is currently loading up his U-Haul full of guns? That's the plan?" Vinnie said.

"I mean. It sounded more elegant when Moe explained it," Stacie said with a grin.

"What are you hoping to get out of this interaction?" Vinnie asked.

"Right now, our best guess is that Damon is in there checking his supply. That 'lost dog' flyer that went up at the coffeehouse was an order for a huge amount of guns. He hasn't responded to it yet. Our source says that before he does, he will check to make sure he can fill the order," Moe said.

"A guy like this has his inventory in his head. Plus, why bring a U-Haul if you aren't moving the guns? He's going to move your order to a secure place and then call you and tell you how to get it. He's smart. He's staying off the phone until everything is set up in case someone is listening," Vinnie said.

"So you think he's going to pull out of there with a truck full of weapons?" Moe asked.

"That's how I'd do it. He doesn't want anyone else touching his supply, but he also doesn't want to be connected to the deal itself because he knows that's what the cops are going to follow. Plus, we already know he's all about preparation," Vinnie said.

"So you're suggesting we don't go into the murder lot," Stacie said.

"Kill box. In the army, we called that a kill box. Expect both him and boxer-boy to be packing. No cameras. No one coming around any time soon. You go in there, and he's free to open fire," Vinnie said.

"This is the best chance we've had to take him down. We can't waste it," Moe said.

Vinnie looked up and down the street. It was quiet and silent in both directions for two blocks. He started the hatchback and said, "Follow him out of the lot. Wait for my signal. As soon as you see it, call the cops and come running. If either of them get out of the car, I'm going to need your help."

He pulled off before Moe or Stacie could ask for clarification. They watched as he turned left, drove two blocks, and then turned left again.

"I really wish that douchebag cop hadn't taken my gun," Stacie said.

"We could really use Francine right now," Moe said.

"Either thing would be helpful," Stacie said.

There was a rumble from the lot, and headlights illuminated rows of storage units as the U-Haul approached the gate. Moe started the car. She could feel her heart pound in her chest. She was tempted to jump out of the car and start screaming. The truck stopped at the gate, and Damon slid into the passenger seat and Big Tony got behind the wheel. Moe looked over at Stacie, who took her phone out and waved it in the air signaling she was ready to call 911. The truck pulled out of the lot and turned left. Keeping her lights off, Moe eased her car forward. Staying a block behind the U-Haul, she followed it as it roared down the street. There was no sign of Vinnie.

"Where do you think he is?" Stacie asked.

"I don't know. I figured he was going to set up a road block or something," Moe said.

The U-Haul came to a stop at the intersection a block ahead of them and Moe slowed her car, not wanting to get too close until they were back on main roads.

"Where is he?" Stacie complained.

As the U-Haul pulled into the intersection, tires screeched and lights flashed. With a loud boom, Vinnie's hatchback exploded into the front of the U-Haul. Metal and glass erupted in all directions.

Moe flipped the lights on and slammed on the gas. "Call now!" she yelled.

"Yes. We need help. We're at the corner of Rolling Mill road and North Point road. There's been a horrible accident. Please come quickly. Yes, I'll stay on the line," Stacie said.

Moe screeched her car to a halt behind the U-Haul. Racing from her car, she ran to the driver's side of the U-Haul. The front of the hatchback was smashed to a fifth of its right size and completely obscured by smoke, but the engine sounded like it was still trying to run. There was a small spark and the flicker of a fire could be seen under the car. "Vinnie!" she screamed as she ran to the driver's seat.

Rounding the car, she had a better view. The airbag had deployed, but the driver's door was open. Leaning into the car, she saw a brick lying against the gas pedal. She grabbed it and tossed it to the side.

Not thinking about where Vinnie might have gone, Moe's mind raced to the two other crash victims. She felt the heat of the flames from under the car begin to spill out of the sides of the vehicle. Turning her attention to the U-

Haul, she tried to peer through the smoke. Beyond the smashed glass of the door, she could see a figure lying across the dashboard. She scanned the collision point and quickly realized there was no way to get into the U-Haul through the driver's side.

Adrenaline coursing through her veins and her heart pounding, she ran to the other side of the U-Haul. Grabbing the handle of the passenger side, she tore the door open to find Big Tony unconscious, lying across the dashboard. A gash in his head was filling the dash with blood.

Moe stepped into the truck and felt for a pulse. Tony was breathing, and his heart was still beating. She looked out at Vinnie's car. The fire was growing. She undid his seat belt and leaned him back. He groaned in response.

"Hey, big guy. We need to get you out of here, okay?" she said, putting her arms around his chest. She heaved, and he groaned, but she only moved him an inch.

The flames took to the inside of Vinnie's car, and it became a bonfire. Moe could feel the heat radiating from it. "Big guy. You need to help me," she said. She pulled again, and again Tony groaned but didn't move.

"Alright. You asked for this," she said. Closing her eyes, she grabbed his arm and looked for something that might help.

Her head was pounding. She felt like she'd been hit with a hammer in the temple. She could feel the snot running from her nose. The world spun in circles around her. She closed her eyes. All she wanted to do was sleep.

There was a smack on the canvas next to her head, and a male voice screamed, "TWO!" She opened her eyes. The world continued to spin. Where was she?

Another smack. "THREE!" the voice screamed.

The fuzzy world started coming into focus. Across the ring she could see her manager. He was screaming. What was he screaming?

Another crash by her ear. "FOUR!" the voice screamed.

She focused on her manager. She could see his mouth moving. "Get up! Get up asshole!" he was yelling.

Another smack of the mat. "FIVE!" the voice shouted.

Wait. She remembered. She was in a fight. She shook her head. Her vision began to come back. A man in black shorts stood over her, smiling. The son of a bitch was smiling. Rage surged through her chest.

Another smack of the mat. "SIX!" the referee screamed.

She pushed her gloves into the mat. She wasn't done. She was going to make that son of a bitch eat that smile. You don't get to knock Big Tony down and not pay for it. She pushed herself up to her knees.

"SEVEN!" the referee yelled.

She went to one knee. Grabbing the ropes with her glove, she raised herself up to standing. "I'm good! I'm good!" she yelled with Big Tony's voice.

The referee looked her in the eyes.

She pounded her fists together. "I'm good! I'm good!" Big Tony yelled.

Moe opened her eyes and let go of Big Tony's arm. His eyes were open. "I'm good. I'm good," he mumbled.

"Let's get out of here," she said. Putting her arms around him again, she helped him slide across the seat and out into the fresh air. They walked ten paces, Moe supporting as much of his weight as she could. The ringing in her head from the fight she'd seen in his mind was only offset by the sheer adrenaline of the moment.

Once they were at a safe distance, Moe helped him to the ground. "I won that fight. I won that one," Big Tony said.

"I know, big guy," she said, as she sat down next to

him.

A sharper voice came from behind her. "Now, isn't that sweet. So heroic."

Moe jumped to her feet and turned. Standing in front of her was Stacie with a gun to her head and Damon's hand over her mouth. Her eyebrows were knit together in anger. Moe could tell that she wanted nothing more than to rip his heart out.

Damon pushed her toward Moe and kept the gun on them both. "Car keys. Now!" he demanded.

"Fuck you!" Stacie said.

Damon laughed. "It's the car or your friend's head," he said, taking aim at Stacie.

"Okay. Okay," Moe said, holding her hands up in surrender. "They're in my pocket," she said, slowly reaching down to her side.

"Hurry the fuck up," Damon demanded.

Moe held the keys up in the air. Dangling them, she smiled and tossed them to his feet.

"Dumb bitch," he said, pointing the gun at her with a grin, but before he could pull the trigger, Vinnie ran from the shadows, brick in hand. Using it as a hammer, he clocked Damon in the back of the skull. Hooknose collapsed. Dropping the brick, Vinnie grabbed the gun and turned it on the fallen criminal.

Stacie and Moe ran to him. "Are you okay?" Moe asked.

"Yeah. A few scrapes. I jumped clear before the car hit," Vinnie said.

Sirens rang in the distance. "Here comes the cavalry," Stacie laughed.

Moe looked down at the struggling Tony and then at the unconscious Vinnie and then at the U-Haul. She walked over to Hooknose, reached into his pocket, and removed a key chain with ten keys on it. As she looked for a padlock key, she jogged to the back of the van, Stacie fast on her heels. She unlocked the door and pushed it up. Stacie held up her cell phone and said, "Okay Google. Flash light on." Light filled the back of the van, revealing crates of guns... every kind of gun one could imagine.

Moe closed the door and relocked it. Running back to Damon, she pushed the keys back into his pocket.

"Did we get him?" Vinnie asked, red and blue lights illuminating his face.

Moe smiled. "We got him," she said.

Vinnie put the gun on the ground, kneeled, and put his hands behind his head. Moe and Stacie followed suit. "You owe me a new car," he said.

"Anything you want. You earned it," Moe replied with laugh.

CHAPTER THIRTY-SIX

Moe walked through the police station with her chin high and purpose in her stride. At the same time, she stayed in step with Detective Mason and Detective Keller and didn't stray from their shadows. Since she and Stacie had entered the five story headquarters and passed through security, she felt as though all eyes were on her. Still, her heart raced with glee.

When the doors of the elevator closed, Detective Keller finally broke her silence and asked, "Is it true you read minds?"

"Not exactly. I can relive people's memories," Moe said from behind the detective, who did not turn around to hear her answer.

"Huh," Detective Keller said.

"It's real. I've seen it," Detective Mason said, also not breaking his gaze from the elevator door.

"And you're her grandfather's ex-partner," Detective Keller said.

"Yep," Detective Mason replied.

Keller glanced at Mason and said, "You know it's against regulations for you to give family and friends preferential treatment in contracting. It's an ethical violation."

Without returning the glance, Mason replied, "Write me up then."

The quip made Keller laugh.

As the elevator door opened, a renewed sense of mission came over the small cohort. They stepped into the hall, walked around the corner, and into the bullpen in silence, knowing there were a thousand ways their mission might go south. The room was a grid of paired desks filled with computer monitors and paperwork. Cops laughed, drank coffee, and chatted about their cases and their weekend plans, as every office does at the beginning of a workday.

Moe spotted their targets right away. Ambrose and Mitcham's desks faced each other. Neither were seated. Rather, Mitcham seemed to be entertaining a small crowd of other officers with a story about some arrest he'd made.

Ambrose saw them coming first. His spine straightened, his shoulders squared, and his chest puffed out as if he were preparing to defend a verbal attack. Mitcham took another second to catch on, but once he did, the jovial expression on his face was replaced with grim anger. Their response brought a smile to Moe's face. Controlled terror was exactly what she was hoping to see in this moment.

Without hesitation, Detective Keller took the lead in the conversation. "Gentlemen, I'm Detective Andrea Keller with internal affairs. Let's step into your captain's office please." With the last word, she marched past them toward the glass door at the back of the room that read "Captain Shultz." Pushing open the door, Keller walked into the office without waiting to see if Ambrose and Mitcham were following.

Moe, Stacie, and Mason filed in behind Keller. The

office wasn't much. It had a window that looked down on the street below. A small plant sat in the sill, reaching for as much light as possible. The captain was a heavyset man with thinning grey hair who looked like anxiety and too much time sitting behind his desk had gotten the better of him. He greeted them with a disgusted, "Goddamn it, Keller. It's Friday. No one wants to do this shit on a Friday."

Ambrose and Mitcham slunk in the room after Mason. Although they still carried the look of indignant victims, they kept their eyes low, refusing to look at their captain.

"What did you two fuck up this time?" the captain barked, leaning back in his chair.

"Captain Shultz, this is Moneta Watkins and Stacie Howe. They are private detectives who have brought evidence today to present to you," Keller explained.

"And what the fuck are you doing in here, Mason?" the captain demanded to know.

"I'm just here to watch," Mason said with a grin, as he placed an evidence bag on the desk in front of the captain.

"Captain. This is completely out of line. We haven't done anything," Ambrose began to complain, but was cut short when the Captain held up his hand.

"Shut up, dumbass. Save it till your union rep is present," the Captain said.

Ambrose closed his mouth, rolled his eyes, and went back to looking at the floor.

With no joy in her voice, Keller explained, "The bag in front of you contains Ms. Howe's personal firearm. Not only does she have a conceal-and-carry permit for the weapon that Officer Mitcham and Ambrose confiscated from her, your two officers did not check the weapon into evidence. After the complaint was filed by Detective Mason, he and I made a thorough search of Officer Mitcham and Ambrose's office space and discovered the weapon being inappropriately secured."

"I found it in that one's desk this morning," Mason said with a grin, as he motioned his chin toward Mitcham.

The captain closed his eyes as if he were in pain and said, "You never come in here with just one thing, Keller. What else did these dummies do?"

Stacie removed four black and white glossy pictures from the file folder she'd been carrying and placed them on the captain's desk. Taking them up, the captain glanced at them, glared at his two officers, and then set them back down on the desk.

Looking at the two officers, Keller continued to explain, "In these pictures, taken by Ms. Watkins and Ms. Howe, you will see Officer Mitcham engaging in romantic activity with Cher Silverstone. Silverstone was the eyewitness in the Charlie Michaels homicide case, in which Philip Mitcham was the arresting officer and the first officer on the scene. Ms. Howe and Ms. Watkins claim they can prove this relationship began before the murder, yet Officer Mitcham failed to disclose his personal relationship with this witness."

"Goddamn it," the captain muttered to himself, as he scratched the back of his head and sighed.

"Captain, you have to understand," Mitcham began to argue.

Again the captain raised his hand to silence the officer. After another long sigh, the captain said, "Go ahead, Keller. Do you thing."

For the first time, Detective Andrea Keller smiled as she said, "Officers Mitcham and Ambrose, Internal Affairs has opened a case into your role in the Charlie Michaels homicide case. Additionally, a claim of harassment and conduct unbecoming an officer has been filed against you."

Turning to face the two officers, Detective Mason

added, "And to be clear, I filed the claim. So don't get any ideas about reprising against these two fine women. You want to try and intimidate someone, come and find me."

Captain Shultz gave a forced smile and said, "Now it's my turn to say, pending the completion of these investigations, the two of you are suspended without pay. Give me you badges and firearms, and contact your union representative. When you call him, tell him you need a good lawyer."

As Mitcham and Ambrose removed their badges and guns and placed them on their captain's desk, Moe looked over at Stacie and was moved to see a smile on her face and a tear in her eye. Putting her arm around her best friend, she gave Stacie a light squeeze.

CHAPTER THIRTY-SEVEN

Watching Dorothy Lumpum present a case at trial was like watching a master sculptor shape a piece of marble. She held then entire room in the palm of her hand. It likely helped that the court was filled with a friendly audience. The pews were packed with men and families who'd been served by Malcom and who had come to show their support. On the front row, behind the defendant, sat his friend and partner Marvin Jenkins in a fresh bowtie. Next to him, directly behind Malcom, was Malcom's fiancée, Katie Scrasdale. For the first time since Moe had met her, she was not dressed in black. Today she was in a green blouse and white skirt. The colors seemed to bring new light to her face.

When Malcom had entered the room, the crowd had burst into cheers. As this was a hearing, there wasn't a jury, only a judge who was perched high behind her oak bench. It had taken her four full minutes to wrestle control of the room back from the crowd.

Dorothy had begun her plea by launching into an explanation of the State's initial case against Malcom. She'd then picked apart the defense offered by Malcom's original attorney, hinting, but not directly stating, that

Malcom had not had proper representation. Then she began an introduction of new evidence. She first entered into record an affidavit from Josh Rudd, the graphic designer at Connections, stating that Josh would be willing to testify that he saw Malcom calmly enter the building, unlike what the original eyewitnesses had said. Dorothy made sure to make note that no law enforcement officials had come to interview him. She next entered into evidence an affidavit from Jordy McGill that spoke to Charlie Michaels' state of mind and that both his wife and his receptionist were present in the building shortly before the murder occurred. Dorothy also made note that, again, the police had made no attempt to interview the new witness, even after the witness had gone to the station to offer her statement. The judge had received both affidavits with a stone face, reviewed them briefly, and then handed them to her aid.

In a clear and commanding voice, Dorothy said, "If it pleases the court, I would like to call to the stand Tai Murphy."

The judge nodded.

From a pew in the back, the young physical therapist stood and made her way down the center aisle. While the room bored holes in her back with their glares, her eyes remained locked on her shoes. She climbed into the witness stand and looked down at the ground.

A bailiff approached her with a Bible in hand and held it out. Tai placed her hand on it, and then he said, "Do you swear to tell the truth, the whole truth, and nothing but the truth so help you God?"

Still staring at the floor, Tai said, "I do."

"You are now under oath, Ms. Murphy. Any lies you tell in this room will be prosecuted as perjury," the judge said for good measure.

"Yes, ma'am. I understand," Tai said in a mousy

voice.

The judge nodded at Dorothy, and the attorney stood. "Ms. Murphy. You work at AABA Physical Therapy. Isn't that true?"

"I did work there. I quit three days ago," Tai said.

"But you worked there the night that Charlie Michaels was killed?" Dorothy asked, refusing to be distracted by unnecessary details.

"I did," Tai said.

"How close is AABA Physical Therapy in relationship to the Dream Homes Realty office that Charlie Michaels was killed in?"

"The buildings share the same parking lot and back alley. We could see their entrances from our offices," Tai replied.

"Would you please describe for the court what happened the night that Charlie Michaels was murdered?"

Tai took a big breath and bit her bottom lip.

"Ms. Murphy, we're waiting," Dorothy said.

"I don't know," Tai said, shaking her head.

"You don't know what happened, or you don't know if you want to share the events of that night with us?" Dorothy asked.

Tai swallowed. "The second one," she said.

The judge leaned forward and said, "Ms. Murphy, often speaking the truth is difficult. You do have the right to remain silent if you feel what you share with us today might implicate you in a crime. You cannot be forced to testify against yourself. Do you feel the need to plead the fifth amendment?"

"No, ma'am," Tai said.

"Well then, this man has been sitting in prison for months, and I've been sitting on this bench all day. We are all ready to move on with our lives. We've already had several of the original witnesses' testimonies contradicted. I think it is therefore time for some truth to be told, don't you? Let's bring things into the light so we can all move on," the judge said.

"Yes, ma'am," Tai said. There was a catch in her throat like she was about to cry.

Looking at Dorothy, the judge said, "Ask again."

Dorothy showed no signs of pleasure. Rather, she plowed forward with the mundane, effortless power of a bulldozer pushing around mud. "Ms. Murphy, please describe for the court what happened the night of Charlie Michaels' murder."

Tai sighed again. "Well, Cher and I had finished up with our last clients, and we were sweeping up."

"Cher is Cher Silverstone who provided testimony in the initial case?" Dorothy interrupted.

"That's right," Tai said, nodding. "It had been a really full day and we'd been closed for, like, forty minutes. So I was sweeping up and Cher was wiping down all the tables, and that's when we heard someone banging at the back door."

Dorothy nodded, indicating that Tai should continue.

Tai looked up for the first time, locking eyes with Dorothy, and sighed again. Then she continued, "Cher was wiping down the tables and someone started banging on the back door. At first it freaked me out because no one comes in that way, but then I heard Tiffany yelling, so I figured she was just coming over after her shift."

"Tiffany is Tiffany Brown, the receptionist at Dream Homes Realty?" Dorothy clarified.

Tai looked down again. "Yeah, that's right."

"Please describe your relationship with Tiffany," Dorothy said.

"She's my girlfriend. Well, she was my girlfriend. This all kind of, I guess, got between us," Tai said.

"And how did you meet Tiffany?" Dorothy asked.

"Cher knew her in college. They were friends at the University of Kentucky. They lived on the same hall freshman year. But then Cher had transferred to the University of Maryland to be closer to home. So, when Tiffany moved to town, she stayed with us for a few weeks before she found her own place. That's when we started dating," Tai explained.

"So you heard your girlfriend, Tiffany, banging on the back door and calling for help. Then what happened?" Dorothy asked.

"So I went to the back. I thought maybe she wanted to go to dinner or something, But when I opened the back door, she was. Um. She," Tai froze at the memory.

In a soothing voice, Dorothy said, "Take your time."

Tai looked up at the attorney and nodded. She took another deep breath and exhaled it slowly. Looking back down at the floor, she said, "She was covered in blood. It was all over her. In her hair and all over her clothes. And she was crying. Really hard." Looking up at Dorothy, she continued, "I thought she'd been attacked. I thought the blood was hers. But." Tai seemed to freeze again at the memory.

"When you saw her at the back door, what did you do?" Dorothy asked.

Tai looked up and tears began to escape her eyes. "I brought her inside, and I tried to calm her down. I was checking her out at the same time, to try and figure out where the blood was coming from. That's when she started saying that she'd been attacked. That Charlie had attacked her. And that she'd had to defend herself. And then Cher came running back, and she asked what happened. And Tiffany started explaining it all again. And then Cher just took charge. And she said, 'Get her out of here. I've got this.' Then she took out her phone and called her boyfriend."

"Thank you for sharing that Ms. Murphy. Would you mind explaining to us who Ms. Silverstone was dating at the time?" Dorothy asked.

"She was dating a detective named Philip Mitcham. He was coming to meet us after work. We were supposed to be going to dinner," Tai explained, tears flowing freely now.

Dorothy, interjected, "To clarify for the court, Philip Mitcham is the detective that arrived on the scene and arrested my client."

"I'm picking up on that, Ms. Lumpum," the judge said.

"What happened next?" Dorothy asked.

"I took Tiffany out the backdoor. I didn't know what else to do. And I took her home and helped her clean up. There was so much blood. And she couldn't stop crying," Tai said, trailing off at the memory again.

"Thank you, Ms. Murphy. We appreciate you sharing with us the truth of what happened that day," Dorothy said. Turning her attention to the judge, Dorothy said, "I'm done with this witness, your Honor."

"Thank you, Ms. Murphy. You can step down," the judge said.

Tai stood, but didn't move. Looking at the floor, tears rolling down her cheeks, she said, "I'm so sorry."

"Thank you, Ms. Murphy. You can step down now," the judge said again.

Tai looked up at Malcom.

He nodded to her in reply.

A new wave of tears erupted from her eyes as she sobbed, "I'm so sorry. I'm sorry. I'm so sorry."

The bailiff stepped forward to escort her down from the stand. She wept all the way down the aisle and into the hallway. Moe could hear her faintly crying in the back through the remainder of the proceedings.

When the commotion had died down, Dorothy removed a red handled knife contained in a sealed plastic bag from a box on the floor. "You're honor, I'd now like to enter into evidence the knife that was used to stab Charlie Michaels." Handing the knife to the bailiff, he took it and handed it to the judge.

The judge examined it and then handed it to her aide.

"This knife was found," Dorothy began, but she was cut off by the judge.

"Ms. Lumpum, we could continue, but I'm ready to deliver my verdict," the judge said. "Could I have the State's representative at the bench please?"

Dorothy sat down and patted Malcom on the back.

Malcom looked back at Katie, his eyes filling with tears.

The young attorney who'd spent the entire hearing in silence stood and approached the bench. After a few quiet words exchanged with the judge, he went back to his seat.

Looking down at Malcom, the judge said, "Mr. Sennack, the State of Maryland has done you a great injustice. It is clear from the evidence presented today that you are completely innocent of this crime."

The room erupted in joyous cheers, which caused the judge to begin banging her gavel.

Once the room had calmed, she continued, "I'm ordering that you be freed from custody immediately. I'm also issuing warrants for the arrest of Cher Silverstone for perjury and Tiffany Brown for murder. On behalf of the state of Maryland, I apologize for how you have been treated. This state owes you a great debt for this injustice. Mr. Sennack, you are a free man."

As Katie wrapped her arms around her fiancé, the room again erupted with cheering.

ABOUT THE AUTHOR

Jeff Elkins lives in Baltimore, Maryland with his wife and five kids. A graduate of Baylor University and Truett Seminary, Jeff is the author of more than ten novels. To follow Jeff's work, visit his website VagrantMisunderstandings.com. Sign up for his monthly newsletter to receive a free novel and a free short story.

If you enjoyed Fight, look for these other books in the Watkins and Howe series:

Grab

Steal

Made in the USA
Middletown, DE
26 March 2020

87265074R00165